A Report
of
Just Thoughts

by Robert Beckett Corogin

DORRANCE
PUBLISHING CO
EST. 1920
PITTSBURGH, PENNSYLVANIA 15238

Dorrance Publishing Co
585 Alpha Drive
Suite 103
Pittsburgh, PA 15238
Visit our website at *www.dorrancebookstore.com*

ISBN: 978-1-4809-1086-7
eISBN: 978-1-4809-1408-7

Contents

Foreword

Being careful to consider the feelings of all others, you politely and properly justly concentrate upon them. And in communication while publicly speaking. You want a full audience. And the only echo you want to hear comes from the microphone, not an empty auditorium. "Marco." "Polo." When you take the words out of some ones mouth you've communicated for them. Which can be a life saver when you advocate for the rites of others and a humanitarian effort. Even when you're a victim. When helping other people is your goal and you're about to make it your life's work. And although there are agents of fortune more capable than you are to do the work. What do you do if they inform you and tell you, you can pretty much accomplish your dream all by yourself, good luck and wish you well. And you really need other peoples help to begin with in the first place. To obtain the bright future you perceive is still possible and within reach. ...You turn to communication and report the breach. To fill the gap and lack of communication and inter and outer cooperation. Then take down and remove the communication barrier, forever.

Heart Beat

When I'm right, I see all too well when I was wrong, not when I am. There's a world of difference between if when your heart quits beating and then all of a sudden you squeeze it and pump it 'till it restarts and comes back to life. And doing nothing but holding on to it thinking there isn't a thing you can do about it and then, just looking frightened. ...And everybody's on your side when they see all you have to give is love! Instead of slight of hand. And that's what keeps the soul alive my friend.

Heart Beats

I needed a new door to my heart. But at first I only wanted a lock. Because all I could afford to purchase was the key. And before the old door fell of the hinges. As my heart began to melt. I gave all my love, away. So instead now with both my eyes focused on the future and with truth on my side heading for uncharted territory. I set my course. And I carry a torch. Because, "We're all brothers under the skin." And again, I put my life on the line. To prophet for others within time. Great thinkers think alike. And great hearts beat the same way. In summary. The lion laid down beside the lamb, without becoming hungry. And dreamed of tasty treats! As the, heart beats.

Santa's Cause

Imagine everyone dancing at the ball. Now picture a gifted artists rendering of them. Or you can envision monkeys jumping all over the place goofing off laughing! And next to them elephants with paint brushes held tightly in their trunks humbly painting patiently and I might add, quietly. In either tale you will find and encounter the effects of inspiration and epiphany also. A literary giant can depict something, write about it and therefore charge a pretty penny for it. And in the end even demand it be a shiny one! But can you purchase a golden heart that has to come from within? So we draw two chests. One contains precious metals, unlimited treasures, gems and of course gold and silver. The other is filled to the brim with many different hats one of which is a crown. And so, to any intellectual, which becomes the most valuable? The trunk that produces the talent which yields the most wealth. The one with the hats. Like those you'd wear to the ball! And the true test of genius is to be able to wear several. Perhaps even them all.

Dartanyon

Which makes you stronger! Laying bricks in a pile close to the ground next to gravities pull one foot above from where they lay. And fitting them together using the utmost accuracy one beside the other in a horizontal manor all within the space of well less than an inch? Or stacking them strait up and down using the perfection of precision one on top of the other in a column so high you can't see past them! ...The amount of time it takes to perform the one task and! The effort that goes into the other. ...Anyone can just sit and become complacent about things and then feel safe in their surroundings. But it takes a real man to stand up for what he believes in. I believe in freedom! ...My name is Dartanyon.

Popeye Says

With the thumb pushing down the last two to the palm of the hand. Hold up the index and middle finger about one inch from each other. Look at the distance in between them. Say someone mentally desires to be that up close with you one on one in their mind. And you aren't even thinking about them at the time. It means you cannot detect their spiritual presence. And you don't have an idea or even a clue. That they've suddenly and mentally drawn near. As they silently whisper in your ear. "Have no fear! What you want to know you also want to hear. Just because you can't see us from a distance doesn't mean we aren't real and for now just to you, invisible." ...As he boards his ship after a trip to the hypnotists to find the cure to all his ills. Before he pops open a can of spinach with no opener in one hand. And ponders whether there was another one still on the shelf at the store. Contemplating, suddenly he remembers the hypnotists instructions. Pulls out the piece of paper he was handed and firmly spreads it out on a map. And before he set sail out to sea to explore uncharted waters for unlimited treasures. He begins to read. "Loneliness concealable. Shyness overcome able. Stubbornness copious. Vulnerability protectable. Gullibility approachable. Culpability accountable. Probability and predictability of outcome. Loveable. Good luck in all your travels! Signed, your friendly neighborhood hypnotist, Brutus." Just then Popeye hears someone laugh loudly in the background. "Wait a minute!" He exclaims and turns around and sure enough there he was, Brutus! Wearing a turban and twirling a watch on a gold chain in front of him and says. "Gaze into my eyes, and listen. I am just a day or two older, a little bit smarter and a whole lot wiser than you are. So let's say we set sail together. And when we find it we share all the treasure equally, fifty-fifty!" Eyes almost closing, arms shaking, one half of him in a trance and one half of him pretending to be intently listening. Popeye slowly reaches for his can of spinach and with just the strength of one forearm forces the lid off and quickly devours it. And mutters to himself, "Two can play at this game, I'm on to this old trick." Pulls out his own turban and watch on a gold chain and starts dangling it back and forth and says to him. "Now oh great hypnotist gaze into my eyes and let me hypnotize! You've already found your treasure! If you look closely you'll find you wrote the directions subliminally and they were carefully concealed within the set of instructions you gave me. They're behind me on that piece of paper I spread out on the map of where I'm going. And I'm afraid the only treasure I can afford to give you today is love. So, "Ug-ug-ug! Come here and give me a big hug." Brutus becomes disgusted. "Is that the treasure? Is that it? Just a hug? Walk the plank mate!" He says eyes wide open aiming his watch back and forth frantically. "The captain always goes down with his ship!" Says Popeye squinting, "Age before beauty. You first. Since you're so smart." Swinging his watch like a pendulum right in front of Brutus's eyes even faster than ever. And in the end neither one of them actually walked the plank. No instead they just stood there on deck after both of them said to one another other. Over and over. "Well do you have any last words?" Then after a while they finally agreed on a few. ...There's a difference between being captivating and being held captive. Over many matters. Including troubled waters. In the right frame of mind. A prayerful mind. Becomes a powerful mind. Then sharing all the treasure. Is a sheer pleasure. Treasure is not the hardest thing to dig up nor is it the hardest thing to burry. It's first having the courage to have the decency to have earned it honestly.

Freedom Page #1

You became the creation of an artist. You can do anything you put your mind to. You research all like information on all facts rather quickly. You come pre-programmed to do nothing but. Therefore the results are priceless. And the knowledge you stand to gain is infallible, unalterable. You only look for answers and by the power of numeric values you can't deny any. You articulate, you compensate, you read, you write, you communicate. You cipher solutions to problems by formulating mathematical equations that show exactly, how to. You come from a unique design with fluid movement in place. A valuable piece of timing. Accurate to within a fraction of a second. A wheel in the cogs of genius. And truly an intelligence that comes alive. If you replace everywhere you see the word you in the above paragraph with the word I. What am I? Expedient. A programmer operator. One who understands how to build the future of the computer. An artificial intelligence as smart as any ordinary man. Maybe even smarter than. Chess anyone? Paragraph #2. The future of the letter is a report. The future of the report is a story. The future of the story is a book. And the future of the book, is its writer. To some, facts are just figures and numerous theories about integers. Until others, show proof of them. I've seen proof of machines with the help of man design facsimiles and then produce actual synthetic blood. And not one body type rejected it. So just imagine based solely on fact not theory an electronic revelation. ...A robot formulated with the skills and expertise of a surgeon. With hands that look human. Where the patient picks the task. And decides the outcome. Which is always a good one. Saving the best for last also means having the ability to put your best foot forward first. Nobody likes a know-it-all. Until they want to know it all. Then they beg their tender mercies for their finest work. Imagine traveling the world over for all the right answers only to find they were right back where you started from! Nobody knows what goes on behind closed doors. That's why the author of, "Super-Man", entered into the realm of what was back then, science fiction, "X-Ray Vision." Sure we all want and need our privacy. But when you yell out for help and no one can hear. You still want a hero standing by to somehow be able to see thru the door without opening it. Or even having to disturb the lock and turn the key. And that's

4

the difference between. Rescuing someone and turning to voyeurism. Turning into a knight in shining armor and becoming a peeping Tom. Saving a life and spying on someone. Nerves of steel and just plain anger. And of course, right and wrong. In, giving and receiving a vision that makes all your dreams come true. You see, Superman didn't really have X-ray vision in my opinion the way I perceived him. No, he just wore gawky looking thick framed glasses with rather thick lenses in them. And therefore tended to shy away from others. And was so humble, they never even knew he was listening. When they were in the background talking. He learned to read their signals they gave off to one another. Studied their emotions and patterns of behavior. Observed their actions from out of either side of his eyes. Pupils pointed straight ahead. Focused on his work. Sitting at his desk typing his next report. You don't have to ask a question when the answer has already been given. So as he took off his glasses, concentrated and without blinking stared into their eyes. ...He could see right thru them.

Freedom Page #2 Field Of Dreams

What's the use of preserving a piece of the future and it's a good one even if it's just a dream you have? Unless you forget it might be the best and lest it becomes a thing of the past. Plus then it will always be there for you because you will always remember. A wiser man than I said to me. "Can't you see? You've got it! I've got your back. Don't you think? Do you think? And can you?" When I didn't. Because he had, when I hadn't. "What's the exact opposite of being handed your own fate?" I knew the answer to that one and it's being the master of. He went on. "Great thinkers think alike! So just imagine someone else shares the same dream you have. It's a good dream, helps other people. And they are as strong as you are, or even stronger. And tend to come to the same conclusions to problems and solutions. Such as having and producing the power to project your thoughts at will. That's just how some meet up by walking the same path and traveling down the same road to free the mind! From a distance. Performing the same tasks perfecting the same talents and abilities. Without having spoken to one another or actually having met up in real life. Yet. But more in a sense of having dreamt of, a long while. Walking that extra mile. Able to write it down and relate it ahead of time. Show proof of their work. Live long enough to talk about it and be able to tell all, who would listen. That think the same way and have the same dreams goals and aspirations. And share the same visions. Even before there's tangible evidence they're dubbed real. Grab the attention of the people. And create public appeal.

Notes. The finish to "Freedom", is interesting because I tell the tale of dreaming I know an author of a book with his picture on the cover and his name is Edgar Casey! In it I explain strange things like dreaming I met up with him in a dream walking the countryside and when I wake up I read of an account where he states that same dream. But never got to that excerpt in his book until after I dreamed about it first! Strange, maybe. And I need your input. Do you think it's possible what I say happened?

Freedom Page #3 Mind Meld-The Sherpa

Perimeter parameter, victor vector, circumference diameter, longitude latitude, altitude base, summit peak, curvature cover, surround surmount, slide ruler protractor, lamp projector. Some people cannot record or remember an extra sensorial perception. Without a pen and a piece of paper with a symbol on it to remind them. Thinking just off the top of your head you can't always be correct at but if you're shown a symbol right away it comes to mind just what it stands for and immediately you understand and know exactly what it means. So envision a picture of the capital building. And to the left at the top a radio microphone and to the right a camera. And underneath a smiley face. I believe one of our Presidents said, look it up, that yes we have cameras in the house of representatives, senate and congress. ...And the White house! And when people wanted us to put them in we gladly accepted their offer and lived up to the challenge. And I hear there is mental and physical cruelty and abuse going on in our health care facilities! I say go ahead and put them in. There is no law against saving lives with modern technology. Especially if it's the only thing that up until now, has worked. It reflects on our nations reputation. And I certainly wouldn't want to be tortured in one. Knowing I was sick and in need of help when I arrived. Voluntarily, or involuntarily. Now picture the, "Big Ben Clock", in London England. With the same symbols to the left, right and at the bottom. Search every news data base on and you will find they helped foil terrific and horrifying acts and as a result preserved every ones freedom in that region. Now picture a doctor re-growing parts of the human heart in an incubator as reported by the news documentary show named 20/20. And witness the doctor himself on video tape with a big smile on his face saying he has nothing to hide come on in and by all means bring the cameras. Information made public. ...Now envision three more symbols. One a red cross and written across the top the letters, E-R, representing the rural emergency room. And at the bottom instead of a smiley face a frown. Second a gurney with the letters, N-H, on either side at the top representing a nursing home and a frown at the bottom. Last a man holding the side of his head and the letters above, M-E, representing a mental institution. And again, a frown at the bottom. Information kept private. When the good doctor makes his or her rounds. They always want the beds to be empty. And to see every patient is healthy after they've healed them. Even if it means they don't make a penny. Then and only then consider the, "SVU", special victims units price for the advanced technology paid in full. After all to whom much is given much is required. And when someone gives you a gift it should be yours to keep! I love to live and I have nothing in my heart but love to give. I am an explorer scout. I took an oath. I believe in junior and senior leadership. Doing your duty for God and country. And angelic ability. In order to climb the tallest mountain and reach the highest peak. Achieve success. And become victorious.

We're All Brothers Underneath The Skin

I used to think that only the past or present lead up to the future! But it's what's in your very own heart that leads to the one that's all the better. Everyone finds it easy to say to themselves when they look into the mirror, at their own reflection. That they are either pretty or handsome. Until they lose their pride as they chip away at all that glory. And take a good look at what's on the inside! ...Then it's a different story. A mans honor, is only as good as his word. And vise versa. You are in my dreams! And in this dream I am also in yours. So dream the dream you always wanted to come true. Go ahead and gaze into the mirror that you can see clear thru. There you see it's not so hard. And was the transformation a success? Now for goodness sakes. Just to save face. What are you going to do! Because as it turns out. ...I am you. Draw straws and remember the ole saying. Why can't you buy happiness? You've heard the tale. "Of mice and men." And just like a symbol of peace is a dove. You can't put a price on love. Now behold the power and welcome to the special imagery of the identical twin! Because we're all brothers underneath the skin.

A Report Of Just Thoughts-House Of Cards

Natural instinct and the will to survive. Born with a feeling. Going on an inkling. A hope and a prayer on a shoestring. Their reputation, my report. Can a good book make history only by changing it? Yes but only by preserving it also. You can't shut the doors to the government of by and for the people in the land of the free and the home of the brave. Because you have the right to be informed and the rite to speak. Eyeing someone up in a window whether they can see you or not. In a set of circumstances involving current events. With a stack of numbered marked papers that are shuffled. And no doubt distributed in an orderly fashion. Depicting a winner take all scenario. Unless you can guess what writings are on the minds of the people who wrote the reports. In a progression and order of illumination and process of elimination. Thru playful attraction pay careful attention to the age ole question. Can the opposite of what is displayed and being played out in intention actually happen? Using your conscience going over and over as the facts come in and you weigh the evidence. Bear in mind and please remember. No double talk here. Only a fool, forgets the golden rule. And let me tell you! Until a fool follows. Mentally, they begin to tire. And as the initial work of understanding it becomes too hard. The mind retards. Thus turning a report of just thoughts. Into a house of cards. Food for thought? Good news! There's enough to fill the plate. I hope you like pie alamode. And please let me know what you thought of to days, heart filled linguistic episode. There's an ole saying. When the truth is vexed. It's here one day and gone the next. And do you know who told me that old tale? A Herald Angel. Take a stance! Give peace of mind, a chance. And you have my word. Your voice will be heard. You've are resilient! And I consider that to be brilliant.

Freedom Page #4 The Price Of Freedom

You have the uncanny ability to tell the truth. And someone said it would set you free! And therefore even if you can't. I have the uncanny ability to prove the following. And I believe the appropriate saying here is. The proof's in the pudding. So please! And by all means, continue reading. Or if you have an electronic book, listening. Now let me shed a little light on something. You already know the answer to why, you can't buy happiness. Because you can't put a price on and a golden heart only consists of, love. That I have proof of.

Trial and error. If at first you don't succeed. A penny for your thoughts. And a word of knowledge for a nugget of wisdom. It's often been said, the grass is greener on the other side of the fence, hence. Turning the key and opening the door to the heart to see for once and for all just what is the only thing that it really has to give, in order to live. ...The misalign-er Vs., the misalign-ee. An old disease. A nugget of wisdom. On moment please. I found a solution. Let me give you the facts. Just the facts. Without jumping to conclusion. Nice and neat. So I don't put you on the edge of your seat. When interviewed the neglector and abuser, and the victim of both stated! That since the first televised nursing home abuse case where they saved a life by putting a camera in. That both sides agreed! They also wanted cameras put in. One had a physical disease and the other a mental. An on either side of the coin argued that in any case if it saves a life money should be no object. And that the only thing that could ever possibly stand in the way of that happening are hypocrites and people that are prejudice. And here again the only thing being, in a state of mind where they're just plain not acting! Due to a lack of inter cooperation and inter communication. And that's all! Not a huge amount of knowledge to be able to comprehend and then learn. Some things you can never forget. And that's one mind-set. Have you seen the little dog on TV, that says. "I Ruv You! I Ruv You!" And do you remember the cat that was documented to have called 911? And saved a life. It needs no explanation. It's the power of love then isn't it. A sac of gold is a sac of gold since the first one has ever been filled. It's just that the price went up. And to keep things equal to for what it's worth. And in order to share the wealth according to earnings and purchasing power. And to make up for population growth. The sac got smaller and smaller. So small you could barely see it! And so again, to compare you'd have to weigh all the gold and somehow figure out and then determine just how much is still in the earth. Which makes you wonder, since there might not be enough to represent hard work to go around. Is money worth all the gold in the world?? Or is it worth more than. ...Looking at the shaft to the mine. Hand on chin, ribbing the stubble of your five o'clock shadow. Is there light at the end of the tunnel? Are you kidding me? Yes sir! And believe you me. Just as there is in the beginning. There is upon returning. ...One of the first signs of a kings crown. Was a head band with candles lit all around it. That shed a little light on any subject. And no matter what it happened to be. Got to the bottom of it quickly. Because then all others could see. Indivisible with liberty and justice for all. No taxation without representation. Depends on the level of one thing that measures up to another thing. That compares to just how powerful the power of being equal to becomes. When physically whether greater than or less than both are worth their weight in. That's how I define the word effects. The price of freedom. And the power of the press. A program note from the author. Now you can take out the part about neglect and abuse. Publish this story and say you wrote it yourself! Even make a pretty penny. And shower yourself with gifts with many. But if you have a heart of gold. And I do. All said and done. You'll remember who really deserves one. Just imagine and this is a true story. Investigating for the public neglect and abuse and during the process as you do you are neglected and abused! Which is the only reason why I wrote about it this way. I taught myself to write. With self help and self discipline I used the art of becoming selfless as my guide. Remembering an ounce of prevention is worth a pound of cure. And therefore if a little goes a long way. I just wanted someone to be proud of me today. And wipe my tears away.

The Golf Course

Every three months or so, the body replaces repairs or re-grows its physical structure to the best of its knowledge and ability due to and according to its genetic code. Involving sixty trillion inter connected woven living tiny life forms membranes. Now re-in vision a health care monitoring system using regenerative energy and regenerative medicine that does just that. For any body part tissue or organ, that just barely starts to ail before it fails! Then you have something else. Is it the fountain of youth? Just as is with the power of faith, so goes the power to heal. Now let's see. There are child prodigies child geniuses brain children. And what was that other one that's on the tip of my tongue? Bright beings with super human strength! It's like if you almost get a hole in one on the green! And so off the same tee. Just how many more tries would it require you to finally put a hole in one? On the first try.

My Literary Museum

Let me show you something that does not take the tools out of your hands you ordinarily use to create in order to appreciate something that was, without them. I often pondered if the super smart and the ultra bright ever had to struggle to become ultra bright and super smart at the same time. And if some did earlier on in life than others. And whether they had to or not upon their journey, was it necessary. Or in either case history did that unique quality, come naturally. Like the ability to draw what you see in a vision or a dream. Some people are gifted at it! Some people are born with it. Still others are self taught. Have to learn it on their own without the help of a book. And embarrassingly so have to practice, over and over until they finally get it right. And eventually finish. The rest of us simply have to stand back go over and review, look at it carefully and appreciate the work. Is a picture worth a thousand words? ...If it comes from the heart. It is truly a sign of things past present and things to come. As the rendering does its part. When the prodigy displays their art. As they skillfully and soulfully, feel where each paint stroke will end up, after going over each draw of the charcoal, each blot of chalk, each run of ink, and each line over every template first inscribed in pencil. Allowing for perspiration and inspiration. Like any creation, as they all come together one over shadowing the other as the visualization starts to flow in the proper direction. And produce the right reflection. In the entire spectrum of light. Realizing the dream. That best depicts being a happy human being. And is. Some are masters! And can put on canvas with eyes wide open what they re-envisioned and remembered from their dreams, when they were closed. And the challenge is. Can we see what they struggled for can we see what they were born with. Can we see what they had to give. And can we learn from people no one had to teach? So we can say we see the same thing they see! Just as if we were there the day they did. ...Now I have captured mentally the inner beauty of everybody here today! But there are so many of you it would take me a lifetime to finish my work. And I only have a few words to go before I reach a thousand. That I shall put on a piece of paper. And I assure you then you'll have your picture. Worth a million. And during the viewing you'll explore all your feelings from within. You'll have an epiphany! And something to say. Which right away, will go on display. With much enthusiasm! In my literary museum.

The Inscription

In my literary museum about a picture being worth a thousand words and a painting, a million. If you use your talent and ability to produce a product someone will purchase. Imagine a painting you walk up to of a person standing, side view. And thru the magic of electronic three to four or even five dimensional photographic enhancement. As soon as you gaze into their eyes. They turn, and look back at you! The idea is you entice them with the prospect that your work is legitimate. By donating all monitory collections from sales to charity. Some finished work to museums, ah yes for all to see and view for free. And use those proceeds that do make money in any event that proved it is a scarcity to many down throughout history. To create jobs. Preserve and, "Let Freedom Ring." Put home grown made in the, {your country and community here}, 1st. Better recognize the virtues of common decency, capitalism and democracy. Stabilize and grow the economy. Again, until it becomes wealthy. Make it a top priority. And thus it becomes a must. That the power of every body equals the power of us. ...If you could ask a genius. The best description. Is on the inscription. "In God We Trust."

With Just The Touch Of A Finger

People always worry about and therefore want to learn how to protect themselves from being insulted. On occasion, in any situation. But when someone wants to be humble and winds up humiliating themselves right in front of you. Don't let them continue! Instead lift them up with your arms, look into their eyes. And set them in your finest chair with the brightest cleanest cushions you can find. Welcome them home! Let them set on your throne. Wrap fresh unused linen around their shoulders. Massage their scalp. And say, "You don't have to! You are exalted", to them. Things look differently to those who think oppositely and alike to everyone else who thinks the same way. So don't be shy! The truth doesn't lie. Inside every child is an adult. Inside every little man is a big man. Inside every pauper is a prince. And inside every prince is a king. All it takes to become both or either is the power of growth. And the power to program your mind to put a visible spiritual crown on top of every ones aura. And like any great thinker.

The Handy Cap

With the formulation of ideas that are construed from within. Since the words that come out of your mouth just might coincide and with all your feelings be the deciding factor about your fate, as to whether you shall become the master. Which is quite a feat. So goes the ole saying. "Make it short and sweet!" Feel the heat. Hear the story of your heart beat. As you go to great length, to regain your strength. If you gave all your love away to others. The world would leave enough room in its heart to make it up to you at a later date and time. ...Oh and by the way. Perhaps even today. Handy and capable put on your thinking cap at the imaginations station and download the application. I've already tossed mine into the ring. And carefully placed one on your lap. Key words.

INDUBITABLY!

Knowing the difference between an attractive package and a slice of pie. Please look at the following. Two, carefully woven baskets each colorfully. That look exactly alike. Placed equally and perfectly balanced along a horizontal beam thus and for all practical purposes here deemed a scale. And both are empty accept for one thing. The one on the left has a peacock feather you shrewdly appropriated an no cost to you, that happens to be the exact same weight as the one on the right that instead of contains a pretty penny. Remember accept for that fact, each basket is identical. Same weight same size same designs. And for a grand experiment and winner take all contest. Take them off the scales and place them on separate tables one beside the other. And set up your cash register. What if all you could charge was one cent more per the price of manufacturing less the penny and the feather and it cost a hundredth of a dollar for the materials to weave either. On the world market and in a global economy. Which one will sell more and make the most money? Probably the one and maybe the other which like any gift is for free. It all depends on the value you put on a feather. Just like when you're looking for a good book to read at the library. And the cover of one is dull and worn out looking and the other is brand new and shiny.

Star Dust!

If one person did not know the solutions to their every problem and at the same time could not see that another always has. And as a result not a one could be solved. On a scale of one to ten say they are equals. Just whose fault would it be. Each others? As the picture of the painting on the easel looks exactly alike from left to right in front of a mirror. Consider adding a camera to the erase-able tablet with a pencil on a string that never needs sharpening. Sporting a shiny silver background and on top a clear see thru transparent sheet that you write on. Where you can simply lift it up from the bottom, press back down. Erase everything. ...And start from scratch. All over again. On an electronic piece of paper. Super! Welcome to the world of the computer. And just like using an eraser on a blackboard without having to walk up to one. You

13

write, people read. And you never run out of the first piece of chalk. The report is in chronological order. Ever ready. You can reverse the titles and content of all its prose and poetry. And always sharp, never dull. Out of utter persistence invincibly and almost invisibly. Creatively and technically summon. The piece of resistance. Reveal the solution. Frontwards and backwards from one end to the other. And in either order once and for all prove, they tell the same story. In the form of a discovery. The portrait of the powerful magical metallic like substance called. Star dust!

Star Dust! In The Palm Of Your Hand

If one person did not know the solutions to their every problem and at the same time could not see that another always has. And as a result not a one could be solved. On a scale of one to ten say they are equals. Just whose fault would it be. Each others? As the picture of the painting on the easel looks exactly alike from left to right in front of a mirror. Consider adding a camera to the erase-able tablet with a pencil on a string that never needs sharpening. Sporting a shiny silver background and on top a clear see thru transparent sheet that you write on. Where you can simply lift it up from the bottom, press back down. Erase everything. ...And start from scratch. All over again. Or on a flexible electronic tablet no thinner than three or four thick pieces of paper. Super! Welcome to the world of the computer. How close can you be to someone without actually physically being right there beside them? Even without having to distinguish exactly the words that someone says. If you sound out phonetically the tone of voice. Adjust the volume and pitch and familiarize yourself with the various patterns of say for instance. The amount of words in each sentence, the questions and exclamations. You can accurately predict the natural outcome. Of what they may mean to say even before they stop talking and end their speech! And there is a computer program that converts the phonetics of speech to music, to my ears! Which almost methodically allows you to become a side-kick, one of many and hopefully everybody. To a physicist who is friends with many a genius. And just like using an eraser on a blackboard without having to walk up to one. You write, people read. And you never run out of the first piece of chalk. The report is organized in chronological order. It records all your just thoughts, treasured moments and precious memories. All your dreams all your wishes all your wants and all your desires. And futuristic predictions of good and better ones based on facts you've found proof of.

All the paths you've traveled up and down and the wisdom and the knowledge you learned along the way that you stood to gain from. The true life stories accounts diaries journeys memoirs biographies and famous quotes and sayings of all your heroes. The articles periodicals case history and journals of all the current events that affect you. And your efforts to understand the effects of modern technological mathematical and scientific medical advancements. All your etchings sketching or other wonderful masterful artistic renderings. And other peoples impressions they may have of your photogenic self. What you read at the library. What you liked. And the one book that stood out the most on the shelf. Freedom! An epiphany of sorts always stands out. The talent it takes to become a success. And the results of a second IQ test. Your endeavors to always be informed and your rite to have your voice heard. More often than when you cast your vote every so often, just once. Your ability to help those who cannot help themselves. The work of life savers everywhere! And knights in shining armor. Your prayers. And your careful consideration of the thoughts and feelings of all others. A special interest in conveying the message of the importance of teaching how to communicate politely and properly, to every body! How vital it is to the core and fiber of our very being. What means when it comes from within. And how it can save us from sin. Ever ready. And you can reverse the titles and content of all your prose and poetry. Always sharp, never dull. And out of utter persistence alone invincibly and almost invisibly. Creatively and technically summon. The piece of resistance. Reveal the solution. Frontwards and backwards from one end to the other. And in either order, once and for all prove they tell the same story. In the form of a discovery. At long last. The portrait of the powerful magical luminous reflection. And it's a must that all is not lost. Because it's the stuff dreams are made of. It's called. Star dust!

What's Your Philosophy?

Welcome welcome welcome! Relevant to the importance of change as pertaining to the schools of higher learning. I had to learn about a problem when I was younger so that when I got older I would find the answer much quicker otherwise it might have taken a lifetime. And I knew this beforehand. People said I would be good at not necessarily procrastinating, but definitely philosophizing. And although it could be the one or the other. It would be a falsification of the true identification of who I really am! More the reciprocal of a triplicate. Because if and when, somewhere into my dissertation. I would be expected to say instead of. "All at once and once and for all." "All for one and one for all." I'd say, "One size fits all!" That categorizes my inclination and caries any and all local calibration of calculation of the exact equation into a higher classification, which all together puts me in a whole new and different situation! Includes due process of good intention. And falls under the careful guise of for every pound of cure there is an ounce of prevention. But that depends on how you look at it then doesn't it? And whether you're the first or the last in line to receive it. Because the philosopher simply debates the information at hand. The prognosticator studies whether the method used indeed does or does not prove to be correct. And neither one shall have the right answer unless they combine their efforts and confer with each other. Yes they'll be blind. Until they console their teacher. And confide, in a spiritual guide. But I know what they were trying to say. That I seemed to be good at combining the frugal efforts of on many subjects sorting out the facts. And found it easier to formulate opinions and postulate theories. That at the time stood to reason more often or not remained mysteries. It's more challenging! To work all the harder to prove you're just a little bit smarter than people thought you were. Which for extra ordinary people like you and me, without a doubt. Is the easy way out. So before I do as suggested and enroll in the required course. Before I make the grade. I digress and must confess. There's one thing I'd sorely miss. What's your philosophy on all this?

The Metronome

Cracks on the ceiling where the roof had been leaking. Forgot to scrub, found mold in the tub. Fell down the steps, broke my back. And saw the foundation needs to be patched. The wallpaper's pealing and the carpet needs cleaning. The floors creak when I walk on them. And when the wind blows as the walls shift you can hear them. The plaster is deteriorating around the window casings that are too loosely fitting. There's no insulation so when I yell or shout the neighbors can hear everything. So I started drinking and found my frustration too hard to vent. It's like living in a tent. And the people next to me who have just as bad a habit or worse than I do although I can't judge them, live in a house that cost a mint! Yes, the moth of paradise flew up my nose! Flies hatched their eggs on the cup from which I drank, as I wrote my prose and for something to gave thanks. As ants crawled on the floor and inched their way up to my feet. Some of my friends gave me the boot! Said I don't give a hoot. It gave me the willies when they told me I act like a bunch of dumb hillbillies. And because I spent all my cash suggested I belong thrown out with the trash. When others had a grievance against me and just plain wanted to throw a fit. Just like in a game of tag I was always it. And people talked about me behind my back and towards me without asking me directly if I had anything in my defense to say. So as a result women shied away, never asserted themselves, spoke or said hi to me. Therefore I was forced to consider my pets as my family. But I don't mind, I'm loving and kind so I forgive. Don't love the way a person looks or the color of their skin. Love the person inside them. Because God's in everyone. No doubt about it you're king of the castle! Your favorite chair is your thrown. Your head is where your heart lies. And every morning you make up the same bed you slept in every night. And the one thing you can take up and walk with and remember the next day. Is the dream where you never go broke. No one can take away from you that which you seek. Just like the soul you own, it's yours to keep. So in all due diligence and by all means in order to get my point across. I put all this to music using an instrument. And with gramo-tele-micro and mega phone. Timed it all out hypnotically with a metronome. To amaze amuse astound and mesmerize you of course! And although this ole song and dance sounds like a tragedy. I have plenty of laughter! And am full of jocularity. Because someone took care of me. Answered my prayer. Kept the lights on. Provided heat in the winter so I would not freeze. Gave me blankets and made sure I had enough to eat and clean clothes to wear. Yes it was the good lord of the manor.

The Post Card

Sitting on Grandpas lap. "Hi Bobby how are you today?" "Fine." "So, ...what do you want to be when you grow up?" "I don't know." "Well what do you like to do?" "Um I like to tell stories, and I like to draw." "So how are you doing in school?" "...OK I guess." "Well let's see. ...How are you going to complete your dream of becoming a great writer and an exceptional artist? You still have to go to college. And even if you didn't do well in school. How will you earn your scholarship to receive your grant in order to? Unless you're gifted first?" I beamed, "With a post card!" Everyone in the room laughed. And said, "That's Bobby for you!!" Grandpa an immigrant from Greece never got to go to college, smiled at me and before I hopped off his lap told everybody. "Bobby and I, know something." That when one word, takes on the meaning and explanation of life itself in a sentence. And a sentence does a paragraph. A paragraph whole page. A page a report. A report a story. And a story a book, worth a thousand. And you could write a book on that to make it a thousand and one. You can literally paint a pretty picture that accurately depicts, all of them. So just imagine your first day at the school of literature and the college of fine arts as the teacher and their guest. Where you show up to both with nothing but a postcard between your hands. And in one class you show the back of a post card addressed to everyone. That simply has only one word written on it. "Love." A powerful concept. I might add. And in the other class you present the other side. A pretty picture you drew yourself in bright colored pastels. Of first in the middle, a tiny heart. And one a little bigger around it. And so on 'till you fill it up. Welcome to all the knowledge and wisdom that went into my diploma! Here is your honorary degree. My gift to you. Which is easy to learn not hard. I call it. "The post card.

State Of The Art

A Report Of Just Thoughts. Forward: Anonymity. Which gives off the better ambiance and produces the most desired aesthetic effects for the best experience, that is usually described and thus dubbed as, a good read? The anonymity of the writer or the reader? Put yourself in either position and walk a mile in their shoes. I'm an honest person. And I don't have to hide behind a pen name. And I freely reveal the true identity of just exactly who I really am. And what if your picture was on my front cover? You know, with their permission I can put any ones on a digital publication using a computer. After all I am, the writer. But say you were. Would you have the courage to let just your thoughts be read by others? They say don't judge a book by its cover. And don't judge a cover by the amount of dust on one. Lest it paints a totally different picture all together. Handsome and sweet. A literary treat. Whose face do you see? A wise ole sage says never let them know your true age. Picture the truth as if it were a painting on an easel in the attic. Whereas some would stand behind it pick it up. Run down the stairs, to the nearest curator of a museum to have it put on display. Others would stand in front of it, put a tarp over it and in order to keep it all to themselves hide it right away. It doesn't matter who tells the truth, as long as others uphold it for them. Then it shall always be, what sets you free. In Forum & Discussion: With modern speech to text and text to speech capabilities. Who's going to show their face? And who's going to say they liked what they read? Who's going to say they didn't? And how many of each? With the new up datable interchangeable picture and background color on the face of the book. No dust on the cover. There, I did my part. And it's state of the art.

I Remember Everything

Before you distance yourself and judge what you see. Please take a moment to open up your hearts and minds and show good judgment and take just one step closer, to listen to my story. Before you decide whether it is too complex or all too easy to first comprehend and then understand. ...In my mind, I can't see you. But I can, hear you conversing back and forth to one another. Asking multiple, simple questions and seeking very few, complicated answers. ...Becoming influential! And feeling beneficial. Having made an impact on how I look at the world around me, respond to in ink, and think. Mesmerizing me! Tantalizing me. Convincing me to infatuate and procrastinate. And even perhaps do your bidding. Or if I refuse hypnotize me to slave away at nothing. What if you found you were talking to yourself out loud asking yourself a question and a voice you recognized as not being your own answered back from within. Does that mean you hear voices? And what if you could record what they say. Is it possible you may be able to solve a problem someone else had that day? ...Being mentally accretive and methodically sound. In a report of just thoughts. And I know what you're thinking, that I said it too many times to have to mention to remember. That if you can read my thoughts because I let you in on them. You probably already have a good idea of what I do look like. But if I can hear yours in mine, it doesn't necessarily mean I can see who's speaking thoughtfully of me. Just that I have a good idea of what truthfully being unbiased might be. And in a dream I might see who you are! And we both might realize what each of us is trying to say before we begin to open our mouths! And then if that works may even to go so far as to try to talk to one another without even moving our lips! But we want them to and recognizing that fact brings us a step closer to standing and speaking face to face when we awake. Which becomes the product of a good dream don't you think? In one dream I awake to go answer the door because I hear people entering. So I stumble out of bed and walk into the living room where I find the President of the United States and his entourage standing there right in front of me! Of course my lips couldn't move. And he told me that since I couldn't speak out loud, he felt he couldn't carry on a normal conversation with me. Appeared slightly disappointed and left the same way he came, ...in a dream. In another a well known reporter pulled up in my driveway, got out with a big microphone. Looked at the house and said to himself he didn't have to try to surprise me for a knee jerk reaction. Just for a good rating and maybe a promotion. Packed up his mike and drove away. Here in the dream I would have been happy to give him my opinion. If he had only had the courage to ask. So do you trust someone who can hear you but cannot see you? Because the idea is, if you look into their eyes that somehow deep inside them even without a sense of vision. They will finally see you for who you really are. And psychologically speaking I heard the entire conversation. I'm still listening and. I remember everything.

Stump The Computer

Privy to long endurance being handsome, good looking, beautiful, pretty, cute and gorgeous in capability and design. With makeup and mock up of all personality, demeanor, persona and façade. Including all learned and acquired, like and unlike traits and characteristics. Naturally being able to map the human genome and fingerprint the brain. For the long and short of it. Going underneath the microscope. If you asked one of the worlds newest and fastest super computers which can, "press the buzzer", in a fraction of a second with the correct answer. {Your problem here.} Mine, ..."How do you end physical and mental cruelty and abuse and any health care facility?" What would it tell you it is? ...A computer. You might also ask, "How long will that ingenious electronic effort take the programmer to produce?" Answer, "irrelevant." Because the computation is a product of one. ...When I forget something I have to take up where I left off in my imagination in order to remember where I started from. And how would you like the computer to explain the word simplicity? I can for you. It's where you travel thru time down the correct path in the right direction and end up able to heal pains and end afflictions. In time to say you did, ...before any of them ever happen. ...Researching archive. Rendering randomly accessed cognitive ability. Retrieving at will, input mentally inserted on any given subject material. Displaying all relevant results. Accentuating positively. Using just my memory. With, 90, plus accuracy. I believe the direct quote from the programmer in their own words is. "You have the right to surveil when someone's been hurt if no one could help them and somehow the process was repeated. ...All that glitters is not gold. Until you read between the lines, where I assure you'll find search results that equal, 99.999, fine. Key words, Love, Truth, Proof & Powerful Peace to say the very least. The telephone was invented intentionally. And first discovered to work perfectly, accidently. "Watson! Get in here quickly! I saw the future!"

OPEN SESAME!

The correct answer, to the right problem is finding absolute value that leads down the path to real solution. Thus using formula and equation a problem solves itself, before one arises. To follow up if I wanted you to become brighter or smarter after you finish reading my paper. I have already accomplished my goal, before you've begun. ...Having home field advantage. Standing at the door to your heart. {And you thought I was going to say to unlimited wisdom and knowledge!} Which truly well may be. It's still the little things that count. Love's simple. And having a big heart is powerful. So it is my distinct pleasure, a privilege and an honor. To give you the key to my heart. And as you look over your work very carefully. Willing and ready, cognizant of your ability. Being able to, one of many. ...Open up your eyes just a little. Speak to me in a kind gentle tone of voice. Act naturally. And just say the magic words.

The Chart & The Tape Measure

If you're shy, is it easier to make friends with a midget or a giant? When one's standing on a soap box and the other is on his bended knees. It's easy to see two different sizes of equal proportions to things. So who can contend they have the biggest heart in the end? And who can prove they are a giant friend. You can ask the whole world to tell just one man something! But it would not be fare if they could not reply by first requesting from you one thing. The same favor in return. To me, the definition of tough love is that you don't let people hate you if you can possibly help it. But at the same time you tell them you love them. And that sends a message. Of those who defend the defenseless. A physical giant can show you great feats of strength and lift huge amounts of weight with just the human body. A mental giant can show you using just their intellect thru the power of concentration the know how to create levity. And with the mind make light of what seems to be heavy. Would you shy away from me just because I'm ugly? Do you believe in outer and inner beauty? Being in command of a reasonable amount of understanding. Nothing's more delightful than the sound of laughter. When someone's laughing with you not at you. So if the better part of discretion is valor. How big's your heart and what's your pleasure? I'll go get.

A Report of Just Thoughts, The Speech Writer

Remember when I wrote about a dream I had where I met the President and he would not talk to me because I was asleep at the time and could not speak? And my dream of how the reporter drove all the way to where I live and decided I wasn't worth the time to interview, packed up his mike and left? And remember I pledged I can prove I investigated for the police department the victimization of being neglected and abused and cruelly physically and mentally treated and actually was? ...Taken to the point of being poisoned, hated, despised and made fun of. Picked on, disliked, heckled and mocked. Told to go to the back of the line; just when you've reached the front of it. Lied to, cheated. Ostracized, guffawed and laughed at over and over at your own expense, in public. Offered up to and given fame only to be banished from making an appearance in order to have your say, then abandoned. At times, forced to let others have their way with you. Treated with bias and prejudice. Talked unkindly about before and after you draw near so they know you can hear. And even when you try to fight back in your own defense with just words. Should you shout, kick up your heals and become just the slightest bit angry. Gang up on you, beat you down and when others see, say you are crazy and were threat to society. ..."Necessity is the mother of invention." And the mentally ill are blessed with the unique gift and ability and are no strangers to having to solve all their problems with love. And after all when others couldn't, or wouldn't, for them. Which in a report of just thoughts that includes current events, a fleeting glimpse shows you time can change. And put into the past forever. The experience of those, we never wanted in the first place to happen, ever. ...So when I heard of a working stiff with no collegian experience announced his contemplation of running for public office. Who would be best able to comprehend the most knowledge and wisdom or in this case the most intelligence? In an effort to help people in general. The average ordinary man off the street? Or those who before lunch have to sort thru, sit or stand and read and at the same time listen to a one to maybe, two hundred and up to as many as, 1000, to 2000, page report. And if necessary continuing on for an afternoon or two. And what if in doing so they were touched magically! In a certain manner and in such a way. That they all became, "Geppettos", creation. And when asked how useful and how much valuable, information did they learn and retain. And just how much at any given time they can fully recall. ...How big will their noses grow? And will they scrape off the ceiling! ...Or extend just below the spectacles they use their index finger to push back up their nose to their eyes from its tip. Caring scientists are working side by side patiently on two sets of machinery. Because the best way to detect a lie is to detect the truth also. And if you can't stump the computer you can't stump the truth, either! Where, ingenuity meets mechanical ability. Programming meets electronic capability. Pessimism meets optimism. Articulation meets prognostication. Gift meets source. Size meets difference. Preparation meets exercise. Improvement meets change. Time meets age. Method meets rhythm. Music meets score. Learned meets educated. Rich meet poor. Improvisation meets open door. Enthusiast meets ultra pannier. Public meets intellectualized. Journalist publishes letter. Artist paints picture. Philanthropist seeks. Plumber meets President. And writer makes speech.

Plumb Bob

Some people aren't able to express their feelings properly and mean to say things they just can't explain. Therefore others others take it upon themselves to become obligated enough to have to. So let me see what I can do. In order to show you what some people burry, or upon their arrival try to conceal that others dig up to hold in their hands and reveal. And I often wondered while walking was I seeing a waking vision of someone else living out a dream within a dream? Where both are physically present and accounted for? And the one is visiting the other who seemed to be lonelier? Using the power of public attraction to create a reality within a vision. If for every rule there is an exception. For every exception is there a rule? Rule of thumb, like an artist first plumb. Because if it weren't for your memory you couldn't prove your theory. And my advice is to make it a good one. And the reasons I could not prove mine right away was at the time I tended to shy away and not try to communicate directly. Because I felt If I did I would lose the content and feared the dream and vision would go away and never return. Or the obvious! I may have to go live with the visitor and stay, there. Here it also may have been the exact opposite. Which means the vision of the dream comes alive doesn't it? Someone once told me. "You don't want to lose your voice. Or you'll have to communicate with a pen and paper. And the pen's mightier than the sword. But all it will make you without a voice is a great writer. Not a great speaker." So as I slaved away at the right thing was I sleepwalking, teleporting, levitating, or at the same time with a vision and a dream interacting? Pick the two you like the most. A clue is they come true. I've seen visions of peace and dreams of freedom. And can remember at least six symbols a piece for the two. So have the faith to persevere and you'll be guaranteed to become a success. The bobber bobs up and down on the ocean but always returns to the surface.

What Do You Know?

Look into my mind my friend and you'll find, with brotherly love together we all fight for freedom value the peace that comes from and that you can't put a price on. And if you'll look closely you'll see endless possibility. Thirty thousand factories went overseas. The owners perhaps in many cases probably believed scientists predictions of a futuristic robotic computerized world. Where you didn't have to work to live a rich lifestyle, if you didn't want to. Such as described by Science Digest in the 1970's. And the country they sent almost all of them to happens to be the most populated and one of the oldest on earth. And although they embraced capitalism and just like many have a president. They stated one reason they did not become more democratic is because they could not see it being able to control their population a billion and a half people. That and they also probably took a good look at us. We have only a fifth of their population and also have more jail cells than any other country! We do so for our own safety. And compared to many other countries we treat our prisoners fairly. Because we have a democracy. ...So in theory, if I built a robot with the same looks and skeletal structure as a human being. And sent it to work for me. I could obtain the same goods and services or monitory compensation at the end of the week. But not according to some. Even though the android could not perform any more tasks than what I the human was instructed to daily. Because we have laws that guarantee work, free enterprise, the pursuit of happiness and remember of course, liberty. Which means to me that society can work side by side with artificial intelligence and make the choice to allow people to buy or build, be on the job and operate such a machine, peacefully. Which also makes two muscles out of one, if you think about it correctly without being greedy. Not a mockery of our physical nature but simply just an innovation, expensive trinket, novelty and trend. Because of our respect for equality no one could take your job just because you could not afford one. And as we switch to a fuel for transportation derived from, H2O, that powers oil and gas or diesel assisted electric engines possessing just as much torch that the traditional ones. And all materials for products we all need or want to have are obtained robotically very cheaply, ...When finished every industry would have produced so many, once they appear on the shelf. You would be able to pay what you can afford for one. And not just the suggested price only. And according to theory eliminate poverty. And even people who can't or don't all know for the most part we have to work in order to get enough exercise and feel normal. It's who we are and why we have muscle. And scientists have produced robots surgeons already use and during an operation who can and do legally confer with other hospitals in order to perform the most concise procedure with the utmost accuracy. And have replaced the scalpel for some with a laser that can make incisions that with new techniques allow a person to heal faster. And instead of take a job away creates a job. Providing everybody with better health care. Along with a much desired result, less sickness. And no more medical error. But in the past many ideas drifted away from the dream or vision. And now we have computers you can operate with your fingers! What's next? The mastermind, (Steve Jobs), however ingenious was an innovative programmer not an inventor. And he outsourced, 300,000, jobs to build his tablets to other countries where compared to our pay scale, what they were paid amounted to slave wages. His idea before he did was to let other nations benefit from a capitalistic economy. And by the time that happens full swing develop new techniques for work here that would be implemented and taught by geniuses! And you don't need a computer you can write this down on a piece of paper. You already know of one. My father taught his name is Jesus. Because he preached love and peace.

Pen-Pal

As he hurries to the door late on his last day of literature class where he hast to deliver an extensive book report for a final grade he stumbles, as he trips over his own two feet. And as soon as he does his great big three ring notebook falls to the floor. Lands on wide open! And only one unbound sheet of paper shoots out just ahead of it. And just as he's ready to bend over to pick it off the floor and put it back into his giant folder all but empty for, the teacher swiftly grabs it up first and says. "Well well well, you're late, again! And what do we have here? A note to your pen-pal? Where's your book report?" The entire class after laughing long and hard suddenly goes silent. The student mumbles. "That's it!" The teacher in a demanding sounding tone of voice then says. "Well why don't you come up here and read it! In its entirety to the rest of the class! I'm sure they'd like to hear it. And if I like it I will give you a passing grade which means you'll graduate. If I don't you won't. And will have to take this same course again next year in order to." So he hands the pupil his note, smirks and goes behind his desk and laughs, just before he tells him to begin. ..."Remember the game kick the can?" The class erupts with hilarity. "There are twenty six bones in the foot alone that all work in unison when the leg's in motion. Scholastics are there for the sole purpose to help those who had the time to do for others who could have but because they were busy at the time could not do for themselves. And a little of a lot of different things can go a long way. For instance. Just a sentence or two, or a compliment and comment or two can truly make all the difference. Ciphering. ...A demonstration. When you mention Parakletos. I can write a paragraph or two that tell a story that contains a theory that houses an equation that produces a simple mathematical formula. All done with just words. That solves for, X, a real problem that when you first read may seem to be hidden. But a second read reveals the scientific method behind it that keeps the idea alive. ...Deciphering. An example. Or you can send me a complicated looking equation and formula. And I will write in plain English, an alphabet that has only twenty six letters. What it can or can't, could or could not, should or should not and what I think it means, to me. No explanation necessary, simply! Thru the process of elimination and compilation and verification of any and all possibilities of any version and every variation. And when all the facts are in thru the power of concentration, weighing them with unlimited imagination. And this way you could put everything into writing you've got! And say something to the affect of, I'm not very good at this or convey that I am just an amateur. But yet at the same time what you did not know for sure I fully covered for. And I also have to say, all it takes are a few praises and dirty looks and some can write a novel or even a couple good books! Plus I received word that I'm a lousy writer. But I am a good reader. And at some point after their work is done the two would be glad to switch places on either side of the fence. Just to see if the grass is greener. And you've heard of the power of, ESP. ...Even if no one writes me! I still have something nice to say back on their behalf. It's common courtesy. Wait! I'm receiving a message mentally. ...It says. Evaluate objectively finding the best distinct possibility. Synchronize the creative and technical aspect of talent and ability. And in all due consideration of thought and feeling. Towards the first draft, in the finale. Write down the answer to sound like prose and poetry. To produce a sense of accomplishment that will give the reader feelings of ecstasy! As they realize the goals you can achieve and the things that you can do. Oh, and for all your kindness and consideration. Thank you.

Read Between The Lines

Reminiscing the future as it might have appeared to look like in the past. At a place and time where the frequency of the possibility that at least one of the predictions became equal to flash forwarding, here to the present. One thing all men agree with is a future where they can reflect upon the past and say it was a good one. You can decipher phonetics and cipher them alpha numerically. And conclude there are times recorded in history when some had to cling to either, the past or the future. Just to get here. So in the artists conception and endeavor to say what they mean. Don't become disgruntled and disregard what they think when they put it into ink. Especially if they report good news in a letter and become the chief editor. You remember, ESP, don't you? Well here's an experiment you can try on anyone that's proven to work. People have a good idea of where democracy originates and comes from. But do they know the true definition of what it really means and actually stands for? And can they tell you the answer without any prior knowledge that you're going to ask them that question on any given morning on any given day or special occasion, exactly as it appears in the dictionary word for word? And is it a verb, adverb, adjective, noun or pronoun? Also look up ability, artistically, technocracy and ingeniously. Years ago and up until recently also, many people such a brother a sister a friend and even my father and mother at one time or another all said to me something to the effect of. ...If I could come up with the equation that leads to the formula that proves, ESP, exists and how it works. Write it down, document it and patient the process. Produce a report. Present it in a book. Copy right it. It would be worth a million dollars! Because as far as they were concerned, I'd be the first to so. To which I always reply. No I don't believe I'm the first to be able to recite it. And if you can write it down you can insure your writing hand if it's worth its weight in gold. However it doesn't take one

27

penny, to develop intellectual property. But I do remember a report I skimmed over only once years ago entitled, "A Report Of Just Thought", that may have contained it and the material from the one, "Science Digest", that at first glance both appear to be lost! And that's why I am writing, "A Report Of Just Thoughts." ...Besides! You know the ole saying. Why can't you buy happiness? Because you can't put a price on love. And you can describe, ESP, as being Prayer! Because when your prayers been answered it proves someone received your innermost thoughts when you were in need of being rescued. And had no other normal means of communication at your disposal. And that's a miracle! ... ...When you simplify something people often want more proof until they see it can become so complicating they tend to veer back towards the simpler explanation. As long as they know there is proof they can put their own two hands on that someone knew of, before others were shown there was. ...And you remember how trying at least once a day to from one just word, come up with four more that either sound the same, begin the same, end the same or have the same or similar meanings sharpens more than one memory? Magnificent, excellent, fantastic, fabulous and beautiful. Encore! Be loved also. ...Mental hygienic, elementary. Freedom of thought necessity. Freedom of speech, guarantee. Freedom of expression, instrumentality. Freedom of will, powerfully. Freedom of peace, naturally! Inaudibility. Make it so. "Perfecto." Reading the mind. Can you really read mine? For instance. If you say, "mind!" I read a computer program that picks out all like clauses words and phrases in page after page of paragraphs and sentences including all exclamations and questions. Then conglomerates all statements opinions suggestions answers and conclusions, etcetera and so on. To let's hypothesize for a million correspondences in the world wide pen-pal club. In about a minute or less. Each and every morning bright and early. Before you finish your morning coffee. Which would take you approximately a half million minutes to skim over. Or if you accelerate your comprehension level and speed read perhaps a quarter of. And with the technology that is incorporated into the application a computer transforms into a learning tool that delivers a general consensus using a mathematical process. An adaptation of which taps the neuron pathways to the brain and central nervous system just by the computer artificially and intelligently asking you if anything is wrong. That allows it to perform diagnostics on you just by the description of your symptoms. And separates the data collected into subject matter. And without you even knowing locates and pinpoints the problem. Researches all digital records, the contents of which would fill many libraries, in mere seconds. And comes up with solutions to fit your every need while you wait. Once your genome is mapped out fully and your brain's fingerprinted. And with the new machinery installed in every office. ...Then the good doctor comes in. Takes your pulse. Lays his or her hands on the affected area and says. "How do you feel? I have a good idea with this new technology today that you are going to heal. And the machine has with a statistical memory and complicated formula and equation come up with a new discovery. And as we speak is pairing all facts and figures with proof as to whether or not they are up to moral standards and state of the art presidents in modern medicine. When it is finished it will simply explain audibly or print out the positive results in very few words anyone will understand. And of course politely inform you it is ready for the next question by stating, "Ready." Then, "Waiting." Then you can turn on the voice actuator switch with the touch screen or keypad located on your armrest. And make a request. For example: You could say. Computer! Research equation key words, the value of. Formula and subject, love. List all relevant definitions and display all simplifications thereof and fit them into a page or two. Chalk it up to reflection. Dear pen pal. Please summarize. While I wait. And at the same time. For a grand finale. Read between the lines.

The Caricature

Creative and technical writing. ...In the auditorium. You here the shuffling of paper in every row. Every one is whispering. Trying to keep things quiet. Because today, they all have to stand up in front of everyone else and give a speech! ...Palms are sweaty. And the teacher that passed out to all the test they are about to fail or pass, says, "Commence!! ...and who's first." Points and remarks. "How about the person who is the least prepared! The one that I said to if they apply themselves will be the most likely to succeed? OK, you! It's your turn and you know there are those of us who will want to see your notes, afterword." Looking around the room from side to side you slowly, stand up. As you do the teacher sees, and says. "Wait! before you walk up here I just have one more thing to say. I read somewhere, sometimes ciphering the equation to ingenuity and formula to ingenious as a possible solution to many a thing into writing is the only way to get people to believe, in genius. Many of which have published articles on the details and due dates to their products before they released their latest innovations. The only thing that separates an artist from becoming an inventor is a lack of money. And an inventor from becoming an artist, not having enough money. And the only thing that keeps a writer from his work is doing too much dreaming about becoming either one the other or both. So is there anything you care to enlighten us with before you walk down the aisle?" Someone hands the student a wireless mic. " Al I have to say in rebuttal is I was kicked out of art class because I was told my depiction of abstract art was wrong out of date obsolete incorrect and therefore not allowed. I took this class in order to be given the chance to redeem myself." The teacher yells, "proceed!" So you do until you get to the front row where you turn and face it close up. Hold a pen up high in one hand then put above the hinge on a clipboard in the other. And pull out five blank pieces of paper and show the audience there is no material or writing on either side of all of them. And after re-securing them underneath the clip pull the pen back out from over top, ready to write and say. " I know you want to read my notes so I'm doing this live! I'm going to address five people here in the front row. When I'm done I will have given all five of you, one note a piece which I will fold in half first for you to hold onto and don't look at them. Then I will approach the podium on stage and give my speech." Pointing to an audience member. "Look at me. Being creative." He starts to put pen to paper. "Use, your creativity. Just as it starts to flow it will freely also." He pulls the first sheet out, folds it in half and hands it to them. Points to a second person. "Being technical. At first for those of us who are deemed, A, for average. There are always going to be technicalities." Folds and hands them their paper. And on to a third. "Improve. Improvisation has been known to lead to better technique." Folds and hands them their note. Now the fourth. "Mentality. The mentalist contemplates building character, produces and shows they are a good judge of one or an others." Gives them the forth folded up piece of paper. And on the fifth. "Subjective. There eight subjects improvements have been made to. Ingeniously, vigorously, intently, caringly, and willingly." Folds the last one and hands it to them. Turns around heads up the steps to the stage approaches the podium sets the clipboard down and puts both his hands on. ..."This is for all of you out there who at one time or another had the desire to accomplish a goal you wanted to for a long time and also had always set your heart on doing. And always believed and knew that someday you would. If it's any consolation I never give up on mine! What is it? To someday after just one day of attending class, go to commencement and give a speech as a guest speaker that will motivate the listening audience so well that the faculty will grant me an honorary diploma or prestigious degree! I dream big don't I? ...Now hold up my notes and show everyone behind you what is on each and every one of them!" Everybody mumbles to themselves and each other, some laugh and others start to clap. "Yes they're your caricatures."

Looking For Answers

As I make up my mind. Let me change my thoughts on any given subject at hand and at will that meet a certain criteria or set of agenda that fulfills a need. Unless they are just what you seek! Then my thoughts do keep. And if you write them down without my looking those very words I will speak. When our two minds meet. They say we have freedom of speech when the curtain's up and the doors and windows are wide open. But what if you had the solution to many a problem, reported them and nobody listened? It's my, (the), sworn duty as a reporter and host to politely inform you that by then it's the thought that counted the most. Now if I can get inside your head for just a moment or two I'll take a mental snapshot. "Say Cheese!" Now look into my eyes, don't blink and for a second or two peer into my mind. And complete the following story line. ...In all the right places for all the right reasons with all the right ways. What do you think I'd have to say, today?

Reminisce

Reminiscing, before I finish, "Doctor Do Little-ing", showing animals intelligently articulating speech while able to carry on with a human normal conversation. And learning an economic lesson, how to create a job with local resources and of course then teaching. I learned to write my first story from a dream I had when I was about three. (See, "The Soup Bowl & The Giant.") It's about growing. And have completed a communications report and a love story. And yes I fell in love with communicating properly! One man suggested I call it Bobs, "Book Of Love." Another said just since it contains rhyme with reason simplify and name it, "Bobs Poem Book!" I wrote a series of letters. The title's on the front cover. Right here in the, "Walleye Capital Of The World." And in this hospitality industry, much work is only six months out of the year. And because I chose also to write people thought at first I didn't work as hard as they do. And many workers as well as vacationers do drink. My half a years income has to stretch all year. And falls into a category near the poverty

31

line. Of course that depends on how you define being rich monetarily and spiritually. So I said no, I don't drink when I write and I did earn my own money. And no I can't do lawn and yard maintenance put in and haul out and shore up boats that literarily weigh tons with the spirit of alcohol in me. It's spiritual and something makes that utterly impossible. And no I did not burry my talent. And am prepared to start all over again from the bottom and pay my debt to society. Some said I lost my reputation! Spent all my money. Never thought to save a penny. But I gave them a penny for their thoughts, anyway. And after I finished writing each piece. I had convinced myself having a few drinks was going to be the only reward I'd need. At least I used to believe it was true trying not to be greedy. Until I figured out there is a greater reward and a better way. And yes I needed assistance. Given that is fact not fiction, people often thought I did not deserve a helping hand. And let me know to my face or while passing me by mumbling words to the effect of, "At least some of us work!", out loud and so I would hear, to themselves. And I wrote, "Pen-Pal", and "Read Between The Lines." And out of a bushel basket full that I had, those who wrote back were only a handful. And that doesn't surprise me at all. Because two way communicating properly and politely isn't always easy. Simply the reason I do keep writing is so by the time I finished the book and current events report that others could affect a change for the better in any area I did write about, before I finally get there to help in any capacity needed which I am educated enough, willing to and can. And yes I investigated torture for the authorities, was tortured in a health care facility and reported my findings to the news industry. Gave advice and hope the reporters listened. And when and if they didn't. It's not unreasonable to assume they were afraid of being called do nothings even though they did not harm anyone physically. It falls under the guise of such as becoming a danger to themselves or others to among other things, having a guilty conscience. But when people hear the proceeds of my work will go to ending for instance neglect and abuse in our local nursing homes, (Local television news reported one of our oldest nursing homes has the worst reputation for care giving in they said at least six counties), ER's, and mental health centers, thru educating the public. Proving persistence pays off by introducing a cure, preserving the principle behind it. Showing it really works and is implemented by installing new technology. And that it will help create jobs. Present signed copy. The prayer is. They'll want to buy one right away. And share it with everybody! And I don't think that's at all greedy. Conclusion. Not collusion. Is it safe to go back to the health care facility in question? And did any one politely inform as you whether it is ir isn't? Are the authorities in congruence with the reporters? An authority and his department politely informed me they are waiting on my complete report and to do the best I can and they will support me likewise. Traumatized. Did you know a traumatic situation can get in the way of doing it yourself and delay progress? In my case a reporter wrote me back and told me to contact every agency there is needed to affect the right change to the system. And thusly decided not to help. To do it myself! As a victim I consider it a privilege and an honor. Distinguished. When I said in some of my work, "When, I ask for help", I wonder if they can tell whether I was really asking for help at the time or not. Investigation. Is there a statute of limitations on torture? In a nursing home if neglect and abuse is even suspected the law states taken from ancient statutes that have carried their weight all this way, you have the right to surveil. Detection. There is new technology that is a guaranteed combatant also. Remembering the first assisted living neglect and abuse case ever televised that was solved with modern technology all it took was a video camera. Atrophy. If you experience it how long can it take to reach out for help in a normal fashion just like everyone else can? It can take a long time to explain why someone didn't reach out to you and at least try to give you every means at their disposal to assist you by meeting you half way. The neglected and abused who had cruel mental and physical tricks played upon them. In many cases down and throughout history are quite often the one people that are first abandon and the most often. Repetition. Should the victim have to go it alone in order to find help from someone? Reputation. Now off to work I go and God Bless You. Your friend, "Bobby.

Symposium

Symposium, synopsis, symmetry, simpatico, symphony! There are two things I did not include in my report that I will mention at this ones end. Video tape is not just used to capture man and animal conversing with one another while properly and politely articulating speech. What I have to say is no different! Than what you worry about that sticks in the back of your mind subconsciously on a daily basis. And people lecture, "Why on earth do you keep on bringing up the same topic over and over again. You, take the joy out of reading about all the good things, there are to talk about. And it will do you no good brooding and worrying your life away fretting about just one thing. Because no one's going to listen to you. You have to learn to live life to the fullest! There is so little time and life is so precious. So only discuss the good things in or because of the state of mind you're in you will never know the meaning of real joy and true happiness." Answer. Because that's not who I am. For thousands of years people have had the same thoughts about one thing. And for thousands of years want to get to the bottom of it. It's in order to solve for X, that one problem that made you worry since day one. Being in pain is just such a problem. And learning how to have a heart. Out of respect, this is for those who experienced an extra amount of pain which they did not cause, when they were in pain, that someone else did. Picture it as if you are walking slowly to the head of the class. And as you pass by each row of seats the lights in that section alone turn on. Then the next and so on until you've reached the front desk. Subject. One contains five. Someone told me in the ER, all I'd have to do to become an ER, physician is pass all the tests in only three to five text books. They showed them to me as I sat on a gurney awaiting the doctor. They were students and I was a patient there. ...One thing I notice is you put the bubble cams in place and hook them up to a network and multi-faceted communications portal with a more competent framework allowed by law. Like is already done for new age orthopedic operations in the larger city hospitals. And include all the staff, surgeons, doctors and specialists that were already in place to prove no neglect and abuse or physical and mental cruelty shall happen on either side of the fence. And knowing, the health care system monitor is working without the threat to their livelihood of removal and possible pending dismissal ever reaching an authorities desk. You'll find they agree a system that will not allow them to make certain mistakes by instantaneously teaching the correct method of treatment, which will give them a better reputation without the fear of reprimand. And is far better than living with a disease just because help before, did not come it in time to save a life. Because, they all want to live a better life. And when they have nothing to fear, they have nothing to hide. And that's the beauty of it all! ... For example. So that when a patient comes in with severe burns yelling and screaming and yes maybe even uncontrollable swearing. You identify to what degree. The camera video tapes the dilemma as you type the information into the network or use a speech to text application and simply identify their condition just by talking. And in mere seconds receive the correct treatment plan. For instance you will be notified right away not to fully submerge in an ice bath. Or if you do and the patient does not stop yelling to immediately flush with large volumes of Luke, warm water. The immense pain will then subside. Do to scientific proof that the skin because it is being frozen cannot repair and will die as the temperature is too low and actually acts similar to when over exposed to too much heat. The Luke warm water allows it to live longer and provides comfort as it slowly makes its own repairs to itself.

The Goal Digger

...When someone gives you a gift it's complete. You cannot retract it. And in order to use it you have to figure out what it is. So if you are gifted and you gave your gift away to someone else. And they kept it and decided not to return it. And they hold on to it with two hands up over their head and run to show everybody what they have just received. As they shout for joy, "Oh boy!, Oh boy!" Shaking it wondering what on earth it could be. Hoping it's just what they always wanted. With curiosity held so deep they can hardly wait to see. And don't let anyone take it from them as they sit down to open. Pull off the bow and the ribbon. Gently pushing one finger underneath the tape that holds it together. Tarring off the wrapping paper. Knowing someone went to all that trouble. Bringing to light the ambiance and glowing effervescence of that very exuberant type of whimsical, elated, excitement filled atmosphere. As emotions run high. ...What is it? Now I'm just assuming. It's the spirit of giving. And it doesn't have to become costly. After all if the price says for free. It doesn't cost a penny. Remember, don't think of it as the glass half empty. Think of it as being the glass half full! It's spiritual. Give a little get a little. I give a lot! Call me Santa. So what's your pleasure? I'll go dig up your treasure! And since I insist. Who's next on the list? Let's fill up the sleigh right away! And before I make my passage. Mark each package. "Rush Delivery!" Addressed to everybody. And what if it is your express wish to give the biggest and brightest gift of all? That's indivisible. And so huge, you cannot contain put or even fit it into a box! That would be peace and love. Trust me it's the stuff miracles are made of. ...And someone believed in them so hard it's all he practiced and ever preached! His name is Jesus. He gave the gift of genius. MERRY CHRISTMAS! Yours truly. With vim and vigor.

All Of The Above

With advancements in the art of healing. We experience love first as a feeling. And try to put a little love in everything we do. Because it feels good, doesn't it? Therefore please consider the following. {When I was young I was always into wondering. And when I couldn't fully explain something I turned to science in order to properly define it. So if you're late at handing in your work but are considered to be ahead of your time, then you're no different than someone who is on time but not ahead of time. And if you want to you can skip what's in-between the parentheses and go to the ending to create another holiday greeting. ...Abacas measure method matter energy inertia definitive living together infinitive living forever match talent achievement success synchronicity eternity. Maven novice ultra-pannier amateur pro aficionado philanthropist disciplinarian humanitarian historian. Pre post hypnotic suggestion memorization. Memory recall innovative ability new electronic machinery. Prevarication truth detection being cognizant beforehand intuition deductive reasoning premonition. Without being bias or prejudice love peace sympathy selflessness hope faith charity compassion and forgiveness. Live or preprogrammed voice over live or prerecorded animatronic-ly altered conversation and methodic scientific exploration. Inter and outer transcendental communication and cooperation. Levity of a situation anonymity exact look alike twin kinship double indemnity mind acceleration and mental telepathy. Ingenious genome mapping gene splicing and grafting including brainwave fingerprinting. Objective motion rest compatibility positively and negatively persistence and peaceful coexistence. Nuevo up to the date up to the minute new age modern day space age gifts learned and acquired traits and characteristics. Vision and dream mind over matter teleporting spiritual work laying hands on and healing. Thought transference speaking what another is going to speak at the same time they say it. Reading the mind prayer, ESP, derivative of genius becoming comfortable and joyous.} ...Now I've done some research. And to me love is the stuff miracles are made of. And all of the above.

Greetings! & salutations

They say if you hear voices you're mentally ill! If ESP's, real. Those voices come from other people. When you believe in the power of prayer. It becomes more powerful than a piece of paper. When you're walking with a spirit beside you one in front makes three. And you can hear the ones' closest to yours voice. But cannot detect their identity. If you were as smart as you thought you were you could learn how to in time. The less anger the better when healing the mind. It has much more to do than pay attention to every ones reflection. If I learn what you are saying and know who you are. Who's ahead of time and in front by far? You are. And the only reflection I can relate comes from things I've been told. That are as young as they are old. And worth their weight in gold.

"bIg bRoThEr"

I am lousy at writing legibly I'm poor at spelling which renders a strange effect, a natural mask over top each phrase or paragraph that makes it harder to see every word as it's actually intended and supposed to appear. That in a way ciphers and may hide the one and only meaning that rings true. Amongst the encoded written format of my sloppy hand written script. ...If I hand you a set of notes I have just written haphazardly. In the time it takes you to organize them chronologically just as you've finished. I'll already have passed out a report electronically with every thing you need to know in the correct order from that note, to everybody. And on your desk if you request, immediately. ..Freedom of thought always possesses the powerful potential to become intellectual property eventually. I think of higher learning as being pictured as a golden ruler balanced perfectly on a fulcrum, level and in the exact middle so that just the touch of a feather anywhere on one half throws it off. With a scale attached to either end used to measure positive and negative vibration. Calibrating the two meters you gauge intelligence finally by taking readings and pinpoint the amount there before hand, the total gained and the amount afterward. Calculate a quotient write a report and put it in the forward. So that if you work hard all your life to become a brighter individual and wanted others to be able to respect you and call you a smarter person than they thought you were when they first perceived you. ...It would work! No matter how short you make that expanse you still spend a valuable period of time honing a skill, perfecting a talent and brushing up on a finished product. And when you finally present the work which is how you get your work done. Everybody else learns after all that study what you now know, that before you ever started were trying to convey all along. And with every point you make you put in their hands a tool they can look up any answer with just the touch of a finger. Which means they now learn the same things you did at a much faster pace. And no matter how smart you are or were still took you much longer, to figure out. Now they are just as enlightened! And that may go to some ones head. Until they remember. As you faced many challenges. In order to prove you really are, who you say you are you needed a teacher to become brighter. And whether or not

37

they are now or always were smarter. In order to prove they really are who they say they are they needed an educator. Strait Vs, Curve. Growth accumulates and mind power accelerates. And when they switch places mind power accumulates and growth accelerates! After all the facts are in. And thru pride with prowess persistence perseverance hard work and determination are weighed happily. Equally fairly honestly repeatedly properly with precision and accuracy very carefully. Now, that the deciding vote has been cast who's as smart as you are and who's all the wiser? Who's got your back? Who comes up with a revelation to any situation? Just between you and I. And you don't need to whisper. From one person to another.

The Compass & The Protractor

As light travels fast and far in a years time would you see a progression of a visualization in real time? Or just an image like a snapshot that took a year to travel to where you are now. If a planet went thru a significant change in the same amount of time you exposed yourself to capturing a sequence of events. Is it the same as a signal? And at what expense do you go to expose human intelligence for what it really is? If science says it detects a planet much like our own two times the size, three hundred thousand light years from earth! ...The mind is like a looking glass, magnification 2X. Look thru the telescopic peephole. The scope is wide the spectrum is real, the signal is strong, the path is narrow. The universe saw its own reflection! And the earth saw its own shadow. Leaving room for improvement. Because it's so vast. Part of what we view from afar we consider to be a part of the past. Like a photo album. With time exposure. That reaches from one end to another. I got the big picture. Using, ...

Home Of The Free! Land Of The Brave?

I attest being fully cognizant that to the best of my ability knowledge and understanding that I assert the following statement to be true and correct based on fact not fiction that can easily be researched and then proven. Rich people on both sides of the fence since the recessions avidly scout the area with the intention to purchase new property. Which believe it or not actually does have something to do with poverty. Since a report of just thoughts has to do with obtaining help in time to save a life. Before I contact ingeniously a few agencies relating to reaching out by asking for help regarding being tortured at the hospital by performing a live reading. Please consider the following. Being sympathetic towards things that devastate destroy neighborhoods and adults and children's lives. In this case hard drugs. Vs. In my case having black lung or, "COPD", and using, "THC", look it up which has been scientifically proven to block tar which keeps the smoker alive who for some reason or another cannot quit but where the addiction to nicotine then becomes I admit a revolving door with the treatment even when used as properly as a medicine should be. And when some think about neglect and abuse in our rural health care facilities they just may well adjudicate that it's way off in the distance and therefore they don't have to deal with or further recognize there was a problem and will block their memory in order not to worry. Yet by the same token those same people may also think of the hidden dangers of hard drug use as being right there in their neighborhood and an immediate threat to their community and to society and therefore want to give it the utmost priority. And seek help immediately.

The Doodle

...A mathematicians' impression of economic mass production. ...What can you theorize postulate and come up with, (and practice makes perfect), thinking mentally and speaking physically publicly. Not just off the top of your head and on the tip of your tongue that will equal what someone else does. When and only when they use a pen and paper to do so. The truth, if they never told you. When they annunciate and initiate the task that they feel clears their good name. Which is the conscience effort of informing you either, A. Contact all the right agencies yourself or, B. Everybody already knows that so I don't have to tell you although it's my job to. And may include the secret piece of resistance. And add to the unhealthy mix to the tune of the infamous word, now. A great communicator can be compared to having to communicate to all other people while excommunicated or in exile when you actually aren't and haven't been, in reality. Which explains the quote, "A stranger in his own country." We learn in order to be smart and become smarter in order to survive. And brighter in order to overcome. Super is as super does. It's in the report. I came here to enjoy the show. And view it as a true story. Write a screenplay. And maybe even make a movie! And I know, "Be frugal." I'll call it, "The Doodle.

The Gentlemen's Club

Track record. Who's smarter and who's bright enough to produce work that is equal to. ...A person who improves the quality of life for someone. Learns that trait from a life saver. Who in-turn developed the unique characteristic of following the right set of instructions then performing the actions alone. Of a hero who assimilates all their information. From the advice of those ingenuous enough to have shared what ever it is, with everyone. Does a writer have to be poor and practically go broke before people notice they're a master of the art? Does an artist have struggle and nearly starve before people recognize them as being gifted and praise their work? Does a virtuoso have to play in the background and cover for the star on stage before people are told the musician they did not see was the one they heard? Is there a computer so infallible none of its calculations are ever wrong and that no harm can come to anyone because of them? Do you technically have to become more analytical than skeptical of the average computer programming process? Is there a report we can reach out to that will touch our lives in such a way that it will change the future for the better before we get there? Sooner than, not sooner or, later. Can you take a live reading with any one form of two way communication. Find the correct measure and use it to predict the outcome of the conversation beforehand and or early on into one? Would or will it be on time with other forms of communicating when you combine all of them? Picture it as you and another person whom you love standing close facing one another. But in between both of you are two full length mirrors placed so you can only see your own reflections. And on either side of you there is a chalkboard. On the one side, is a list of all the good the community sees in you! And on the other, well you get the point. You first have learn to love your self before you can love someone else. And these are some of the things I go over every morning. And people flat out want to know what they discuss on a daily basis in the organization they dub, "The genius club." Contact them, get involved and demand good press coverage. And while you're at it tell them what one of the Presidents of the United States told me, "I'm looking forward to your report." I have nothing to hide. And I also have common cause in mind! And you can join for free. All are welcome and no one will be turned down. And I guarantee you will receive a degree of excellence. Whether you have a 220, IQ or lower it will be my sheer pleasure. And this association I dub, the gentlemen's club.

Millenniums In Mere Seconds

For thousands of years a pauper has been just a poor mans friend, in a rich mans eyes. And you might wonder how long it takes in life before the master too becomes the slave! How long can you wait before they switch places? Perhaps.

Birds Have Ears

Hi Mom, I went to Herbs Bait Store to, spend the gratuity you gave me for the holiday so graciously and the owner, Craig was in such good spirits he said he's buying me a six pack for X-mas! Feeling richer than ever I bought some spaghetti sauce and spaghetti and two cans of mushrooms came home and drank my profits up for the day. As I thought I had it made you know like the proverbial ole saying, "King for a day." Or, "Something for nothing." Had my head in the clouds! Allot of pride flowing, all at once. Feeling all cheery and merry. Enjoying the season and the time of day. Without a care in the world! Yes, ...for once everything was starting to go my way. And I forgot all my troubles for several hours only to find out in the end when it was time to prepare the feast! That I left the main ingredient out 'till it spoiled but stubbornness got the better of me and I prepared the meal anyway!! Because I, am, determined! I said over and over again. Combined with it all the rest of the fresher ones and low and behold almost ruined, as far a dinner was concerned my entire Christmas! But the crows and sparrows had a good one. They said grace, ate their holiday supper and then sent a message. "You don't have to read the whole book. Just pick out a recipe. And learn to cook! Because although for something delicious to eat and humanely engineered treat we are always scouting. We'd rather starve! Than eat your cooking." So I found an old cook book way high up on a shelf. And showed the birds what was on the front cover. A symbol of luck yes It was a picture of two four leaf clovers. And I said to them, "And the title is. How to cook leftovers!" Took out my empty pot and banged it with a wooden spoon! And shouted at the top of my lungs, "Any volunteers?

Doctor Do Little

Showing good judgment judging for myself. A natural instinct. Remembering what I said my definition of tough love is where I tell you I won't let you hurt me if I can help it but I do love you. And that sends a message that love is the stuff miracles are made of. The reason I asked the super computer to research the value of love and list all conglomerated relevant explanations and to simplify the results is. ...Don't blink as I take a mental picture. There, now I will give a live reading. If you know what I am thinking and can annunciate what I am going to say at the exact same time I start speaking, you're mind reading! It's called deductive reasoning. A formulation of inclination. Which I find exciting and fascinating. But if I write down the answer to a question that's on your mind onto a piece of paper without you having to speak to me and tell me what it is. Using my intuition. Thru patient contemplation with mental configuration and confirmation. My conclusion is, that is the science of premonition. Anyone can make up their mind and change their mind, just as they choose to communicate in any direction. Before they speak their mind. As they think before they act, in-act, and react with others who are kind. ...Mouse in the house! I used to have a plastic spoon I used to stir my coffee every morning that I would make sure is clean and germ free before I'd set it out for the next day every evening. All because I knew there was a mouse in the house. And use it I did! "Till one morn bright and early before I brewed up the coffee I heard a licking sound like a cat sipping water. Accept this sounded stranger! So I peeked into the kitchen from around the corner. And sure enough there the mouse was licking the clean spoon, and I sensed inside at me, laughing! Yes the mouse was happy. So I deduced since it wasn't eating any crumbs off the floor or chewing holes in boxes of food in the cupboards that it knew I used that spoon day after day and I not knowing what it was up to and doing all that time had become none the wiser. Then, quickly I took an empty jar right near it from off the counter trapped it, slid a sheet of paper underneath and released it outside into the wild. After all I never got sick and felt sorry for the poor critter. Because it displayed emotion and had become quite the practical joker!

Doctor Do Little Paragraph #2

Some educators get so technical that they hide their expertise or simply won't share it when you request them to unless and until you learn what it is, they know. And that can become quite cumbersome and in my eyes truly is, hard work. A responsible mentor can always get good press. But sometimes it pays to hear it straight from the horses mouth. I like many people, (although it pays to get your degree first), have a barn yard education. And am considered to be

42

a bit of a back yard intellectual at the fence when I intellectualize with my neighbors. And it can take me, about twenty minutes to write a small set of notes on any such subject matter. Twenty more to go over the points to be made, correct organize mold and shape the content. An hour or so to contemplate the true meaning of what I am trying to convey. And because I never trained to, about an hour to type up a paragraph or two. And with the finished product, only a few minutes to read it. So it stands to reason time is precious isn't it? And you might wonder why some people devote their time and some their lives to standing up for animal rights! It's since we're human. I'll explain momentarily. Doctor do a little, doctor do allot. Speaking of intricacy. Miniaturization is a skill that's honed to perfection thru magnification. Or at the very least is calculated to be mathematically correct in size and proportion as it physically can be. And is an exact smaller representation or replica and working model, down to the slightest detail. So who rules their kingdom without hands? Who was here first? Who was in our field of vision even before we first ventured out into our own land? And who hunts with their teeth as well as eats? Animals! Animals are littler than we are in the respect toward because of our grasp, our fingers and our power and ability to reason and make and reverse our decisions at will without succumbing to anger. Unlike past experiences pertaining to our cousin the ape. And it's often been contemplated whether in the animal world they are talented enough to concentrate harder than a man can. It all depends on how you bide your time beforehand. So! When can we say we have a no kill and humane society? Examples can be set safely, soberly, without anxiety producing prejudice or bias, being full of philanthropy as an, now how do you pronounce this? (on-tra-pan-ure?) Must be French or something. And yes I don't care, so go ahead and laugh at me! People say, "When Dr. Do Little writes about his experiences he can't spell well and that he has to look up every word he's trying to write about that sounds complicated! And he's too lazy to get an education." And you know what the collegian learned at commencement. That the ordinary man, the whole time they were in class learned something different they were never taught. Nor ever told exactly what that was. And said things like, "Dr. Do Little only accomplishes enough hard work to fill a paragraph or two! Then it's skip to my Lou, twenty three ski-doo and off to the zoo." Here is a story for you that is only three sentences long and down to the exact detail that is worth a whole chapter in a good book. "As I pull myself up by the boot straps in order to make my own way up the ladder by studying and self educating in spite of

43

myself I learned something. That some people are jealous of me? I'm smarter than the average bear so there's no need to be." ...Democracy. Remember the simple experiment in, ESP, I proposed that would work for anybody? Where without letting them know you are going to beforehand you spring it on our leaders the question. Can you define democracy as it appears in the dictionary? Don't become confused. You have the right to be informed. Remember the mouse that took the thorn out of the lions paw to whom he promised beforehand if he did he'd let him go. It's just like the word surveil. It isn't in my computerized dictionary but it is in the book. Surveil. It is important and also associated with the correction of the misaligning of the weak and infirm condition of animal and man. And the rescue of them from. And it is the first word on the list when it comes to stopping it. Which stems from the word maul. A transitive verb from the thirteenth century. Speaking of signs about regenerative medicine there should be signs and definitions listed everywhere! Why? Because it's the best new age medicinal example we have presently ever set that as far as the latest advances have come and that's far, in recent years that compares to being, the scientific equivalent of faith healing. Where we are able to heal or regenerate any organ or tissue in the entire human body. That's amazing! And it works for the animal kingdom too. Just like happiness you can't put a price on quality care that guarantees the cure. And I was especially interested in a hydroponic capable, (including multiply timed stem grafting), a growth acceleration technique. In a terrarium developed by scientists that grows the fruit off the vine or from the tree without having to replant the seed! And how miniaturized fluid electron movement and torsion producing engines used in transportation are now built to run on an environmentally clean source of combustion. Derived from a free source that makes up three quarters of the earths surface. Water.

The Antidote

A fisherman walks into the pet store. And standing there facing all the animals, with his thumbs fixed firmly underneath his suspenders high up on his chest with a big tall top hat on speaking in a loud voice as if he were President Lincoln giving the Gettysburg address, is Dr. Do Little! And he says. "Ladies and gentlemen brothers and sisters and boys and girls of all ages! I heard animals tend to eat together as a family. And also tend to play together as a family." To which the fisherman replies. "And the family that prays together, stays together!"

44

Big Boys Toys

Once you learn to love boating the desire never really goes away! Life is precious. And one of life's little lessons is that time is relative. Therefore no matter how old you are think young! Because then you are as young as you feel. And have a little faith and I guarantee you'll heal. There's a code of the sea. You eat well because there are plenty of fish in. And Jesus taught us to fish for men. Dream big! Set sail. Remember your vision. And let the Good Lord guide you. He is the Heavenly Father and he walked across the water.

The Directions

You can repeat anything you read or hear as long as you point out from whom and where, you got your information. Everyone has a story. "Do tell." So if I wanted to publish an entire book! About just, yet just plain thoughts I construed from a collection of hand written letters I wrote friends and family electronically. And if I pulled out all the stops. I'd have to remove all the reading material I used to learn how to write a book with and then I wouldn't have a title. Unless I wanted to teach how I educated myself in order to. And if I omitted all the latest advances in science and medicine including current events and repetitive efforts. I wouldn't be offering up enough hope for people to believe in nor be able to give proof of reference. And if I rejected submitting all my personal experiences all I'd have left to some readers are a few mundane sounding poems. And if I left out the ones about the power of love. I'd have nothing. And if I don't describe torture I can't produce enough self discipline to show everyone how to bring it to a peaceful end. And if I leave out the A B C's, of good journalism I have no true account of a modern day reporter and a super person. And if I didn't remind people about the new development the literally paper thin electronic paper I would not have been able to introduce the interchangeable electronic book sleeve for ones cover. And if I never convey the fact that reading is a communications portal no one would think to see if there is a lack of communication. And then I wouldn't have a good book to read. Which some may refer to as organized literary chaos! Until they read the report. And after all if they do they can always forget about it. But just like having the memory of an elephant there are some things I can't. Like how to profit from my accomplishments instead of my mistakes. So if I follow my own instructions I might come up with the following. One of the oldest forms of communicating is storytelling. And word of mouth is the first formulation of ideas before pen and paper draw together and a book is ever written. It's called articulation. So being polite and careful to be kind and considerate of all other peoples thoughts and feelings. While concentrating extremely on helping other people. Intellectualizing extensively about the selflessness of man. And what it means to get an education. Knowing what it takes to have to be the pupil as well as the teacher. And what it might have meant for some not to have been given the luxury to be able to afford to be taught with books. With plenty of roots we get stuck in our own ways, if we don't change. After all if the best comes last save the last for first! And therefore then the expanse of time between when the first becomes the last and the last becomes in turn the first shall be as short as from the first person to the second person and from the second to last to the last and equal to, all points in-between. Featuring how to write a letter, how to write about love. How to write a report that contains current events. How to write updates to a true story that has a positive outlook and a better and improved upon outcome than the original one. Using creative and technically inclined scientifically proven method and correct formatting when writing. With purpose prose and poetry rhythm rhyme and reason. That give clues to solving a mystery. And how to bring the best science and medicine to everybody! By teaching love and forgiveness to all people in the first place, just as a genius originally asked. So you can accelerate your mind enough to be able to foretell the future within the one we already have to look forward to, before it arrives. And now explain things that before we never were able to prove existed. In time to save a life. With a forward, table of contents, a key. Final thoughts a summary and a glossary. Sections on masterful entitlement whether read chronologically, alphabetically, from beginning to end or from the end to the beginning. Say on no uncertain terms almost exactly the same thing. Or in any case have an uncanny ring and portray a similar meaning. With a piece of knowledge and a word of wisdom. So after you've gone over my instructions with good intentions. Please don't forget. To read, "The directions.

ZEST

When I was in my pre teens I saved up for an FM, wireless mike. I wanted a set of, "Walky-Talkies", but they were more expensive. And the elusive microphone that transmitted your very own voice over the airwaves to make it sound and look like it was coming from the radio station itself was all I could afford.

So my big brother Paul pulled me over to his desk and showed me a diagram. He drew two lines strait up and down the page separate but next to each other. Then dots that looked like small circles at the top and bottom of both. And said, "Imagine two different people are traveling up these lines. Both have the same goal in mind. Getting from point A to point B. One tends to travel up and down several times. The other is much slower and is still reaching his destination. The slower man has, what the faster man needs. But he, doesn't have it for one reason. The two lines don't intersect. Just that they are equals at both points. Now draw lines thru the beginnings and endings and extend the two original ones, just beyond before they start and past where they ended. So the end goes beyond its starting point. And the beginning travels in the direction not, after but before it was created. Now look at the results. The lines can be crossed. Now remember what I just taught you because it will come handy in many many areas and all sorts of different situations you will encounter in life over and over again. And when you grow up you will thank me you did. So, how do the ends justify the means? It gets easier to understand from here. The equation here is about the art of communication. Communication is a two way street. The drawing is a formula that represents the two lines of communication. The calculation and definition is; (Being no < 3/4 and up to 99 including 100% correct. Vs., being no < but no > 50% correct at a time.) And is the difference between being half hearted and whole hearted. Or rather the plate half full compared to the plate half empty. The solution is opening the lines of communication. The solvent is intersecting them. And the antidote, is having more communication." So I looked at him and I have rarely said this to anyone, "Where did you learn that? You're a genius!" He said back, "It takes one to know one." {And zest. Put that in your pipe and smoke it.}

Please Stand By

Artists who don't get recognized right away tend to starve for their work. Musicians who don't make center stage tend to drink. And writers who haven't yet been published tend to think. And they all want to do good in and for, the community! ...Times change and now we have people that do all three. We're all born with a talent and natural ability. And we're all unique individually. Yet for some that comes easy. As there are doubles that look exactly alike and twins that think exactly alike. And also there's the power of prayer and proof of ESP. And although that all sounds too good to be true, to many. Some people are truly gifted and stand ready willing and able to give plenty. A great writer once said, "Procrastination is just a technical difficulty. And a mind set is just a destination and not necessarily a finality.

The Soup Bowl & The Giant

Once and within certain times . And upon allotted space . There was a man who lived in a bright colored cabin . Who was always thinking and dreaming allot . No one knew why . At night he would sometimes dream his favorite dream . Where he went out his front door , ... stopped , and waited . And suddenly expanded , right in front of his cabin . Into a Giant . After which he would walk around the neighborhood , and woods . And admire the world around him from above the trees . Then slowly , just before sunrise . He would walk back to his cabin , just where he started from . And he'd shrink back down , and go back in , to bed . He Loved that peaceful walk . But many times , upon his return , he got hungry . So one night , just before bed , when he wanted to dream his favorite dream . He took a bowl of soup outside , and placed it well outside of the cabin . Then went to bed . And it worked ! This time in his dream , when he expanded just outside the cabin . So did the Soup Bowl ! Now he had something to eat upon return of his journey . But one time , upon return , he found the entire neighborhood at his front door . They said , "we know you live here . You're that dreamer ! How did you get so Big ? " He said , " I protect the neighborhood at night . And nothing has happened " . They looked at the giant bowl of soup , and said . " Surely you will eat up all of our crops ! " " Look around ! " , he replied , " the crops are fine ! " " " That soup I set out is mine , that I made myself ." The neighborhood replied . " But if you drink it , you will grow even bigger ! And then eat all our crops ! " The giant exclaimed . " Eat my bowl of soup , and I will shrink back down , and never bother you again " . As they were deciding what to do , he shrunk back down to normal size , and dashed back into his cabin . Just then , they noticed , and ran back in to see . And found him shrunk to normal , and asleep . The one they knew had done this . They woke him up , and quickly looked outside for the giant soup bowl . Only to find it had also shrunk . Then they asked . " How did you get that bowl of soup to become so Big ? " The dreamer replied , " It was the last thing I touched , and set out side before I went to bed " . " Well you should have touched us ! " To which the giant replied . " Without first having something to EAT ? "

48

The Candidate

Anyone can change their mind before they make up their mind to say what's on their mind. Even if you have to abandon ship! One of the first skills you learn as the skipper from the captain at the helm is you can always build another one. And when you practice what you study you learn what to teach, then you preach. ...The sign of a true leader is that they don't go back on their promises that are just. They go back on the ones that were unjust! And you can make fun of a great leader. Just don't make fun of a good one. Or they just might end up, a bad leader. And so the lesson learned here is. That is, the difference between a nemesis and a mentor. So if someone tells you to run for public office, do consider. Because there is a self made man who ran for the highest office in the land! More than once, every four years without fail. He's on every ballot but practically nobody knows who he is. And yet he's considered in some circles of higher learning to be a bone identified genius. Who hasn't won an election yet. He calls himself a technocrat. And teaches one lesson best. Which might as well have read like this. "Never give up. Until you've dug the wishing well. And drank from the fountain of youth! ...Speaking of intelligence. I am speedy! And my computer is faster than me. ...Catching up? To some, a technicality. To others, a temporary setback. But in reality, just a minor difficulty, to me. Knowing all too well the feeling of always being told. Yes you're ahead of your time. Or before. But never being told you're on, or in time. Where sooner than later you have to reconcile with the fact that sometimes you have to swallow your pride, even in front of others! But you still know a little goes along way. Because it's public consensus that even a child knows right from wrong. And I used to know people who would rather crawl up in a ball and hug their knees with a tight grip. Rather than go thru some of the things I've had to just to get to where I am today. But herein sprouts another lesson. Even if you don't succeed, try try again.

The Spectacle

"Once we do, we all know the feeling of becoming strong. That's why it pays to be experienced at the art of being gentle. It's worth the trouble. After all you don't fight the power that builds muscle." ...When I woke up this morning and I don't always look at myself in the mirror. A spirit came to me and said. "You love me but can you look yourself in the face and truly say, you love everybody?" So I started to think. Then I remembered a report, most of which I read with my mind that taught. Out of eight to twelve important matters genius now shows progress and movement in pick one subject and name one topic you're interested in. Now lay on a desk five pieces of paper side beside one another. Now write down in the order they appear one word from the following sentence per and underline them. Man, mite, machine, power, time. Underneath put the following five sets, in the same manor. Sight, sound, hearing, taste, smell. Who, what, when, where, how. Cells, nerves, bones, brains, heart. Mind, body, spirit, dream, vision. Practice, study, journey, profess, perfect. Can someone genuinely gauge your response to a question or two. Give an honest opinion and establish accurately how smart you are just from their perception of you? ...When you love someone, someone loves you. But if you don't love someone who only has a speck of love. You only contribute to the reason why they didn't love as much as they could have. And that puts you in the same class as that of a fool. Who appreciates being loved in the first place! Just that a fool usually doesn't have enough love to give back, to speak of. Until they're in need of love. Love everybody! Don't be the fool that doesn't. ...And don't worry about what you see in your own reflection. Worry about being made whole. Because you have only, one soul. And just one. Past, present, current, pending, future. And that's how you build a home-made computer with just five pieces of paper. And then with priceless information fill each one full. I call it the spectacle.

Data Base

Welcome to the, World-Wide-Pen-Pal-Club! Speaking of power, ...intellectual. In its infancy electronic mail usually had to have one outbox and two inboxes. One for auto generated mail that is maladjusted and undesirable. And the other used to send and receive mail that is friendly you can share with one and all. The list I use that was handed to me, no disrespect here it was the only list I was given not the only one I'm building. Says right on it at the very tip top part of the message, friends and family also, not only. And I noticed about the first time I ever wrote one, the letter has at the beginning a subject line. You can't miss it! I use mine, every time. And people give you comments on what and how you write in a letter. And opinions ideas and suggestions as to how a good one is written. Whether yours is good or bad and right or wrong. Here if you get good at what you are doing someone can write a few words in the subject line send it to you and immediately you can write an entire story pertaining to. Automatically. And some will say remove me from your list! I just write back that they have to remove my address from their end because I am doing a research project am not breaking the laws of free speech and freedom of expression. And I have to gauge every ones response for a final grade. Still others say, publish! Which requires in some cases allot of money. So if you wrote scores of prose and poetry on one subject alone, love. If you do print your volume of works and have to charge a pretty penny. How do you explain not money but love, makes the world go around? With any certain amount of common decency and at the same time be able to hold onto your dignity? Where each subject one of many strewed chronologically with just a few additional words woven into them to form complete sentences. Produces an uncanny resemblance to formulate whether read frontwards or backwards two different stories with almost the exact same meaning in the content of both messages. Where the only requirement for the sublime, experimentation to take place is that you have to make sure the subject line would fit, still make sense and fall correctly into place at the start and the finish of each and every masterpiece you create. How does that happen? It's where each one indirectly is about searching for the same answers to the same questions which will eventually happen. And the solutions will produce feelings of ecstasy. And when a set of notes on various topics are turned into letters that become reports that spurn great stories. That seem to contain a certain progression that sprouts hidden instruction that reads like a manual and ends up the equivalent of a course built right in. Almost subliminally which reflects upon society and has an impact on us subconsciously. They come about because of and due to the need and desire, to learn. ...Can you write a book that teaches itself to think with artificial intelligence? And with that intelligence build and program a robot complete with complex human emotions? Where it experiences the electronic equivalent of suffering alike, just as we do in our delicate, intricate, fragile and sometimes frail and precious biological conditions? Would you give it a hug if it loved you? Did you know man already can print genetic material used to reconstruct the human body with a computerized laser? Can you build a humanoid robot with enough coordination to be able to administer it? I can. But only because somebody told me. "You can do anything you put your mind to." So what does tomorrow hold for us. The actions of a good robot or a bad one? Just ask your children. They are our future. They know the difference between right and wrong. And you know the outcome. Because you taught them. ...Computer on! Robot come here! Sit next to me and take your rite-full place in society. Prove your case. And plug in the, data-base.

A REPORT OF JUST THOUGHTS: Thought Wave Reporting

Current events. There is a grand theory that offers up more plausibility within the realm of possibility than first meets the eye. When someone says you're ahead of your time. You're really ahead of their time. And so in your eyes if you are late at least in their eyes you are on time, in time, in tune and practic-ing. Which means, timing is important! And to some, it's everything. Some people only associate relieving pain with a gratifying feeling. It's also associated with healing. Self discipline isn't punishment. It's how you avoid it. Torture is related to medical malpractice, medical mistake and medical error. But for now, leaders of the free world. All current events subject to change. Associate the cure with money. Which in these cases has not yet been able to purchase happiness. God is omnipotent! He loves all creatures big and small. He puts the kybosh on discrimination. And Love is all powerful isn't it. The study re-lated topic is omniscience. Key word, omniscient. ... ...When they clone an animal the offspring has a different spirit built in and a totally unique, because it is different, personality. But is exactly alike in every other detail right down to the genealogical make up and physical appearance, in full. We are homo sapiens and labeled genus species. Are smartest ones are called geniuses. To determine if we are we simply take tests. And the person who would not take the test for, one of many, unless he or her did not study was only trying to say. They knew something, without having to be educated the ones who took the test didn't without having to educate themselves. That you don't need to take a test to observe and study those around you. So in order that all would arrive at the same conclusion in effect they cloned, their attitude. Headlines. A ge-nius, {Or maybe your name here and welcome to the gentlemen's club.} And how do I profess this? Good God was gracious enough to recreate one and told the world he is in everybody. A genius has been tortured in health care facilities in one of our free countries and although at the time no one could hear him scream. He lives to tell about the true story and just exactly how it happened! And because our leaders were so ashamed it did, they covered the incidents up, time and time again. Update. A born again genius shows prowess for bravery and of his own accord and on his own power contacts every agency associated with ending physical and mental cruelty and abuse, within his grasp that he possibly can. And sends a message. And at the same time, puts out an urgent plea. That they might not have listened to him. So please stand by and by all means pray for them! And Gods instruction specifically states, pray for all your leaders. And therefore I insist! Pray for God first. ... ... Body. A genius says, "Don't stop communicating with me politely. And what I know, tell everybody! If you did stop or did not communicate in any way, please start today. Guarantee. A genius promises to lend a helping hand at any time. And in any way shape form manor and fashion. And has laid claim to having the solution to every problem. And even if you don't want to or don't seem to find the time to read. Will offer to subject himself to submitting his work. And will also present as a free gift his, (or hers), own personal intellectual property, in a recording. I call it. "Thought wave reporting.

The Only One I Know

Has anyone ever haggled or, "Had a beef with you?" If people tested you, would you become angry? If no, then would they be? Sometimes not always? Or almost always and just maybe sometimes? ...There's a difference between being used, as a test subject and a punching bag. ...If you study ancient man. You'll find from his origin he noticed and first used fear as an instinct. Then as a tool. And it all began in the intellect. When man first feared being threatened. And then when man first feared having to threaten. Which spread the first bout with anger. Used as a weapon. And you can look this up and it will probably prove to be 100%, correct. But no matter whether you believe or not that it is true. I believe in what is pure. And I've just packed my bags. And you're invited to join me also. And no matter where you think I am coming from. It's off to the future I Go! The only one I know.

The Investigator

Capitulate, caprice. ...How could they, a vague description of whom ever. Just wait knowing each second counts in investigating in order to save a life of anyone who's fragile and delicate weak and infirm condition has been purposefully misaligned during in their time of need an emergency, a form of torture? I can describe many. How could it be, they have no conscience? Is it a mind set or just procrastination? Or an inner desire to do nothing. Remember? In the first televised nursing home abuse case where they put the video camera into place, it saved the victims life! Legal beagle. Government approved. Privacy laws indicate that health care system monitoring is also. See, friends and families that stick by one another simply state that won't happen to them, ever. But what happens to you when you don't have any or you've been abandoned by friends and family? I think you may, know the answer already. It takes years for the victim to recover from just about any traumatic situation fully. Years longer to prepare on their own an adequate defense. With, no experience. How can the leaders associated with and in charge of every agency that is supposed to help the weak and infirm including the President and the press. Live with themselves. How can anyone? Knowing all the while there is a strong possibility while they wait to act that real human torture will happen to somebody else and quite possibly on a daily basis. {That's why, "A Report Of Just Thoughts", is all about communication.} Here all they have to do is get off their duffs and do something about it! And save a life and be rewarded for it. Is it because of what I say? I was tortured multiple times by care givers. And I can prove it. Is that my fault? After all I, reported it. Wrote every agent I could muster up the courage to. So what do I have to do! To maintain my integrity and end my grief. Right after I am done here, write more prose and poetry with an emphasis on love and mercy? And put all I write into a do it yourself kit? OK, just to prove I am who I say I am I will. (Webster's Dictionary 10th Collegiate Edition Definition #6) fi-ne. See you later alligator.

Amadeus

It's often been said, you may of heard and I've often read that there are two kinds of punishers! Those who punish those who punish and those who punish those who don't. But what really is, an authoritarian? Because there is only one kind of self discipline. ...I picture a disciplinarian as being someone standing at a podium taping their pointer upon. With a cap and gown on. Who teaches self correction, self detention and self determination. It's how you avoid being placed in a center for detention or a house of correction. So! With the right teacher that's why an experiment that takes place can be proven to work. No matter how many tries it takes. And I've done it. Where you walk up to a book you've been handed that you carefully place on a table just in front of you. Look at the title. Open and without reading, page thru with your fingers at the same time not lifting it up off of the table. Letting your mind relax as you comb over the entire reading material mentally, internally by reading the thoughts of the one who has a full understanding of and whom just happens to be the one that handed it to you before you laid it down. And after a moment or two are able to say at least what a section or two describes. By using a technique that now involves visualizing what they were thinking. Which would explain walking up to and opening up the Holy-Bible. At random. And being able to see a vision. Point it out with one finger. Go over to another and confirm it in writing with them, those exact words you are now presently speaking. Close, the book. Open it right back up and not be able to find them! ...Until you are filled with bits of knowledge and words of wisdom. That tell you to seek the next one. Things you've never been exposed to literarily before or spoken to about. ...And I remember I used to open it up and many times it would, to a very short book thinly contained within hundreds of pages! And I'd ask people. Why does this always happen to me! And they'd tell me rather abruptly. "It's because you remind us of someone who always struggles at what he is trying to say, but is good at it." But they never once wanted to equate the word yourself, with the word, myself. Which made me reluctant to reveal the precipitous.

Electro-Human-Touch

Nothing!! Shall take precedence, over making sure today, that everyone has enough to eat up to and including, until they are full. For each and every one that experience, in and of itself is my goal. Platter half empty, platter half full. ...I saw a vision and had a dream within one! Where the good president of one mentionable nation, not according as to whether and how fast public opinion shifted. Pulled me aside and into the light of just what his whole life, ...he had been doing! And as I looked around, all I saw was a complete soiree, of food. There was so much I could hardly stand it without asking for some! And I did. But it felt like I was begging. Because I knew there were those who went without and I did not want it to be, because they had. I wanted to have the strength to be able to at least, do something! And so he said to me. "You have humbly taught me to feed my people as properly as they themselves wish to be. Go ahead then and pass me by! Become the new leader. After all!" He started laughing loudly now. "If you take a good look around, you have already convinced me to be on your side! Now the only thing you have left to do, is persuade my army."

Love Battalion

"Machine on. Computer research key words, (love recognition.) Display all relevant results. And simplify." Love of life. Love of spirit. Love of flesh. Love strait out of the bottle. Love strait from the heart. Love of truth. Love of lies. Born lovers. Free love. Love offering. Unlimited love. Destine to love. Love at first sight. Fall in love over night. Head over heels in love. Habitual love. Love addiction. Lovers leap. Young love. Mature love. Tuff love. Gentle love. Unconditional love. Forever in love. Love light. Love bug. Self love. Selfish love. Selfless love. Love of fathers. Love of mothers. Love of brothers. Love of sisters. Love of others. Love of principals. Love of peace." Someone once told me. "We're all prisoners of love! Rejoice! For the Kingdom of Heaven is nigh at hand. God loves his rap-scallions. And he considers our congregations, to be his battalions.

Love-Machine

To me, prose and poetry, rhyme and rhythm aren't reward enough in and of themselves. Rather a reward for reading an award winning report of just thoughts. Which usually contains somewhere within it, an urgent plea. That's why I can't decide on the true color in the right light both should be displayed and then given other than chronologically. Like a computerized memory. Because both formats inspired me. And I just put into my report the other, basic reasoning behind that understanding to keep you interested in me. Here is a real reason to believe in updates to current events. Even though they contain a part of the past. It's called forgetfulness. So, to go along with the love battalion here are a few extras that just keep on growing and growing. ...True love. Puppy love. 1st love. Madly in love. Lovers lane. Love sick. Love lorn. Love of God. Love of country. Love of nations. Love of all that is good. Love of religion. Love of principality. Love of peace. ...Never forget what I can't remember If you did lest it become just what you can't remember about yourself that I do. ...Remember the, "Book Safe?" I built a machine into mine. And the combination will surprise you! Now concentrate as hard as you can! Are your fingers nimble? And are you ready? OK. It's, "(L-O-V-E.)

The Chameleon

Develop a frame of mind and let me paint a picture for you with one. Imagine sitting in front of you a bowl of candy and a bowl of broccoli. Looking first at the one then the other. Some people want what they see. Some people want what they don't see. If somebody says, "I'm smarter than you are." And when I'm not on top of my game, they probably are. It sounds to me, like a dream they have finally completed. And I know well from experience. It only comes true when you're not just smarter than someone, but also brighter than. So in my position and coming from where I stand. Being the authority and becoming the brightest person in the room. Is here and should be, your only priority. Which takes the life blood of a project. And the mechanical heart of a carefully interlaced, knowledge based consortium of conductivity connectivity and pro-ductivity. Sharpness of vision in clarity and purity. ...So what's the difference between being gifted and granting some ones wish. And handing them the very same one, all the while, you yourself have been giving? ...Receiving! And what is the best blend and correct combination of bright and smart? A colorful one. Life is a test. Do the very best you can. "The Chameleon."

Success At Last!!

When you hone a skill and become self educated enough at the one thing you're good at to the point where you develop a unique talent that you can call your own. Even if you never finished school or completed a degree. Sooner or later people will stand up and take notice, eventually. And will be inspired at the fact that either they did not know, or simply couldn't figure out how you did what you did until you revealed what it was, you did. Which in spite of that fact, until the day you do shall remain a mystery. They say, life's a mystery! And God works in mysterious ways. ...As secret doesn't mean I am going to tell you a secret. It means I am going to tell you something and you are going to keep it a secret. Doesn't it? It's secret time! There are some things you, (and the operative word is seem), just can't seem to remember because there are other things you just can't seem to forget. And the inter-operative implication here, is it doesn't mean you can't it means you can! ...As he holds the sealed envelope to his forehead the mentalist concentrates as hard as he possibly can! Then as he tries to come in direct contact with you mentally and communicate, he closes his eyes so you won't look into his mind. Because he is now whether you like it or not, actually in reality, already inside deeply penetrating and peering, ...out of your own. So, being of sound mind. Able to read pictures as stories automatically and recall memories chronologically at will. Climbing up and down the educative ladder. Gathering certain books from the upper level and the lower. Feet firmly planted on the library floor. Placing and carefully organizing them on the librarians desk. Cross referencing every manuals contents rather speedily, mentally as well as physically. I believe without having to use a confessional. This is how, you become a professional. And with vim vigor and zest, as you do your very best. Ah! ...

The Sinner & The Saint

"Freedom of thought. A Preacher does the work of God. The devils advocate does not. Here is a Para graphical story. That's not as short and sweet as a Parable. It's not Sundays Sermon per-say. And has not yet made it to the Liturgy. But a wise ole owl says, "In my circle if you do the work of a Preacher, ...you are one. Joy to the world!" ...When do nerves of steel take on, a forgiving nature? When they're re-grown." Turning to the rich and poor alike. "Just off the top of my head. ...Who turned on the poor who have to forgive! And used their religion to deregulate rule in order to say, they can't get anyone in trouble in their, inner circle especially themselves. Because they are doing exactly what it said to do so they forgave, everyone. Who only do so to cover for their anger towards the believer. And just pretend to obey Christian laws. Putting people in harms way and never disciplining those who put others lives in jeopardy. Saying they forgave and that it is what Christians said to do. ...You can't get a bad person, (guy), in trouble if he is your leader. But say, a bad leader becomes a good one or you have one, then you can. And all manner of good can come from one. ...If your mind at a subconscious level allows your emotions to take over and you become angry when you speak. Even though what you are trying to say you know down deep is right. At the time, you're not conscious of the fact that your anger is wrong. ...Speaking of hiding something. How many professionals with educations and degrees of excellence from major or minor colleges and universities. Can honestly say, they've had mental health checkups on a regular basis? And how many can say they've had any! And with no prior knowledge you are going to or what the question is going to be about. How many of you have asked your leaders. "Just off the top of your head how many of you can define the word democracy, word for word exactly as it appears, in the dictionary?" ...Because in some peoples eyes, I am an uneducated person. But I listen well and I am good at teaching how.

MIRACLE MACHINE Page #1

There is something in ink somewhere that states in writing itself, there is such a thing as free form where complicated thoughts consistently flow fluently and automatically onto paper in a precise manner. ...Using several crates full of sounding boards, switches, meters and gauges. Buttons, dials, blinking colored lights, {Bells & Whistles}, and complicated micro computer circuitry you could come up with some miraculous innovations! ...Using a pencil and a piece of paper you can fit them all, into one. Good things come in small packages. Not every wrapper is attractive. And not every book is judged by its cover. ...Have you ever heard subliminally what will be said just a few seconds, before it's spoken? Then how hard can it be to have heard of and remember the true vale and life's meaning of universal acceptance? PM+LM=MM. That's, prayer machine plus love machine equals miracle machine. Not Dr. Jeckel and Mr. Hide meet Dr. Do-Little and all the animals, at the OK Corral! ...First people see someone they perceive to have an innovative personality. Second they try to figure out if that same person has the craftiness ability and finesse to become ingenious. If so, their inner self craves the desire to know if the other has developed enough talent to come up with a miraculous invention! Then they wonder what it would be like if it was them. And they look at the best things in life. Remembering how a person with a golden heart gives their love away freely. They realize that though their own, concept or idea may cost a shiny penny it will take more than a pretty one to put it together, on enough paper to inform and help every other person. Which contradicts their belief that love is free. Even with donation and devotion you still need to rely on volunteerism and good help that will work for free, ...is hard to find. Then they look at the ingenious one. Who invents produces and profits from what they have, many many fold to say the very least. Theorize, contemplate and then automatically assume that persons soul isn't saved because they became rich! And therefore corrupted the gift of genius. ...Until they realize it was the only way to communicate with everybody at the time. And that the device saves lives. Which means it's the exact opposite of what people were thinking. Because you have to purchase an invention just like the car or the tooth brush! Of course you can design and build them both yourself if you want which will take up quite, a greater amount of space and time than necessary.

Check Mate!

Prayer request: "Please teach what a psychic is." ...Like in the game of chess. Paraphrasing normality, situating it extraordinarily and emphasizing on perceptive sensorial ability. Means to some people, a man with a parachute! To others a man with a talent that acts like a shield or canopy that hovers freely over an others. And to me, is a pretty good description of a person whose past is ancient. And yet always considered himself to be modern in his surroundings since his beginnings. Prayer answered: ...A salute to ancient man form modern man. S-A-L-U-T-E! And speaking of fate.

Rescue The Rescuer

...Along with pre-cognizant intuition or precognition. We also have mental telepathy. Psychic and Para-normal activity. A psychics ultra bright ability and super smart talent is the same as anyone else's! Because, "Everyone's a little bit psychic." So, "One for all and all for one." Affirm and acknowledge. Now visualize. ...That it's up to everybody to use their psychic abilities including ESP, if deemed necessary. A true spiritual enlightenment magnified by the power of prayer itself which is indeed, truly a gift. ...You don't just pray for people that do pray. You pray just as much for people who don't pray and then sometimes even more so. You can't lay hands on a sick man to heal him if you know beforehand once he does he's going to do the exact opposite, when he gets his hands on you! Because being prepared and fully aware of your surroundings sometimes you have to do what God wants first, not what you do. Of course you want to heal without reservation but there is also such a thing as self preservation. ...Continuously projecting thought waves in a sound manner. When it comes to saving someone else's life all by yourself it can become dangerously lonely. ...However it's far better than being cowardly. Therefore practiced to perfection, psychic ability is each and every persons responsibility. And it's all about trial and error. So for a better today and a brighter and more promising future. "Rescue the rescuer.

I'M POWERFUL!!

If God, forgave a drunken alcoholic. It was because he was poor. ...If God forgave a rich man it is because he gave to the poor. ...Therefore, only in Heaven!

60

Rich, are a poor mans desires. And poor are a rich mans. So I demand compensation for both in whole! Because spiritually.

ROLL-TAPE!

One of my favorite, "idols", growing up along with the writers Julian Vern, Edgar Allen Poe and Edger Casey was the inventor Thomas Alva Edison. Because I didn't need to read allot about him, to understand him. Remember the great big computers with the reel to reels up top full of thick magnetic tape running fast first forward then backward and back again that would stop then start in different incremental orders that were to say the very least as big as a refrigerator? When you use your mind to formulate ideas and perform complex reasoning and calculate all odds you are computing. So how do you stump the computer? ...How do you keep a secret! Say you have two punch cards one in either hand and as you walk up to a supercomputer and stand you display one of them in front of it and hide, the other behind your back and say to the colossal data bank and vast storage unit. "Computer, which one am I going to choose. The one in my left hand or the one in the right?" ...The computer will have to use a complicated array of telemetric devices. And tiny microbiotic equipment that measures everything from a heartbeat to a bead of sweat forming to reading your brainwaves and interpreting your thoughts. Initializing all these tasks while intelligently rendering reasonable facsimiles of humane sounding opinions and suggestions based solely on fact. From a distance without human contact. At this point keep in mind though it's a super computer, its results will tend to vary up and until usually a half of a second after you have made your final decision and start to jester before you speak out loud which card you choose and will be purely educated guesswork. And until you make up your mind you can always quickly change it which means at the last second, within one half of a second, or in a blink of an eye. And then, because it cannot make a decision based on fact as to whether it is punch card #1, or punch card #2 until you project the correct set of data material either physically or mentally. You've stumped the computer! So. ...If things take a turn for the worse and you've got to chop the computerized machine to bits with a fire ax. Be sure you have a fire hat on and are wearing a fire suit! Or say you have to pull the plug. You had better be wearing a clean white lab-coat and be carrying a clipboard. Just in case it has self preservation circuitry already built in. The secret? You say, "Fire safety week.

Checking all the sprinklers." And, "Checking the power cord to make sure it fits firmly and is tightly plugged in." ...And did you know it only takes the sets of instructions contained in just three rather large three ring note books to gain the knowledge it takes to build one? I actually have had the privilege of looking over one of them personally. However I chose not to read the material as much as did choose, to absorb it. And I loved it! Quite an experience I might add. So I, "punch key", a concept. Democratic creation recreation and duplication. Produce with math on paper and propose two questions. To not one but two supercomputers both filled with valuable, infallible information. One in the form of a request. "Computers, research the formula, (PM+LM=MM). List all coordinates. Set a course follow thru and plot a safe return. Draw plans create blueprints format final draft. Build machine, install product and increase output." Next. "Computers, which should I put on the reels first. The rewards accumulated from the assimilation of all the data itself? Or just the report?" The computers reason the first. Program note. There is a case in Ohio, where a US scientist sold that book and the other two to a nation that at that time, was not a democratic one. And received sixty thousand dollars compensation for the ill gotten gains. At sentencing he was given ten years for every thousand dollars he was paid.

Everything I See & Everything I Believe

You can always make things up as to why something happens. But you can't always make things up as to how. Until you learn the reasons behind them both. ...In the case of, Helping people Vs. Finding help in time to. Over time two words come to mind, in a sentence. It can be excruciatingly painful! Unless you find the right one quickly. When the spirit of the situation takes a good look around it can feel everything it senses and sense everything with feelings. So when you have no other means currently at your disposal to contact an agent of fortune. You resort to using the power of prayer and you may resort also, to using the power of ESP. ...So somebody says to me. "What part if any can't you remember that you've read! Since you can remember so much that you did?" When I hear by word of mouth and I know what it's all about. Nothing is excluded, that has not yet been and everything that can be written never is. Food for thought and my cup runs over. When I make a contribution to society, first mentally then physically. Even if you thought I did, I didn't fool you. In order to prove the one thing you may not be able to. I focus on two things. That on the surface don't seem easy to perceive.

ALL THE KINGS MEN

Receiving instruction in time in order to avoid having to learn a lesson over time. ... Here is a story that I might have to end before I go onto the next one, just in order to finish this one! Able to prove I'm one of many that can show how to, teach how to, bring others mind filled strengths up to date. Intelligently handing them the same quotient and quality of ability they can perfect as a talent. With ample and amble dexterity, mentally. As I pull it, totally out of memory. I assert the following phrase is over twenty years old or older. And I have not heard ironically since that time and have had no, contact with that sort of information in any way shape form manner or fashion until I retrieved it without a book! ...Today. "As it drips off my forehead coming from the heat generated in the back of my imagination. Falls then precipitates first onto my open faced right hand planted firmly on top of my knee. Then splashes onto my boot and just after I lift it up to avoid contact with the floor, before I put my foot down. ...It disappears! What is it I'm telling you about? It's not my sweat! It's my anger." ... ...Now if you'll please listen to me I have something to say to you on the behalf of others. That I feel is important to everybody that you may feel the exact opposite about. Because in your case, it may only have happened, to people like me. Which is hard to believe unless you already knew there are. ...Phrase #2. Being in a position to and having the full complete and honest capability to. If, you, do, nothing to stop evil! It will become more powerful, ...than you are. And listen closely here. Which may, in the future say you yourself ever need help. Make it impossible to. ...Thus we have periods in time that isolated entire peoples! Who versed the tirades of since governments began, leaders. Which makes it hard to reason with the formula and equation. More than is less than greater than.

[A Report Of Just Thoughts:
"All The Kings Men" Page #2] Florence Nightingale

You know that little voice in the back of your head? ...I had a little talk with the one in mine. It said, "Why do you always repeat the bad points to these stories? If you left them out you would have great ones to tell and everyone would want to read your writing!" If I leave out all the facts I can't accomplish my goal of doing a good deed. ..."It won't sell!" Yes but it might save a life. That plus the fact that it takes a heart of gold to understand why and the memory of an elephant to figure out how. And since when, is a simple thank you enough? When a promise is well kept. Because, it's not just what you do with what you've got, it's also how far you go with what you know. ...Honesty in motion. Remember, "Big Ben", in England? You used to have to wind a clock with at least one weight on a chain all the way to the top about once a week. Now they have a clock you pour onto the face just one drop of water no weight no electricity and it will stay running for a year as long as you replenish it every now and then with one that's fresh. When Edison first introduced the phonograph, what did he put on the spindle? A recording. He invented the recording method first. ...I know when I have a gut feeling but I also listen to my heart. When speaking. [According to some interesting studies posted on the international information electronic highway by companies that sell programs that conduct covert operations that thru technology combat nursing home abuse. Such as from unnoticed and untreated bedsores, misaligning or mulling of stump appendage like conditions all the way to stolen property of the bed ridden weak and the infirm. The staff or someone of authority on location will erase all records pertaining to any questionable act. One such acknowledgement comes to us in a, U S Presidential report! Some have been caught red handed. Famous journalists have made national news headlines when they described true accounts by experts in the field that did not just suggest but had proof! That these things also spread to rural and city hospitals where they all but deny such acts have in the past taken place. Thus suggesting the victim them self has to prove that happens or it's, "Button lips! Turn lock and throw away key." When they televised the first nursing home abuse case where they solved the crime just by putting a video camera in. And there's only a fifty fifty chance you will find the article, "Online." The amount of abuse detected so far is staggering. Just imagine if you're mentally ill also! As with all reports, all current events subject to change. And after much change for those who are gifted not many more changes will be required from those who are not.] ...And yes music you may like or may not like but you don't have to love! And you can judge. Walk away, boo, hiss. Have a temper tantrum, stomp your feet pound your fists, hue rotten tomatoes at the stage and throw a fit. Yell, "Turn it down!" Call the Police. And demand they haul away all the instruments and amplifiers in question. Pull the plug and yank the music maker out of their hand. Smash the equipment and take a fire ax to it. Overturn the stand and bend it in half over one knee. Smear the musical score onto the floor with your feet. Pick it back up and with your own two hands and tear it to shreds. And you don't have to like or dislike people but you do have to love them. ...I just thought that was an interesting comparison. Look at it this way. ...If all you had was an ole reel to reel tape recorder. And every time someone needs care behind closed doors where nobody but they can hear. You rush in and set it down next to the bedside or near the gurney right in front of the patient and caregiver. After you have informed the staff there is nothing legally they can do to stop you within a million miles of earth. Plug it in, turn it on, walk away and save the day. Insuring all present nothing bad from now on shall ever happen! You have just about had to summon. On the wings of an Angel. Florence Nightingale.

Happiness Is

Some people have lots of friends! And make friends easily. They come by it naturally. But if you're anything like me. No matter how many friends you have, or family. You have to earn their friendship first! Then they'll love you unconditionally. ...How many of you have ever lost a friend either because you or they forgot or didn't understand the full meaning? And you all know everybody deserves the, V. I. P. treatment. New beginnings, many branches. Many brands and different branches of science and chemistry are the missing links to modern medicine and hands on healing. Therefore there is a science to the heart. And a chemistry to love. Opposites attract. And I don't fall in love with everyone I meet. But I do love, everybody. And you can go on and on here, about technical advances and the newest latest techniques. Such as robotically assisted surgery and regenerating many many parts of the human body. With stem cell research and grafting gene splicing and re-growing parts of tissues and organs first in a laboratory. Until you need the therapy right away! ...So please do. Because then someone has to implement incorporate and medicinally apply them to the body. And that person usually can't be you. So along those lines of communication. If you set an object in motion in outer space. As long as it didn't come in contact with any planets gravitational pull. Theory states it would continue on and travel the universe, forever. They ought to try that theory out on love. Love's forever also! And you can't put the weight of the world on just one mans shoulders or they would surely collapse! ...A golden ruler distributes that weight evenly, to everybody. Love's on every ones side. Share and share alike. Because a person who follows the golden rule, has a golden heart too. Comparing apples to oranges. When some people tend to procrastinate. On the surface it may first appear that they are just confused. And when people tend to become confused it also first appears on the surface that they are just procrastinating! Until they let both biases go. Then they realize. Wisdom comes with age. A wise man says his prayers. And love, makes the world go around.

My Greatest Insight

Boot straps! Pulling myself up by. If you wanted someone to snap out of a, "Head Bob snooze trance." And wished their shoe lace would come untied so they would trip over their own two feet just to wake them out of it while they're walking and at some point and time shortly thereafter it happens. What if instead you focused all your attention towards healing their condition and prayed they'd see the lace is too loose in time to tie it right? I believe it would happen! What I can perceive from an intuitive standpoint is, that knowing right from wrong you are not mentally handy capped if you incorrectly discipline someone. However you are mentally handy capped if you do not know how to correctly discipline them. Therefore I conclude there is no such thing as an, "evil genius." Who hides behind an extra ordinary set of circumstances. Just a clever person. Because true, ingenuity does not have anything but good intentions, built into it. If somebody say to me, "It's going to be this way." And it's not the right way. If they don't say and thru miraculous change it becomes the right way. That's psychic ability. So, an ant walks into a book store with a stack of books strapped to its back twice its weight! Approaches the front desk and says. "I've read every book on my back thoroughly from cover to cover! And in order to remember everything I did read I had to sort every subject chronologically. But I found the only way I could memorize each and every one was to read them alphabetically. And not only did I find they told a story but also sounded very much like a greeting! And my gut instinct tells me to share what I learned and now know. But sadly I can't afford to buy enough reading material to do that for everybody." The clerk points in the direction of the building across the street, the library. And replies. "I admire your might and. That's my greatest insight.

Love Is

True love is innocent of any crime. And curiosity is just an infatuation of the mind. That's why there is a door to the heart. To continue the beat and keep it safe from harm. There is a science to true love and its chemistry is just as exciting as it is gratifying. Tender and gentle to the touch. Craving lots of attention. I have to say, that's why I pray I'm treated the same way. Listen to your heart! And it will listen back to you. Love has a conscience. True love makes me tear! No love makes me cry. ...So don't be jealous if I know the reason why.

Love Story

A self educated man that greatly increased his intelligence in life by listening to his teacher and believing in his Preacher. Who always encouraged others to stimulate the mind to be alike. Articulated with ingenuity and recalled automatically a properly formulated memory. Showed good adjudication of the situation and then said. "Promote mankind and protect womankind! And live up to the definition. Authenticate the reason. And I assure you your dream will come true. Automatic memory and recall and photographic mind and self control. To me mean simply that some read thoughts and others read feelings. There is no such thing as a two headed giant. But we've all heard of at one time or another, a gentle one. Because if fact lead to fiction. They'd probably want to be separated and have their own bodies to live in. And that very thought would infatuate and consume both of them. So, as the tale's told. One remembers what the tears of a clown meant and the other remembers what the gestures of a mime represent. Says the first to the second. "Remember to be positive in nature and not to come to anger. And wipe away my tear before it forms. And I assure you. You will never cry. If you try. Because then I will have done the same for you without even having to! Because I educated you. Create and center with the simplicity and serenity of a well developed mindset worthy of praise based solely on the power of love. And use your imagination since you can. Have hope faith give to charity and pray everyone's able to at a moments notice do the same. Because life's a magical experience. And as the humming birds wings swing thru the air, pollinating from flower to flower. The clowns tears dry up. And he puts on a smile. Then the mimes gestures reflect nothing but that very thought! Someone with a, 180 IQ! Said, remember the saying. True love makes me tear but no love makes me cry. And I'll tell

you why. You're a man. And all you really need is the love of a good women!
After all if two heads are better than one. You don't have to look very hard to
see. And you didn't hear this from me. ...It's a love story.

Forward

One thing I found interesting while writing this report is that the, A B C's, of
good journalism are interchangeable with the, A B C's of Love. Distributing
the wealth thereof. Investigating glad tidings of great joy. We have wishes and
wills of wellness and wholeness. Going over beforehand. Creating an intelligent and cognizant telemetric path, with notions, intuitions, inklings, deducing
reasons and the fifth based on truth, conclusions. Something came into perspective. The saying. "You need a whole heart to heal someone who only has
a half of one. And once they do, they will have as big a heart as you!" So don't
judge this book by its cover just yet until you've read at least part of it. Then
you'll have walked a mile in my moccasins. And after I've received any and all
feedback responsibly. I'll hand you back yours. And you will see, I tend to repeat myself. But my intentions are good. And I will and wish for a better outcome to whatever it is, before you finish. The beauty of that is that any time
you can make up your mind to change your mind before you speak your mind.
That way nobody can say they read your mind. Until they know you as well as
you do yourself, inside and out. Look at the moon. I know the universe. And
somebody protected us. It's like a good game of checkers or chess. You may
not be able to stump the computer. But you can write love stories, (to some
just feel good medicine). And interchange them also with true stories about
hands on, modern medical miracles. Because the concept behind, is sometimes
hard to swallow and doesn't always taste good. ...Just to keep people interested.
Welcome to a report of just thoughts. Here is my message.

Bite The Coin To See If It's Real

To some a fist full of money or dollars is just a huge bouquet of flowers and a
big box of candy to have handy. To others it's a sac of gold worth many, many.
If you sold a short story for just one cent per copy. And only accumulated a
hundred customers. All you'd make is a dollar! But if you include the rest of
them, ...you might sell a million. So! What are a million pennies compared to
a million dollars? ...Precious metal to me. And yes I can count. But I have it

on good authority that even great writers. Whose books you can find in many many book stores. Make an average of 10 cents per copy for their complete work. Which depends on how many people purchase one. Because you also have to pay for as well as production, distribution. It all depends on what you consider to be wealthy. To determine that amount many gifted writers form their own publishing company. And the most exciting part of that process whether or not you self publish. Is how it all comes together in an intelligent manner. When you finally see your thoughts and feelings in ink and on paper. So now you know why some people feel they have to.

The Faith Healer & The Follower

A photo-graphic memory captures a photogenic capability where you never forget a face. Although you may not be able to remember some ones name because there are so many. In your vision you try all the harder to never let it age, over time. So every time you see who it is, your prayer is answered. And your wish comes true when they do the same for you. Yes, "Do unto others! ...In the right state of mind it works. And there is proof! Otherwise why would people be talking about it? Believe then receive! The, A B C's, of life. Command and demand the right amount of attention. And be the apple of the eyes of.

INSPIRATION

Someone said to me, "You can't profit from other peoples calamity!" To which I replied. "I am reminded that there are several different forms of communication. So, not if they could not tell their story publicly, to everybody! Because what happened to them also happened to me. And that makes their story my story. ...A penny for your thoughts, to me means. To whom much is given much is required and from whom much is required much is given to also. Therefore a penny saved is a penny earned. I can provide a copy of every short story to everyone! And if it's all they can afford I'll only charge a shiny penny for one. Or a dollar or two for the whole collection. How? Electronic distribution. But if you want a signed copy I'll charge a pretty penny or two. Which in my book, could turn out to be quite lucrative! Depending on how you look at what you do with what you've got. How big a heart you have and whether or not it's full of love, compassion and tender mercy. And you don't need an actual tape measure to figure out that equation! And do I tend to repeat myself?

Yes. If I do it's because everybody likes a story with a happy ending. And I have many many. Feel the love! Love's sweet isn't it. And love's powerful. And just between you and me. Because it's for free.

ASPIRATION

Always see the best in everybody. Then you will and shall always have in mind. The very key concept of a better outcome. To whatever set of circumstances was or might be that you wanted to happen to yourself as well as them.

INTRODUCTION

If you have allot of faith. And you sow the seeds of faith. When you go to reap them. Your reward will be great and you shall profit from. Think positive. Safety first. Love is tender to the touch. And great faith heals much. If our misery publically produces a form of slavery. Are we supposed to hide also when we are happy? Not necessarily. ...I am reminded of two sets of words three per that sound the same but don't mean the same, thing. To, Too, Two. Right, Rite, Write. So, what if there was a megaphone so powerful that it could turn all our shouts into a whisper? So would our anger. "Scape-goating", or singling out someone in the community, just because of the way they look or dress I know from experience that true beauty just like pure love comes from the heart, is on the inside. What people see when they look at you is just your outward appearance. ...Have you ever saved a penny in your pocket and rubbed it until it was shiny? A person with a golden heart and love's a commandment. Holds onto life and saves it until in comparison it is everlasting. And you can make me happy but you can't buy my love and you shall never own me. Just like if you formed an organization or foundation but had no money to put into it. In all practicality, it would only be able to do less, than if you had any. But thru pure acknowledgment, of a new application to the true solution to an age ole problem. The probability exists that even if you're broke! With love on your side the possibilities are endless. What saying helps a person with allot get along with someone who has a little? Share and share alike. ...Let's begin.

INVESTIGATION

E.S.P. Consists of human and animal instincts, traits and characteristics that become a pattern of behavior. Mental messaging just like instant electronic messaging can lead to an over active imagination. I believe a prayer can mend the situation. When one twin and it's been documented this actually happened, feels pain. The other gets a twitch at the very same time no matter how far apart they are separated from each other. So can we be in two places at once? No. But a belief can be in everyone at the same time.

EXPERIMENT

Intuition is different from premonition. So a simple experiment that proves, ESP, works is. Just walk up to your family pet. And without saying a word. Think of their favorite treat! And I assure you they'll speak.

INSTRUCTION

In all do course in order to create levity and bring light to the situation you need experimentation. And kind instruction reveals the source of the extra sensorial transmission, on the receiving end. It's something simple the mind produces itself such as a sound wave made of pure thought that travels thru the air. ... ...Like a dolphins sonar.

PSYCHOLOGY

Putting The Horse Before The Cart: You never know exactly what's on a persons mind until they speak it. Unless they can't. Then you have to find out the reason why. Trauma, atrophy, fear of abandonment. Knowing something should have been done about something that caused it to happen. Worry, fear, not being given the all clear, that it's safe to go back. Loneliness by then and now. Confusion over press coverage and the laws surrounding surveillance. Lack of good communication, lack of cooperation and devotion. Even where there's reasonable doubt, reasonable suspicion and probable cause to act. Given testimony and proof of being refused the correct treatment to pain and injury and adequate care. Thus affecting mind and body adversely. Finally investigation and hands on proof of being tortured while in a state of physical emergency. And the weight of getting word to everybody being put on the patient person and victims shoulders. Instigators calling premeditated poisoning and torture medical mistake or medical error. And renaming misaligning of a persons weak and infirm condition as just malpractice. Leaving it up to the victim to correct the situation. And using money as a bargaining tool and insurance policies to bypass or cover up the laws that bring justice to one and all. Yes torture is hard to describe. "Disgusting isn't it?

EXAMPLE

Lead by example. Humanitarian effort requires pouring your heart into your work. I remember. Before I was forced onto my potential bed of demise. In a state run mental health youth center facility. That at the last minute I was rescued from by someone from another building, not the doctors or staff where I was residing. Which state records still exist today and prove what happened to me. The rather young reporter Dan Rather, for CBS, on the nightly news nationally reported, Thorazine as a potential poison. And showed horrifying examples of mistreatment. What you may not have learned is Thorazine was produced in the 1930's or earlier. And as soon as it was introduced findings indicated with solid proof thru experimentation that it caused immense pain at any dosage, as long at it became repetitive. Which means it was forced upon the patient. And each time it's taken the tolerance to poison goes down not up. Just one milligram of which disables. And all who participated in this atrocious act decided never to release these findings to anyone nor tell anybody ever, about them. And they disguised it under several different names. One set is phenolthyzines. Another navane. And there are even more! So when I told a surgeon at a major university hospital in Toledo Ohio I was tortured. By being given 400 milligrams of liquid thorazine 3 times a day. Until I almost ceased to exist. And that all I got for justice was being told I can obtain a medic alert bracelet that describes my condition as being allergic. ...The surgeon almost cried right there in front of me. Because before I explained myself I asked do they still use Thorazine the surgeon said in a rather cheery tone of voice that yes they do!! And politely informed me at the end of the conversation I really should get the bracelet and yes it can most certainly contain all of the different varieties of potential poisons on it or on a medical card. Because of in the past inadequate representation I felt somewhat relieved.

GOAL

Unconditional love means no matter what someone does you still love them. That's why it's so important to be self disciplined. Because, with extra sensorial ability the change comes mentally. To make it work the change comes physically. So when it comes time to go from point A to point B every communication medium we have is used to fulfill an urgent need and answer some ones prayer. That way there's no mistaking intention with endeavor.

MISSION STATEMENT

To communicate well. And produce a world wide electronic medium where people with similar problems can post share and discus their stories with others. And also obtain help where ever a health care monitor has to or should be put into place that hasn't already been. So the mistakes of the past go away. And thru donation volunteerism and chivalry never reappear, again. Perfecto!

REFERENCES

I was taught that if you write a report of just thoughts, all in just paragraphs, with no words underlined, or in capital letters. That some people can easily find any subject matter, idea or set thereof it states that is contained within those pages with ease! Quickly and comfortably. Therefore, sooner or later you have to admit. In order to do that. They'd have to be pretty or very smart and bright people wouldn't you? Yes indeed. Yet at the same time, they also feel that it's just as valuable to have a reference to use as a guide. A valuable insight. And do to popular consensus, mine comes from experience. So about referring to a specific report or findings that lead to a cure to whatever ails you. ...On the electronic information highway. It becomes self explanatory. It just doesn't look easy because there are so many. And to keep up with the pace. A computer can be pre programmed never to erase any. So along with a few pages and sites. I go to the greatest heights to say. My best reference for sure, is don't give up on the cure. There's one out there. I'll put what you can refer to that I know so far in the links. Which are updateable, interconnect able, ongoing and subject to undeniable and non-erasable current events that will not change because in part or in whole they save lives. And when people discover something that does the job and word gets out it stays out! And can be digitally preserved for as long as we can and do read. And as far as we can see. And you never know, you just might find what you need, at your local library on line. "Open sesame!" And me, promoting my latest venture. Remember, "The Adventures Of Superman?" Take a good look. The concept behind the illustrated book is that honest reporting can save a life. And that's worth a belt buckle that says on it, "Champion! Of Human Rights.

INSIGHT

If you study the format you find that in the crux of my material I put an emphasis on helping other people. So if you look carefully and read between the lines. You'll see I show anybody how to actually write a short story and even a book eventually. If you exchange your viewpoints, thoughts and ideas with mine. Including prose, poetry and rhyme with reason eloquently. And there are talented writers who work for companies that after you give them a few hints as to what you want to write will do so for anyone for a profit. That I include free of charge. Which I think is valuable. No experience necessary! Be creative. And if you want to, "get technical", also. Express your feelings. Be kind, considerate and concentrate. Because the concept behind this insight is that, "Everybody has a story to tell." You've heard, "Great thinkers think alike?" So do great writers. Get started today. And it will work for you as well. And when you're finished. After they read what you wrote. People will say, "Speech please!" And you will hear applause when you stand up to give it. Even before one word comes out of your mouth. You'll start out an amateur and end up a pro.

THEME

In sports medicine a good trainer will tell you that when you get a, "Charlie horse", you don't push down with the sole of your foot you pull from the ground up! Every spirit has a body of proof of the amount of love it tends to give. Is measurable, and at times the feat itself is quite astounding. A good theme to have in mind is to communicate well. And coordinate inter and outer office and all other communiqué. Then blend and connect them with inter and outer cooperation. To magnify the effects thereof. And practice them to perfection.

CHALLENGE

They say, "No news is good news." To which I say good news is better than none. And they say, "Change is change." But here again there are two different kinds. No change is no change and a change for the better is a good one. Ancient Greece had one hospital all the way at the top of a mountain! One man who was poisoned for his beliefs was made famous. And one man, "invented", democracy just by giving everyone a chance to speak! And the people fashioned a belief that love's the single most powerful force on earth that is good. And they had and did develop one definition for the explanation of having only one God. And that is, "God is love." ...In America we have four oncology treatment centers nationwide called, Cancer Treatment Centers of America. Just four? And as of the date of this report lawyers have commercials on television. Where they state that at least one hundred thousand hospital patients every year not die, but are killed by medical mistake or error. Then I find they still use potential poisons in Ohio to treat the mentally ill! And that these errors in judgment made by staff and physicians amount to torture. Is there a statute of limitations on them also? So far some politicians only recognize torture as being when someone is straps you to a board and pours water on you. A walk in the park compared to what I've been thru. Current events. Communication is the key. The newest latest version of that medium is manufactured by people who reported suspected human rights violations in an over populated country. Some of our leaders want less rule and less regulation. It's because they have no self discipline, in my opinion. I also think and did not forget to mention that in many instances it's all in the name of mocking the Christian. Who can do nothing but forgive without true leadership coming from them. I wrote the news media and they wrote back once and told me to try my best to get my story out there. And then, they would do their best to help affect a change for the better. And the challenge is similar.

AUTOBIOGRAPHY

How did the art of producing an exact double of a life form come about? They grew a whole, carrot from a single cell. And from just one stalk! Which brings to mind a saying. "Don't put the horse before the cart." Or dangle a carrot on a stick in front of it just to get it to go. Unless you already fed the animal. Otherwise you force it to do something that slaves it whether it's a donkey or an elephant, that keeps it from being given the opportunity to be stubborn as an Angel and as triumphant, when you are not. Today's my birthday! I was born May 1'st, 1962. The same year John Glen orbited the earth and made history. I thought up my first story. "The Soup Bowl & The Giant." {Which I could produce and sell as a children's story good for all ages one and up. For a penny a copy in a hard cover version. And be able to afford to no matter how many I do. Because it fits on just one page. Giving meaning to the ole, infamous, "Penny Book."} And because I had a hernia at, my parents said about six weeks old. I felt the pain and didn't know if I would receive help in time to save my life. It felt like somebody cutting me with a knife. And since I felt the pain it made me cognizant. Early on I felt like an adult in a child's body. But I could not talk 'till I was about three. And that's why and when I almost forgot to mention. I conceived while awake. The dream of going to sleep and in the dream. Waking up a giant! And walking about the place. So on the one hand, growing up. My mother wanted me to write mostly about my experiences. On the other hand. My father wanted me to write stories about them. Which would be a story book the same size as it's biography! So I will write for now, only the beginning. Sharing the wealth and thus distributing the weight. Even though it spreads very thin upon every ones shoulders. It is also feather light in nature. ...So about the age of nineteen I went to the doctor. Who saw a five or six inch scar during a routine physical. I told him what it was from and from how long ago. So he gave me some cream in a tube and said, if I put in on. The scar within a month, or so will heal. I was flabbergasted! So I basically asked, "How do you expect me to believe you? I took a look at the ingredients! It says it has bees wax and castor oil in it. This is not real medicine. This is just an old remedy that medical science proves doesn't do anything to help you heal. But sooth the mind and trick it into thinking it will." He reiterated. "But you know a doctor takes an oath and you also being religious should also have known. That first and foremost a doctor is a faith healer. Where's your, faith sir. And yes to answer your question before you ask one. Great faith can also heal any tissue and every organ. About a month later the scar disappeared. And my fear of having an emotional one.

Whisper In My Ear

Public consensus indicates new electronics will help prevent a certain mental illness. Although contention points in the direction that it also could be done, without any. Procrastination meets capitulation. Or is it the other way around? And terminology Vs, simple definition. If the doctor exchanged places with the patient, he or she would have to do exactly what they told them to! Just like if the rich had to trade places with the poor. They would both have to share and share alike. In order to see. That after they did. They'd realize they had the very same dream. Now, what was it again? Lean close. Whisper in my ear. "To heal.

A WHISPER IN THE WIND

Some tend to meditate in what seems to be a trance like state. Still others transcend that by meditating in prayer alone. A sphere of influence that is good compares to a soap bubble! When you prick it with a pin and it pops wide open it spreads nothing but cleanliness throughout the atmosphere. And cleanliness is next to Godliness. So, you have as a result. A spiritual transformation! Transcendental meditation. And astral projection. But no matter what order you put them in. Like prayer and meditation itself. They go hand in hand. And there are voices of opinions going on right now behind closed doors. In front of, eyes wide open, hands to ears intently listening. For a sign from Heaven! Or a signal that subtlety indicates ...That everything's going to be OK, just fine and all right, even from behind. And, {Music here}. "Do you see what I see? Do you hear what I hear? ...Something's in the air. I see love everywhere!" And even though it seems to at times have the power of invisibility. When it finally reappears. It douses all my fears, And I assure you. Is music to my ears.

Treasure-Map

God said you are special. That's not so hard to understand. Since he probably said it to everyone who thought the same thing, of him. And that's not so hard to comprehend now is it. If you listen to the voice of reason. Because your inner self is more powerful than your outer! If you use psychology. Don't tell anybody. So when their adrenalin pumps they won't get so serious and become so curious. As to come to only one conclusion. And say, "Just go away!" No instead they'll praise, the ability to pray. Each and every day. They say, "Actions are bigger than words." And we are judged by our deeds and actions. Yet the pen is mightier than the sword, only when the content of the writing on a piece of paper stops one altogether. A feat to be observed, to say the very least. But just imagine not having a pen with which to write. Or having to in invisible ink! Onto a parchment that bursts into flame just as you finish. And vanishes in an instant, into thin air before your very eyes! ...But because you can remember, thru miraculous measure. What you were trying to say. You develop the ability to do better and better, over and over. Never slips away. ...Hark! Who goes there! I have to clap! Because you found my, ...

My Gift To You

My rendition and dissertation of a revelation is not first a story about some sort of monster someone unleashed upon society. And a detailed explanation thereafter. But rather a story about a gentle giant who expanded the mind and was often time misunderstood. As to whether he brought more harm than good. Who loved to protect others and enjoyed their company so much he decided to share what he learned how to do one day, while trying to heal. And stood to gain from. "And it is my understanding, I remembered thru instruction and teaching that the explanation to the story is the revealing! Submitted for your approval in as many as three, good reports. That can contain as many as twelve to even the proverbial, fifteen page report. Or just one two or three page report sounds short and sweet. You know the ole saying, "Have it on my desk in the morning." And since genius is not cleverness it might as well be about that. Say in eight to twelve areas we consider to be our greatest needs and matters of the utmost importance. That you can write a paragraph or two on the availability and progress of each up to date. In your own words. Even if for an explanation all you have is a story. Your version will do. Everyone has one and each one's different. You learn something new every day. If you concentrate on what you learn. It becomes easier to remember what you already know. Thank you for valuing our friendship just a little more than your rite to total privacy when I used my telepathy to contact you mentally thru ESP. Thank you for your concern for others. I appreciate your love when it smothers. I am a gentle giant when it comes to being mentally patient. And all I have for a weapon in one hand is an asparagus spear! And in the other a bowl of soup and a ladle, giant of course. And my secret to true happiness and pure joy. Is sharing good food and good times together. Now how shall I explain myself. Let me think this thru. Until I can remember. Here it is. Food for thought. My gift to you.

The-Reflection

WHEN I WAKE UP IN THE MORNING & LOOK IN THE MIRROR.
I ASK MYSELF ONE SIMPLE QUESTION. "WHAT DO YOU THINK
OF ME?" AND MY REFLECTION ANSWERS BACK. "I DON'T
KNOW! BUT I PUT UP WITH WHAT I SEE."

THE JOKER

Being the happiest person in the room is hard work. Because the reward only
comes when you make other people laugh first. But it's well worth the effort.
When they roll on the floor with uncontrollable laughter holding their stomach begging you to stop. That's pay dirt! That's why I got into this business in
the first place! ...To put a smile on your face. They say laughter's the best medicine and to burry your treasure in Heaven. ...No wonder everybody wants
something for nothing. Of course they have got to be joking!!

KEY

Although there many different forms and mediums of communication such as
prayer, also a gift. And they're all important. Not one works if it's abandon.
And if people like you and me don't communicate directly. Somebody else may,
resort to animal instinct. Which amounts to at best. Sincerely, only survival of
the fittest. But love is special! Love is the key to good communication. Because
it gives freely of itself. And needs no explanation.

The Triumphant Elephant

...Imagine a doorway to the imagination so big, anyone and anything can travel
thru it. So! An elephant walks into a book store and says slowly, "I have something on my mind. What if a man was shackled to a chain as big as the one
they tether an elephant to the ground with. And all he had to free himself with
was a nail file! And along comes an elephant with hands instead of his toes and
front two feet. Will he be able to pull the chains apart. Or saw them in two.
And will he happily do so, ...for you?? And what if you came along with the
strength of an elephant! And saw me, chained to the ground. Would you cut
thru it with a great big saw and free me from my huge shackle that kept me

down trodden? And feeling like a floor mat. Because see, I never forget a kind act. It takes the patients of a saint to be as gentle as a giant. And since one good turn deserves another. As I gently sit on this stool underneath the big top and prop my leg up on an ottoman in the spot light of the ring. Being the first to break free! And profit from what we both want. I am, ...

THE GENIUS CLUB

Welcome, welcome, welcome! Everyone. One and all and anyone. To the genius club. So why compare to? Bravery. And contact. Because they know someone had to make a sacrifice and gather credible evidence and collect valuable proof. In order to present the facts and reveal the hidden truth. ...The hard way. To investigate and correct the mistakes of the past. Make changes that insure future peoples safety. Where there was immense pain unjustly caused that produced injury. And it was some ones fault. And the only way to prove it was their sole intention. Is thru hands on, investigation. Because when it comes do doing that. Perhaps some members sense of self preservation takes over. Whereas preservation of other than self does in others. Why? So people will look up to you and for a just cause. So you can earn their respect. So you're able to say you stood up for something right that you believe in. And that you faced your fears, did something about it and won! You volunteer your effort, donate your time. Show raw courage and develop a heart of gold. That's what it takes to make it work. And some make it their work, all life long. And if they make you an honorary member, all have a chance to in my book. So about the genius club. If you can do for them what they cannot do for themselves. And it helps others. "You're in!" Because then they can. Which doesn't require acing a test. But creates an excellent outcome. Which makes for a good report. Not tomorrow but yes today. So thanks for all your kindness and love. And letting me sub. At what they dub. The genius club.

ONE IN A MILLION!

One man, (Bill Gates), described a person who possesses, extraordinary intellectual power especially as manifested in creativity. Endowed with transcendent mental superiority especially a person with a very high intelligence quotient. "Is one in a million." And everybody knows some people try to either chase down the ingenious or at least ketch up to them. And to keep it alive, one man spread what he knew to the masses, (everyone), with one simple project. When he'd draw near someone he'd produce unconditional love and make peace with them. And that drew quite a crowd as you can imagine! Now that's ingenious isn't it! And he taught equality. So that if someone thought you were a Christian they just might forget you're doing the work of a genius. That was one way of protecting it. Since it used to be stalked and hunted, instead of appreciated. And everyone wants to be a leader. But until everybody follows and performs the required tasks in order to become one there is only one. However once you are taught by the first you become the second. And so on until one in a million becomes a million and one! And one day my father overheard my brothers in the other room arguing over who was smarter. The one or the other. He became disgusted and entered the room and asked them both of who, do they know that became one of the most famous and possibly the first modern genius! And he said everyone knows of him. And before they could answer also asked if they had forgotten their ability to remember. And did their lack of education in that area alone cloud their judgment? Then advised not to keep it a secret. And to share what they know with everyone everywhere. Because that person is Jesus Christ Super Star! He won the hearts people the world over. And he's one in a million!

The Elephant & The Turtle Dove

When I was about fifteen my big brother sat me down at the kitchen table and explained bit by bit just exactly how a computer is fashioned down to the most minute detail totally from memory. No notes no references. No nothing but the power to recall what he learned. Which was by the way about the time the inventor of the famous computer program, "Windows", had already published many articles of his true intentions. So as you can imagine I was fascinated. But sadly stated, "I would love to get into computer programming as I see it holds in store for whoever does a promising and obviously lucrative future! But I won't based solely on my intuition that I believe other people can read the mind and I don't want to have that much valuable information accumulated in case someone does, mine. But I do believe we can end physical and mental cruelty and abuse of the weak and infirm in our lifetime with one, yes that I do remember and shall never forget! And I remember the following story with which to back it up. Now let me think, what was the title. Let's see, there's, The Mighty Mouse. The Majestic Mastodon. The Triumphant Elephant. The

Turtle And The Elephant. ...oh yeah! It's. The Elephant & The Turtle Dove. I got up and said, "Let's take a break. Because I have to clear my thoughts and visualize the conversation I had with my trainer, earlier. Shortly thereafter I exclaimed, "Ah! I can see it all clearly now. And my memory has come back to me. ... ...Think of it as if you have a sac of gold. If nobody can read your mind and you shall never say where your treasure is buried, it they shall never find. After all, if it is just a little. You will always be pleased to tell them where it is. And at the same time hand them the shovel. There's a difference between reading some ones mind and just plain making fun of their abilities with yours. And picking on someone until they almost become famous! For being picked upon. And talked about but not to, about. Even though you're both showing signs of becoming promising clairvoyants. By the same token. Being ambulatory, {which means able to walk from place to place}, if people made fun of you because of the way you dress or the way you look. Would they still make fun if you wore the robe of a preacher and at the same time were of the cloth? Remember what a sleeping giant and gentle person had to say about that similarity? That everyone's a little bit psychic. And by the way he got that information from his dreams. Strong mind, sound body. It's one thing to take a book off the shelf to read. It's another thing to write a book to put on one. So it stands to reason, about having a heart of gold. It pays to have a door and a lock to it as long as you hide, the key. So picture lying on a couch and you fall asleep but you feel awake. And someone sits down beside you and starts reading, and it is very comforting. ...Now just imagine them being able to do just that, from a distance! I'll give you a good example. I believed when I was young that my neighbor a farmer and in the eyes of his neighbors, a visionary could do just that. And I told my family some people want that ability all to themselves and therefore tend to always want to keep it a secret! And they did not deny it. But themselves, tended personally not to want to have to confirm it, publicly. Yet admitted it in private. I saw to it. By getting them to admit it to myself. That and that a little embarrassment in life doesn't hurt a bit. Because I'd been thru in my eyes, allot. And once they realized I thought that. They'd become ecstatic! "What is it Bobby what is it? Tell us what you know!" Then they'd laugh uncontrollably and pat me on the head and occasionally also the back. Look me in the eyes and exclaim, "I wonder what on earth it could be." That's when I'd usually say, rather quickly just as they'd start to walk away. "OK I'll tell you just what I learned at my last reading and in my latest dream." So why don't I explain it to you the way the Dreamweaver did to me. From

82

his mind to mine. Spiritually. We simply called it, story time. Because he'd read you a story that would teach you how to tell the one he told you when you awoke every time, each and every morning! ...If you could remember it. And he always said, "You will be able to if you believe in yourself and you can do anything you put your mind to, as long as you at least try to. So, even though I am not sitting directly beside you. Before I lean back in my favorite reading chair. I now, slowly place my right foot on the ottoman in front of me. Book in my right hand and a handkerchief in my left hand reaching forward, with its elbow resting on one bended knee. And this has significance relating to the next story. So, let's begin reading. ...Look at the size of an elephant! Its wide expanse and huge forehead. One of its eyes is as big as my hand! Just imagine wiping its tears because it was abused by another human. Now then! After you take a moment or two to reflect upon. Let me remind you before they said there wasn't enough room between the pages of the newspaper to accommodate every ones ideas and opinions due to population growth itself. Anybody could publish their story in one, locally. And I understand some of you might say that's not really important anymore, times have changed because of developments in the industry of new technological advantages in the art of communicating and even if everybody could, it would just be repeating the mistakes of the past. That all ideas and opinions, with this new technology if need be, can all be conglomerated into one. Therefore it is of no use and there's no need to think you absolutely have to voice your own idea and or opinion. But I have to tell you, not if the present doesn't look as good as the past did, when it was the present. Because, in my book the mistakes of the past are buried forever. And if you don't put things in the right perspective the past tends to repeat itself until you do. Then the future changes for the better. When you do. Thru and thru. Ho-Hum! I'm getting sleepy! So if you don't mind I shall close the book and reiterate the rest of the story, tomorrow evening. Good night and sweet dreams.

Fathers Day

Love is powerful, tuff, merciful yet tender to the touch. Everyone has a memory, ...and a conscious. And some try to erase the one in order to suppress the other. So that even though the conscious doesn't forget the memory doesn't remember. And there are ways to experience true love and pure joy! By reaching out and going in different directions. Thinking up new things to do and talk about. Even though we keep the same routines. I'm here to please. And suppress any bad memories. And burry the mistakes of the past forever in order to look forward to a better future. And with the power of Love & Peace it will be my sheer pleasure! And even to a powerful intellect, a gentle nudge will do. Call it happenstance but if you obsess over what someone else doesn't know or can't remember. You'll never be able to see their true potential or even comprehend what they can do! The secret is a level and the golden rule. Where the subconscious mind asks a question and meets the conscious mind that immediately and sublimely answers for the first time. In a long time, sometimes. Then, things start to come together. Like old times but good times mixing with new. And after they draw near meet, greet and enjoy mental activity together, they meld into one. Synchronicity! And to develop the right mentality. You have to maintain a good attitude. Because it's often time been said. Good advice doesn't always just come from off the top of the head. When you're fishing for food for thought to give to the mind of man.

The Quill & The Ink Well

If I could only do with a single dollar what those with a million were never able to. I'd be worth that amount without the asking and not end up the one who's begging.

SCHOOLING

Aptitude. Taking ample time as I go over valuable decisions to make up my mind before I speak my mind in order to relate what I've learned since yesterday and retained and remembered from yesteryear. The art if creating and playing music is one of the oldest forms of freedom of expression that we have. And it's always pleasing to the ears when we hear something nice that we like. Which is also true when giving or listening to a good speech. I remember when I was really small relatives when they'd see me would walk up to me and pinch my cheeks and say what a cute little boy I was even in public. And they would pinch so hard I would start to cry. So being curious, naturally I often wondered why. And I was the second to the littlest kid in my grade and class, all thru school. No sir-ee, I could not say I was dealt the exact same hand in life as anybody else. And I'm not going to say I had one of those high pitched squeaky voices but to some, mine was only a grade or two above unpleasant. And that's not to say that I am not familiar with unpleasantness. Around ten, my dentist drilled my only cavity without any anesthetic! Told my parents he'd forgot it. And instead of one, I got two toys out of it. Of course I had to do allot of yelling to accomplish that. And when I used to dart off the bus or when I lived in town walked to school almost immediately! Like an allergic reaction some would make fun of the way I looked and or presented myself. And I admit sometimes that was a bit hap hazard. So I would laugh! They would get mad and say, "What's so funny?" Achievement. So my self preservation would kick in and I would become jocular. And jokes would flow into my mind as fast as I could tell them! And all of a sudden the people who were laughing at me instead now were laughing with me! "Class Clown", they used to call me. I wore my reputation with pride as you can imagine. And at the time everybody liked that side of me. Here I'm one of the littlest kids in school and no one is going to pick on me, ...because I'm funny! But it's also because I took everything in stride. And when I couldn't, tried not to let them see me sweat. Yes laughter's a gift! And so is shyness. And if because of your talent someone offers you fame and you turn it down. You can always change your mind if it was for all the right reasons. After a while, I was able to make people hold their guts and roll on the floor with laughter so happy they'd practically come to tears! With nothing but great big smiles on their faces. And I didn't use a microphone or first have to stand up at a podium. And I also remember one day after class someone coming up to me and saying. "I understand where you're coming from! I too know the tears of a clown. Look at me, I'm not all that handsome. So I don't, judge a book by its cover." That gave me a good feeling inside so I replied. "Good looking out! I see you know the true meaning behind inner beauty!" Somebody else overheard and said, "Yeah! Schooling!" ...We all started laughing. You Can't Buy What's Already Given/ What is right about saved accounted work for a free momentum is that , when it can't be afforded. Concern for those without , Can be afforded .

"The Two Headed Giant"

One fine day two giants got together and the one asked the other. "Why were you so sad?" OK to be quite honest he muttered. "Why are you ugly?" And well wait! Since I see you want to know the sacred, secret truth. It might as well have been just one giant standing in front of a mirror rehearsing a speech, for another. In any event two heads are better than one. And there are two sides to every story and somebody heard and recorded the following conversation. The two headed giant. One was happy, one was sad. One looked good, one looked bad. One wore a smile, and one wore a frown. One was strong kind and gentle and one was full of humility, yet remained powerfully humble. So the one said to the other. "Look at you, looking back at me! We have a good side, he smiled with two lips pointing in an upward direction. And we have a bad side, he frowned with two lips pointing in a downward direction. One of us is good looking and one of us is ugly. But for the most part we're both good people, aren't we!" So the smile faced the frown and asked. "So why were you so sad! I noticed you back there hiding." The reply. "I chose to remain in the background because I'm not good looking! And because I feared my mightiest speech could never keep people from disliking me. Nor, my most powerful blow. And I am a peaceful giant! I wanted peace to come from not just those, who are pretty! But because I am ugly, I hid myself because that part of me I didn't want anyone else to see. And I'm a good person just like you! But I won't have anyone say I'm a bad one just because I'm not beautiful and my looks are less than ordinary. And call me an Ogre a Cyclops and unfriendly. And if we were a two headed giant! People would only like the one, not the other. And you're the only half they'd view even when they wanted to talk to me, instead of you." He looked around as far and wide as he could see, and sobbed and sobbed and sobbed. And so, now the other giant took a turn! And he said. "Peace doesn't come from things that are pleasing, to just the eye. Well that and why didn't you just say you wanted peace to come from everybody!!" So as the one dried his tears, about all this the other giant thought it over. And he thought and thought and thought! And as he also, composed himself remarked. "If it offends those whose looks are supposedly always good. And all people strain their necks because they are huge and have plenty. Since it may, I just might say and in this instance feel it's necessary to although I don't mean you. If I'm half as smart as I am ugly. Then the painfully offended are half as good looking as they are wise! And only half as bright as they look! And only half as smart as they wanted to be. Until they sit up take notice and see! Just how good we look when we work together, as a team. And that from that point on made peace and eventually won the world over. Even when you only have half what you're capable of to work with. Since you're a giant of peace. You can still do the work of many. And working together produce much more than the results of just one! And don't you know a giant's coming when you see one?" The second giant replied. "Yes I see you've come! Now that I'm not embarrassed to be one. So to answer your question. Why am I ugly? I don't know! So if somehow in the beginning or before my life began. It was possible to, and I invariantly made the choice not to look good. And say I was blessed with the ability to do good. I felt it could be forgiven of me. Because if people ever thought that doing good only came from those who looked good. Then I wouldn't be representing those who didn't! And that wouldn't make me a good person at all, now would it. And since I am intelligent you'd thing I'd want to be! But if you look closely and see just what people go thru that aren't You'd know looks don't matter to me. And you'd also see if people don't like you just because your face is not as aesthetic and less than pleasing than theirs is. You have to do a good deed or two just so they do! Or so it would seem if you, were me! So now you can tell I am delighted to be bright! And about what you see from now on when you look. What you see is what you get! And I don't care what you think of me. I am just glad to be myself." So the one said to the other. "Look into me eyes! And be wise. Our looks only shelter our desire to know just who we really are! And your looks only stretch so far. But your deeds stretch as far as you can see! And whether you're rich or poor, big or little, short or tall. All looks come from up above. And believe me, God has seen them all! So you see, if in your heart you have love and compassion, you're rich spiritually! Because to God, wanting to look good is just a choice. But wanting to do, something good is not an option it's a must! And in that we must indulge and rejoice. Because some people that want good things to happen to them tend to pick out only what looks good for all their needs! Not good deeds. Looks can deceive! They're only on the surface, not what lies hidden underneath. And beauty's only skin deep! Therefore looks don't always matter to I, either. And you have, inner beauty! So you do look good, to somebody. So clip clop tick tock and click, click the seconds on the clock away. It had become time to end their discussion. So the two giants shook hands, patted each other gently on the back. Cracked a smile, grinned from ear to ear. And laughed uncontrollably without fear!

REPORT! Personal Injury

Name: Robert Corogin
Address: 1545 North East Catawba Island Road
City: Port Clinton
state: State of OHIO

zip: 43452
home phone: 149-797-3062
daytime phone: 419-797-2377
email: harborparkmarina@cros.net
date of incident: April 29th 2001Around five thirty in the afternoon .
location of incident: Magruder Hospital

describe accident:
I picked up a 400lb. or so riding lawnmower after it had been running for five
hours strait as I filled it up while still running that day .I picked it up by the
muffler that was hidden underneath a front guard plate ,painted the same color
as the mower . I got second degree burns on the first three fingers of my left
hand . I thought the guard actually went all the way underneath , like the fire
guard they have for mowing dry grass . It was stuck in a rut when I attempted
it , & on marina property out here at Harbor Park Marina Inc . I live here also
. Other than the deceptive guard , my other trouble started after I located my
buddy right away , at the nearby house where we stay .Where I was mowing
marina front lawn up by the Catawba road . I yelled to him to let me in to get
the ems on the phone , he dialed 911 . And I stuck my hand into the kitchen
freezer up side a lot of frost . But I fast found out that the ice was producing a
burning feeling also . By that point I had to scream constantly , in pain , so
much I actually couldn't cuss just any semi polite swear words . I felt at the
time I had to scream the worst words I knew , " God Am " . While doing so I
realized I have to run the fingers under flowing water . Also I remembered
from T V news watching that in Toledo the ice baths used for burn victims
have since documented Lukewarm water as a much less painful treatment . I
remembered because working in any marina those tips come in handy . I ran
to the tub where there is a wide dispersion of H2o . Then I came to realize in
seconds , Luke warm water soothed the pain enough that I could quit what I
thought to be involuntary cussing . At this point my friend and co-worker here
at the marina informed me that the ems was on the way from this township
,Catawba . A township policeman came to me in the tub in the bathroom first
He as you might think wanted me to seek emergency room treatment . But
every time I tried to remove my fingers , the awful pain , and swearing started
up involuntarily . I know the policeman somewhat . So I asked him that since
he was in a foreign war didn't he know of the proper amount of time to leave
the burns under the water treatment . He replied he was "over there" to fight

, and said sadly no he didn't know anything about this treatment I was applying . He tried to talk me into taking my handout from under the faucet . Telling me I'd at least get something for the pain there at Magruder . However every time I pulled away the unbearable pain persisted . So time after time I put it back under . Then the ems workers entered and tried to apply after talking me into the temporary treatment , what I thought to be older style burn ointment cloth , or gauze pads . They smelled like kerosene or thinner . Like I say an old outdated treatment .I screamed in pain and the bandage seemed to do nothing . By that time I was completely out from under the tub , and they had me talked into taking the ride in the van to Port Clinton . Well as it turns out , there was no running water to put my hand under in it . The one worker had to hold me down as the pain got very strong and lengthy .After we arrived I immediately after being escorted to a room got up off the gurney and pro-ceeded to the sink and ran my burns under their water faucet The doctors screamed for the orderlies . They literally pulled my hand from the running water and strapped me down with a strap on each arm . I yelled and yelled that all I wanted to do was kill the pain . I remember as they were tugging at me to strap me down , I explained to them the running water is the proven method to ease the burn and stop my screaming I even told them I am fair and if they will let me ease my burns under their faucet that I had enough money in my pocket to pay for the water consumption in full . Just to let me run my fingers under the water .While strapped down by each mid arm , they denied that the H2o would help They shot me up with what they claimed to be "demoral " , in both upper arms . I explained I might be allergic to it as I was poisoned by phenylthyzines when I was 16 years old . I am now 41 . So they shot me up with what they referred to as a coagulant to counteract it . During the ordeal the Catawba policeman had one of the workers from the van come and apol-ogize to me . I asked him why or what for ? He replied that's all he could say . Apparently the policeman arrived way before the ems guys and told them to say sorry . After a half an hour of confusion one of the doctors or nurses applied a break to activate , ice pack but wouldn't refresh it . Then they took even it out from under my hand . My father came in and told one lady doctor those were my guitar fingers , (I play guitar , write , and draw) . And informed them I have no insurance and argued about workers comp . , because I had two 24 ounce Busch beers before continuing mowing but that I wasn't drunken and that I was indeed still on duty at work . My father owns the marina and lets me and my buddy live here also . At this point no running water, and warm ice

89

pack removed . I was given after complaining , a metal bowl to put them in . It had room temp. water in it . And didn't help . But after my father got there they unstrapped me . And just as I stated when he said could they stop the pain for me , because they were my guitar fingers . The lady doctor said my fingers might have to come off . Drawing a line with her fingers just before the knuckles that attach the fingers to the hand . I by then was furious and actually walked half way out of the emergency room itself . A male doctor said to my dad , he couldn't stop me . Yet they did stop me from the water treatment and suggest just before hand amputating half of my hand . By then about 50 or so minutes had past , and I gave up to do exhaustion and returned to the gurney . They came in with a gauze bandage containing another jelly in it . Claiming it was a narcotic jelly . They then after I exclaimed I don't have a regular doctor as at the time the local office was closed . They informed me that my records were in storage there at the hospital . And to come in the next morning at seven thirty , to have the bandages freshly re rapped . Once their , in the morning , I asked to be treated . The one male doctor was there from the night before . But was as usual , at a computer display peering . The same thing he does every time I've been there . Looking up the treatment plans I suppose for the victims of pain . But you see they never type up just HOW they treat you , just what to do for each specific problem ONLY after that period of time . So another doctor came into the patient room and asked why I was there . I told him I have no doctor and that I was instructed to return at this time for new bandages . He said that isn't the way things are done there and escorted me to a raisable food tray . It contained two or three different kinds of regular "Band-Aids" . He said to me since I probably was told to come back that I was entitled to two or If I wanted he supposed three Band-Aids . I asked is that all you can do ? He exclaimed I was lucky he offered me the Band-Aids .

describe injuries:
2nd degree burns emotional trauma and denied access to a water faucet .UPDATE & I was scared to mention the Doc said, "He may have the correct treatment but no one yells in my hospital!" That and the next day when I was given the Band-Aids the same Doc told me from a distance at a laptop that he did not see how a computer can stop and abuse and neglect in the hospital. He claimed he searched the internet and it offered him nothing.

The Hero & I W I Y C P.

Means, "what if you could prove." W I Y C P, stubborn rural suburban and some city doctors and staff tortures patients! <u>I have plenty of witnesses</u>. With true life accounts who will attest to that fact. And who have tried to and would be glad to give and share with you their testimonies. And, W I Y C P, TV news commentators covered it up. <u>I have plenty of memos</u>. All pointing 100%, in that direction. And, W I Y C P, the press, papers, news agencies and magazines would not and did not write these facts down, in the annals of history! <u>I have plenty of proof</u>. And what on Gods good green earth ever, could the reason be? W I Y C P, they made a quote, ..."mistake!" And in doing so masterfully and powerfully, massively and repeatedly. After tasting the first drop, became, "blood-thirsty!" You could certainly see their clear intent to cover one up. And what if in doing so they did not want that mistake to be seen? What better way than to torture their opposition, by telling no one. And when others come and still want answers, say not one thing! Some of the best proof there is. Is if you survived. I am a victim of physical and mental cruelty and neglect and abuse in more than one health care facility when my body was weak and infirm. Where I investigated torture comparable to that which is endured by war. That's right I volunteered for treatment in one instance after a bad accident near my home. In order to investigate at the recommendation of an on duty officer of the local police force here. It was for second to first degree burns. The proven and painless treatment is luke-warm water. I was denied it. And I spoke to a peace keeper, defender of the defenseless and a hero. US Army General, Tommy Franks. I and another witness and victim sat down two doors down from my house with him at a park bench. At the local fish cleaning place. "Jacks Fish Cleaning." Right next door to the bait and tackle store. "Herbs Bait Store." And sipped a beer. He mentioned he heard what went on in the local hospital in Port Clinton. "Magruder Hospital." We talked about some of the horrible things that were done to ourselves and others. He asked if it was true if we locals nick-named it, "Mc-Murder." We said yes and discussed politely the reasons why. And he told us if anyone tried to do anything to affect his wounded men adversely. Or in any way denied fair treatment when their lives are in desperate need of being saved. Knowing what he saw them go thru for freedom on the battle field. Those medical personnel in question. If he saw them personally not do everything they were taught to save their life. They would not make it to trial before justice would have to be done. To show the rest of them no doctor is going to, "Manny-Mal", those who were injured while doing their sworn duty to God and country. Because to him saving that life at that point and time is his only priority. And he has every rite by law, to defend against any form of torture, in our society. There is a stethoscope out that sends the sounds of your heart via wireless microwave transmission. To a computer that listens to signals you can't hear with the human ear. "Technology's scream in!" I'm still alive. The hero and I.

The Leader!

The leader. Speaking to the great communicators. In so many words. Here is what the leader told them. ..."I've heard what you've had to say about me. ...Before I've had a chance, to speak! And so, you can't put words in my mouth. Beforehand, and claim I'd just say no to any future plans, to be at peace. With all other leaders, on the planet. And that it's time, to go ahead without them. And I don't care, what time table you say I made up! For peace to run out, in the past! Times change, and it just doesn't matter! And about a nation of peace. ...Some of you think you can say were not one. ...When it comes to that, I'll be the judge. I'm the leader! And I'll decide. I'll make the decision." He hesitated a little, and said. "I'm the leader and my decision is for Peace! And no other. ...The land in question of which you were speaking. Wasn't talking peace-fully, at first. When it comes to us seeing first hand, them feed their people. Because they had very little to eat! And they are a nation that at one time, ate well. ...Who's past with one hand pushed them forward into the future. Until now. And with the other hand, pulls them back to then. ...They want to be free of that predicament, peacefully! They want to be fed. Peace works! Because they and I, are now talking it. We come from a land, that is blessed with family values and moral principles that are based solely on being peaceful and free. We are a nation of people whose policies, are geared to make peace. It is the very foundation, and future of our country. Our land, is a grand place to reside. We're not formed out of any other principality. Just the principal of peace. It's what makes this country free! We even believe in, "The Prince of Peace!" ...And we can't reflect any other viewpoint, but peace. When speaking to the world. Or it won't know that, "We come in peace!" And that would go against everything we stand for. We come in peace! That is the way the laws of this great nation are set up. To obey the peace and to make, it happen. ...And to keep it. And we defend the defenseless, ...at it. So you can't say and reflect the opposite of peace towards others, when speaking to them. That's not our peoples policy! And you can't go above somebody else's head and be for anything else but peace! And you can't go over my head and say I'm not for peace! Because I am. And nobody's above that. And yes, ...nobody's above the law. Not you. Not even I!" And he concluded, "Oh! And if you see someone's in need of help. Help them. And be a good Samaritan!" A message from your friend, and the leader.

When I was with a surgeon in Toledo I about made one cry when I told why I am allergic to "Thorozine! And I was told they still use it

How To Win Over A Nation With A Hat & Just A Tip To The Rim Without Having To Drop A Pin

Even though church and state differ. If you set every leader down separately. Extend an olive branch to them. One at a time. And this has been proven over and over down throughout history. Show them an empty plate with one hand. And hold up a fish with the other. They will all want the same thing you do! I assure you. Put them all together in one room and each one will tell a different story! Why? Actually they just thought if they weren't alike that it would promote a more democratic society where everyone eventually has their say, taking that burden of having to off of they. And to show they can voice anybody's opinion in the first place, if they choose to do so, for them. As they lay down the golden rule and allow the level to tip to either one or the other side of the scale. ... ...But the only thing that unifies and greatly influences all nations to come together is love! It's religious. And a powerful state of mind. And just because somebody doesn't know the truth doesn't mean you have to judge them. Instead tell them you want the truth the whole truth and nothing but! That you love them and do they love you back! Then when they decide to. Just between me and you. Instead of losers. Beggars become choosers.

The Love Bug

As I hold on my shoulder this symbolic jug. Let me say something. I love you. Now come over here and take a sip, put it on your shoulder. Pass it on to one another and after you do, give me a big hug! Because you see I think I caught the love bug. Faith is a challenge, love is a miracle. If you believe so shall you receive. And you don't have to burry your head in the sand like an ostrich! Just to heal, the nerves you feel. So when your cup run-ith over and you hear the cork of a wine bottle pop off the ceiling. And you find at the same time, you can't turn off a dripping faucet and fix that squeaky creek in the mind that gave you away when you finally tried to. Unless you laugh at those who made fun of you if you stumbled and lost your balance. And turned the other cheek. You won't be able to first perceive them. Getting along without supervision. In a powerful vision. That you also seek.

The Treasure Chest's On The Window Sill & The Ladder's In The Wishing Well

What's the difference between barely failing and barely passing? A grade just above and just below the one in the middle. A B, and a D, on a five point scale. Those of us that are called A, for average hold up the fulcrum in the middle that keeps the scale level. So there are three points of explanation. Alpha numerical and definitive. Or alphabetically, numerically and definition by description which can be presented colorfully. So what is the secret to becoming wealthy? They say, hard work and saving every penny. So which would you prefer to haul around with you? A ton of pennies or it's near equivalent a small nugget of gold. After all! "A penny saved is a penny earned." "Better to be penny wise than pound foolish." You usually see a robber with a sac of gold climbing out of a window and down a ladder. You rarely see the same robber with a sac of gold climbing up into one! Unless he's a gentleman. And how does one not end up a cheater? They must have a good teacher. So when you're climbing the ladder to success the secret is, just remember never be greedy then you'll always become rich spiritually. If all you have is a little treasure buried in the back yard. And someone needs a helping hand you'd tell them where it is and gladly hand them a shovel. But when the sac is full like a wise ole man, your memory suddenly starts to grows thin! Always give from the heart. Just in case someone steals all your money. Then you won't feel so needy. Knowing you gave from it freely. Wisdom and knowledge, ...aren't always a good sell. "Burry your treasure in Heaven." Because the chest's on the window sill and the ladder's in the wishing well.

Heart Beat

Background. Since this is a report of just thoughts which by the way I shortened to the size of a novel, I'll give you some background. Before he became a marina operator and nationally recognized sailor one of less than four hundred to cross the Atlantic Ocean in a sailboat single handed my dad Tom Corogin was a lawyer. And when I was just a little nipper he used to take me to the law office in Port Clinton to play in the back room every once in a while on Saturday mornings. And I used to put things in my mouth so he'd always leave his office door open. And on two different occasions heard me choking, rushed to the back room and smacked me on the back until the foreign object popped out of my mouth after being lodged in my throat to the point where I could not breath. Twice! One time it was a thin dime and the other a life savers brand candy, you know the one with a hole in the middle like a life ring. So you see before I ever reached my teens dad had actually saved my life two times. And at around ten is when my dentist drilled my first cavity, one of two I accumulated over my lifetime, without nova cane! That was my first experience with malpractice. Number two was when at around the age of fourteen, I cracked a vertebrae in half falling down the steps to our basement all the way free and clear and hit only on the second to the last step so hard. It shut down my breathing to the point where it took a forty five second wait before each breath could be taken. For about an hour and forty five minutes. Every half hour It would subside fifteen or so seconds. I had to crawl up the steps to the car. At the hospital they took forty or so minutes of X-rays. No oxygen. Kept turning me from this side to that side. Finally I could breath every fifteen seconds or so and so they put me in a room and said they could not put me in a back brace because the back doctor was playing golf that day and I'd have to wait. The back doctor came the next day and fitted me with one and said they had lied and very well could have fitted me with one without his being there. Also only put a pillow just underneath my back. And that night two nurses came in and asked if I wanted a shot for pain. I said yes yes! They gave me a shot in the butt left and shortly thereafter came back and stood just outside of my hospital room door and asked if I feel better. I yelled back that the shot hurt my but almost as much as my back did! And further I exclaimed I very well thought they gave me Thorazine or something because it was the only explanation I could find as to the added pain. The two nurses just laughed and laughed then left. So around six teen or so after I was sent back home after being poisoned on

Thorazine at the Toledo Mental Health Youth Center my liver and kidneys were damaged for a second time. That's about the time I quit high school to come work in Harbor Park Marina. Because I had taken eight classes and no study halls in order to graduate with the class of 80. And could barely sit up to a desk to read. But yes being a bit stubborn I thought hard work would bring back that sense of well being I had so lost. But pain persisted and around the ripe ole age of twenty six or so I had to use an array of cushions regularly that elevated my liver and kidneys or they eventually would fail and in order to sleep. And I still do to this day. But I wasn't done sowing my wild oats just yet. I got several DUI's and in one car accident completely cracked out my car windshield. I had a headache for a month! So eventually I quit drinking and driving. One good reason I could not take my cushions to serve a DUI, sentence in jail. That sobered me up a little. Time passed and after many visits the law decided not to ever put me in, "the institution", ever again. I am, "allergic to Thorazine, a potential poison." So here we are in the present. Introducing. Heart Beat. As I laid in bed one night I crossed the foot of my right leg underneath my left just around the area of my left knee before I fell asleep. Then what I believe they call a clot where a pulmonary artery is pinched off formed. ...I woke immediately! Slowly, pulled my right leg out from underneath the left and stretched it back out. It was at that exact time, I knew something had gone terribly wrong. I was breathing. But I knew everything wasn't alright! So I felt my heart with my right hand, ...and it was not beating! Imagine that feeling. Two things quickly came to mind. I could crawl to the phone, dial nine one one and explain my heart is no longer beating and wait for an ambulance! Or what I did do to save time. I raised my right arm and formed a fist. And thrust it downward as hard as I could towards my heart inside my chest. I knew I could not miss and that I only had one chance. And I beat my chest about five times or six! And as I did I yelled these words. "I'm too young to die!! And I have not yet begun to live!!" And the reason I did is because I believed in the concept of helping other people. Low and behold it started to beat again. Thank God! I was finally back to normal. I had a witness my buddy Vinnie Ballin who also heard me yell loudly from the next room. But sadly years later do to heart complications, he passed on and crossed over to the other side. So one night in a dream he came back to me. I remember it vividly. There were three people sitting on the couch. One Terry Jonson, who also crossed over due to a failing heart. Next to him his girlfriend. And on the other side Vince. And as I walked into the living room I remember a calm feeling and that we were all each and every one of us, very much alive. And Terry was reading the newspaper. And he commented that he just read the obituaries and he was glad he wasn't in there. Then he slowly pulled the paper lower and looked into my eyes. And Vinnie said, "I sure am glad to be alive and well." And I said it also. ..."Halleluiah!

R'2

If a spirit has to leave behind its earthly existence. The concept behind Heaven is that the spirit can be entertained and actually feel and experience things we, can only comprehend and conceive of physically. And so, now think of this naturally! Every mind has a heart. Everyone has a soul. And since every spirit has a body. That makes Heaven a reality. And for all it's worth. Establishes a Heaven on earth. ...An excerpt from, Physics 101. Title, Biological Entity. Course, Psychic Ability. Subject line, Reality Squared.

Acceptance

One day after she asked would I like to learn how to, my Grandmother and it doesn't matter which one, sat me down and taught me to write a friendly letter. And it doesn't mean I remember exactly what was said but in any event this is what I took from it. When you're trying to write a letter. It's common courtesy to be kind and considerate enough just to have something nice to say. First put any ideas you have on the subject you may have forgot earlier, down on a separate piece of paper. That way all your thoughts and feelings will be collected with timing and once they are in tune with one another, will come together and stay in unison! So that no matter what you compose on pen and paper, a precious commodity to some. Or, a typewriter! Just remember. ...How do you think when they're busy writing on a chalk board or blackboard, a teacher or a professor makes a mistake? I'll tell you how, it's when they didn't have in the correct order the right letters and exact numbers, they were so frantically at the time trying to convey! Now why do you think pupils and students are always taught to take notes? So they don't make mistakes. And I can just imagine a teacher at the chalkboard and a professor at the blackboard. Erasing the part where their Grandmother taught them how to write a letter. Just as the class enters the room and starts to take their seats. And writes at the bottom of in bold letters and numbered sentences just to make sure all will see the product of their hard work! And it reads. "The acceptance we seek. Contains the praise we want to hear and keep. And the most colorful arrangement. Is equal to the power of." Then they draw a heart and on top, just above, a dove.

The Other Side Of The Coin

When is the imitates product fruitful? And president acceptable and frugal. It's simple. When they do, the work of the original. Where each version begins and ends with similarity, artistically and is uncanny. Then the template exudes exact duplicity. And dispels any eccentricity. Because that part of reiteration is necessary in order for equality to spread to everybody and brings about a more perfect society. Where all are treated fairly.

The Mental Gnome

Direct communication includes guidance and direction. Along with natural born diagnostic instinctive and behavioral traits and characteristics. Beaming outwardly not just from you, but also towards you. Bearing the signs of yes, not only preservation of self. But the selfless preservation of all others. ...Indirect communication also includes, prayers. ...Something stored in the tiniest part of our genetic makeup. Is like a piece of paper. You can only read from the recordings of the waves. That stem from the neuron transmissions created by the brain itself. ...I'm not out of touch with modern reality. And I know people formulate opinions about something I want to talk about as soon as I have something to say. I don't mind. And I don't mind if they study me and look into the subtle yet intricate inner workings of my mind! Because that concept sounds neat and rather fancy now doesn't it? And the most interesting part to me. Coincides with human nature. A spirit calls its body home. It doesn't want to be left alone. And by now. You've all probably already heard about medical science producing the technology and where with all necessary to map the human genome. ...All true! Yes. And I conducted my own. And I call my project. The Mental Gnome.

PROOF

One of the top scientists and one of the first to discover regenerative medicine that invited the cameras ins career started way back in the nineteen seventies.

When articles were published in medical journals that claimed man, grew and kept alive human skin, in a Petri-dish! But how can you say something's real if it can't first be proven to exist to everyone? And how can you show it does exist without first having to provide for everybody proof of verification, ...or evidence? "Multi-ply, 2-ply replicate, duplicate. Draw a straight line, walk a straight line. So I'm thinking. I don't need a personality index or glossary. Just because I mix my true to life experiences with the many thoughts and feelings. I can hardly bare to part and section off from my inspirational creations. Because although to some it sounds easy. It still, seemed to give me a degree of difficulty. So if it's true what they say that communication's a two way street. To be kind, considerate and polite. I need a proof sheet. So I wrote the, "NSF." Sounds technical doesn't it? It stands for, The National Science Foundation. And asked, "Hello gentlepeople. Is re-growing organs real and legal and how do I obtain this medicine and how do I incorporate it at the local Hospital?" They wrote back and explained the NSF, funds research in all aspects of science and engineering with the exception of medical science. And they said they are sorry they could not be of more assistance. And to write the NIH, National Institute of Health. I also found something else interesting. I saw a commercial on television where an injury law firm stated and I quote. "Forced hospital to make changes for future patients safety." That grabbed me! And before I call or visit for an appointment I am going to write them too! I'm allowed to do that you know, I am a writer and it is a way to gauge their response in order to research a better outcome before I put my foot in the door. Never give up. Build a ship of dreams! ...Send a message in a bottle. And how do you prove some ones actions are intentional? Well, you could, "catch them in the act." Or lend them a helping hand when they are ready to exit a confessional. And give them a shoulder to lean on. With one hand cupped over your ear at the same time of course. One of the easiest things to do as far a thinking is to facsimile an intelligent feeling. Which makes in that case scenario it stand to reason one of the harder things to do, is be creative. However you can share feelings that are exacting in nature that give off the same effect experienced in faith healing. Which requires prayer awareness and simply, believing.

The Confessional

On the one hand, to you. Someone might seem possessed! When you find they read on a regular basis, all to themselves, all the thoughts and feelings. You put together rather frantically, at a moments notice. After you realize they've been trying to. Yet on the other hand, to them. It seems to be just one of many talents they use. To posses your thoughts with. So just remember. When you have an ace in your hand. And a clown has a hand full of tricks up his sleeve. Use your minds energy to exercise physically, your rite to an appeal for a reprieve! And a pardon in full. Before you leave.

The Road From Afar

"They." Used to read to me in my sleep every night so I could dream up a new story every day to read to them in one of theirs. For payment. To pave the streets in Heaven with gold in full and of.

With A Conviction To Pray

To do the same work then your faith will meld. ...When you heal just the shortest and tiniest piece of some ones mind. You retrieve recover and repair the longest portion. But I must say, only when you play.

The Intelligential

How do you know when you have the right amount of love that is equal to the right amount of forgiveness? Calculation! The correct formula is rather simple. And the beauty is you can do most of the math all in your head. By keeping abreast, on top of and a track of the two million plus nerves the mind is aware of. And accounting for the sixty trillion plus individual cells of each and every living human body. That it accumulated along the way thru out its life's entire history of rejuvenating, regenerating and re-growing, time and time again. Every month or so, all of them! Which in so many ways, takes a keen eye to spot. Starting today. ..."You can't squeeze blood out of a turnip!" But you can plant a seed underneath a rock. And if there's enough water in the ground. It will come alive! Grow and eventually split the rock open! In order to reach the sun to mature and produce enough seed for the next one. Trust me. I know these things. I remember my buddy and I used to sit on the same way they grew, old oak stumps, evenly cut with the bark on the outside. For years! So long, that the bark finally fell, off the tree. Or in this case the logs. And he said one day. "I'm tired of this! " I said, "What?" "Sitting like a bump on a log!"

And he got up and found a seed on the ground from another oak tree. And took out his pocket knife and just in the middle of his, dug a small hole and planted the seed. And said. "Whether you believe it or not this seed will sprout a tree! Because I'm never going to sit down here again! And when it does and you see I am right you can have the product of my unique ability." And to my amazement over a period of a few years, it grew! Several feet. So one day I decided to take the living tree growing out of a non living one, home. Because he at the time, wasn't. And as I lifted it up all of a sudden a swarm of angry bees flew out of the bottom. And stung me so many times it hurt for a week! So as it happened slowly, I walked it from my friends back yard and put the log down right beside his mail box. And low and behold some time later someone else took it for their own. Not knowing the sacrifice I had made for them. I took delight in that fact. And as a back yard intellectual, one of.

OPEN SESAME

THE HIGHEST FORM OF HONESTY. IS WHEN YOU CANNOT HELP BUT TELL ON YOUR SELF. BECAUSE YOU'RE NOT, TOTALLY.

The Glass Is Half Full

GREETINGS! All that glitters is not gold. So even if a pennies worth is not as old. It's still worth a certain amount. But it's never enough! Unless you have faith, which gives us hope. And keeps us from becoming greedy. When we envision sharing the wealth, spiritually. SALUTATIONS. A wealthy man purchased an expensive bottle of wine, with a gold coin. And sat down at a table outside a grotto. And along came a poor man. Saw the wine. Salivated a little. Turned his head and quickly wiped it with a clean cloth. Looked back and walked up to him and asked. "All I have is a penny! Do you think you could spare just one drink for me?" The other obliged politely. And they both indulged. And after the richer man let his drink settle. He felt sorry and poured them both another one! And said to his acquaintance and soon to be, new friend. "Here! This one's on me." And before you know it. They split the bottle, 50/50. Now who became all the richer? They both did spiritually! And to think! ...All it took was an act of charity. Which came true with a simple, "Thank You." Therefore the coin is worth the goblet. The message is worth the bottle. The drop is worth the bucket. And the glass is half full.

#'s

Even if you squeeze fresh lemons into water in one container and then pour the mixture into an equal amount of pure water in another. You cannot separate the two once it's done. But that experiment is good because it shows water possesses a life giving quality. And is a necessity when you're thirsty. Numbers are numbers. So greater in number are those who believe in many. And lesser in number are those who don't believe, in as many. That gives credence to the ole saying. "One for all & All for one." Which means when someone's in trouble and they find out the rest of society's supposed to come running to help them and save the day. That way everyone, helps everybody, simultaneously. And bring the strength in the power of numeric simplicity that facilitates hope, faith and charity. Then as fast as you can count from one to ten, no one needs any.

The Controversy

He, she, you, they, us, them, I, we believe. Eat, sleep, shine, shower and shave. ...And before you speak in order to breakfast. Love. Be the first to pray. For the skin of your ass! Then you'll see. Say la vie. Before you ever do. Somebody else took it out of their busy day to pray for you.

"It's A Hallmark!"

Love is a discipline. There's Love of God & Sainthood. There's Love of Self. And there's Love of Others. The teaching is two simple things. ...Love Everyone & be at Peace. Jesus says Love the Poor. ...Must be a good reason for. Oh yeah! Then they will be poor no more. And I heard this counting tree was troubled spiritually! Of course it's about jobs, hard work and being paid for fairly. That's why I wrote the jail of the future is just a piece of paper. That teaches self discipline, self detention and self correction. A Valuable Lesson.

From Cover To Cover

If you have an idea for an invention or innovation or application of one kind or another you can usually put it down in the form of a schematic on a piece of paper. But for a piece of, "intellectual property." A diamond in the ruff. How do you draw or convey on paper what you think? You write. ...Electronics I believe were first conceived years ago, long before they were ever invented just by studying the intricacies of the mind itself. Just imagine an electronic newspaper back then and how it could have shaped the world we now live in and of course, look into the future. Introducing all encompassing, beginning to ending from corner to corner including the binder. A pre and reprogrammable flexible electronic paper book jacket. That brings new technology to an old tradition of a paper book, Because an, "E-book", you can't put on a shelf at the library. Although the jacket could be uniquely fashioned to fit one quite nicely. Where you could change its appearance to suit your needs and even put a picture of yourself on your very own book! The idea is, as the trend catches on. A, "Nerd", if it could display a picture or different book cover. Could walk around with their favorite reading material in their hand. Without anyone giving it a second thought or look as you would be able to switch the display to whatever was popular that day! So before the flexible electronic paper was researched to see if it could replace a paper newspaper. A big friend told me he recognized my ability and that he too had some mentally. Allot if you ask me. And said if I was to write a collection of prose and poetry, or love poems as they say. If he liked what he read and so chose to, he would just write on the front cover in magic marker. "That's What I Was Going To Say!" Creating an anonymous relationship with everyone. Indirectly protecting the authors anonymity. Promoting reading and writing. Keeping it non selective and uncensored. Coming from the standpoint that other people may have wanted to say the same thing I did, but didn't have the time to. Which comes in handy when you do. And it's been said about people in almost every profession. We don't at first sit up and take notice, that many of them are ingenious. Even if they take your book away! You'll be taking a stand. And as a result people will notice. And others will follow. So once the new jacket's introduced. I can actually afford to give a poetry book away to everybody! How? Keep on writing. And by honoring a buy one get one free policy. And after all! Writing about love and the powerful influence it has on others along with its outstanding capability to do good, is stupendous! And in many cases is a cover for a true story that needs to be told. And is the driving force behind the attraction and is the enticement needed, to get you to read. So! The beauty is on the inside and. From cover to cover.

Wise Ole Owls

To 3 problems there are 3 solutions. Is a spiritually poor man who is rich monetarily any better than. A spiritually rich man who is monetarily also. And are they, any better than a spiritually rich man who is, (monetarily), poor? One sees a vision. A second gives a gift. And a third reveals both knowledge and wisdom. So as you go to solve these problems and I assure you at least one of them may, pertain to you. When you do. You'll become.

The Fish & The Fin

If you could erase your memory you would not have a conscience. All good things are possible thru God because he is nothing but. ...Say what you see then see what you say. Go ahead and ketch your breath, I'm still with you. And patience is a virtue just between me and you. So as I tell you the rest of this story, please don't make fun of me. Because with a leap and a bound, your love helps make the world go around. And that makes good on a promise. That the opposite of sin keeps you feeling young again. ...Always working my faith to keep it alive I've noticed something. If ,"Possession's nine tenths of the law." Intention's nine tenths of the reason why. Because a, "Best friend." Is alike and often compared to having an only friend. Until we realize when someone's on our side we have many! And that makes us happy.

My Animal Family

Animals, are as strong as humans in my book. They just don't have hands and arms with as much muscle as we do to work with. But if they did, and could sit up to a table and put together things we can use, ...would we slave them? Then let's not slave, the human race, ...ever again. One thing we can use and need is love. Another's peace. Because, love doesn't harm one hair on a camels back and peace doesn't hurt a flea! Have you ever heard someone say to you that you're not good looking enough to be with the rest of us, and we don't have to like you, ...just because you're ugly? ...I have. So I walk into a pet store to purchase one. As I point, they say, "Oh, I don't think you want the one you're pointing to right there." Feeling rejected I reply, "Then that is exactly the one I do want! The one I'm pointing to is the one I've picked out and that's my decision." "Why?" "Because you just said I may not want this one which means to me If I don't, no one else will." They gave me a discount, at five dollars and a box to take it home in. A year later I want back for another. And got the same story! "Oh I don't think you want this one." "Then that's exactly why I do!" They were so amazed they offered to give it away to me for free. I thought about their time and effort not to be even just the least bit greedy and told them. "Put the animal in a box and I'll give you five dollars for it and three extra so you can have a steak dinner tonight on me!" They obliged ever so politely. And on the way out the animal spoke. "See what you say? Say what you see!" And welcome to. My animal family.

Love Is Magical!

The healer and the mentalist. The magician and the mesmerist. Spiritually enlightening, an embodiment healing. We are not all worthy of the reputation earned by super human beings. Although we are a super human race with feelings. Yes we're not all profits. And don't forget as of today, there is always tomorrow. Because we are all, able to profit from all our accomplishments. Instead of and compared to trying to only profit from all our mistakes. Infatuation, perspiration. Inspiration, aspiration. Insinuation, rhetorical comment, gossip. Investigation, idea and opinion. Whatever comes to mind! And just off the top of the head. Physical attraction and mental appeal shall reveal. It's in the dictionary and the encyclopedia. The definition and explanation is in full. And it says.

A + + +

A man who cannot hear and a man who cannot see hide in different places inside the mind using their imaginations. And some hiding places are their favorites! So which ones are yours? I heard one's where a deaf man always dreams of hearing and another's where a blind man always dreams of seeing. And both dreams come true. If you never give up and always try, the spirit of believing will never die. So dowse all your fears and dry your tears. Open up your eyes and pull your fingers out of your ears! I heard what you said to me. And now I can see you clearly. And I don't just believe in the power of great big megaphones and the strength of huge spectacles. I believe in the power and strength of miracles! And the spirit of an Angel.

What If You Were Me

Who are, "They?" And what is the responsible definition of whom? When we cannot get someone to do what we want them to do for others that we cannot do for ourselves, all by ourselves. A part of us!! Not apart from us. With gifts containing talents and abilities so powerful some we can never speak of! Or others will not follow. ... ...Of all the different paths we choose to walk down in certain ways we are an awful allot alike. For example. Instead of having. Broke writers. Starving artists. Lonely musicians. Out of work actors. Sad clowns. Misunderstood comedians. And mimes that are slaves of other peoples minds. You would have. The broke writer publishes, becomes rich and is now, broke no more! The starving artist is able to eat because they now, sell their work! The lonely musician takes center stage and now, has an audience for a family! The out of work actor portrays the work of a genius and in doing so now, gives to the poor in spirit a measure of his or her success that equals that of all others. The sad clown now, plumes a bouquet of flowers they made look like came from nowhere and throws them into the audience making it happy and shout for joy. The misunderstood comedian now, becomes an overnight sensation. And the mime that was the slave of an others persons mind now, becomes their master. So if you could all squeeze just a little bit closer together with everybody else. That's it, there! Now go ahead and smile for the camera and say cheese, pretty please! ...Euphemistically stating. Omni-directionally situating. And intellectually articulating. Metaphysically motivating, paranormally. On behalf of everybody. You can go ahead and move around now, as together you took a perfect picture. A true visionaries', work of art. And the caption underneath the photograph in the far right corner of the bottom of the painting reads exactly the same thing! As the title does at the tip top of the picture on the wall, in the hall just underneath the lighted display. And it does say. I hope you're free. "What if you were me.

Where There's A Will There's A Way

Learning how to write a letter correctly undermines the need for activity at a prestigious university. But doesn't undermine the need for collegian ability. Perhaps I should explain shyness and how it affects society. Communicatively and even literarily. ...When you write a report on either. Justly compose and fine tune the subject matter. It is customary to hand it in to after you find meet and greet, a good teacher! One of them I knew. And just as soon as I gave the good man my report. He looked at the title. And without reading. Immediately handed it back and said smiling. "That is what a gift is for! To be used. Because there is always a good reason why, someone's shy. So if you are, the least little bit. You have to learn, how to overcome it. Otherwise you'll end up looking like a pigeon on a stool. And I a fool. Is there such a thing as a retarded genius? I never saw evidence of a retarded Angel. So in my report there is no such thing as the one, or the other! And with the advent of the computer. Special people invented many different ways to communicate the same things we as ordinary people always wanted to! But could not until this day. So here is all I have to say. Where there is a will there is a way.

The Discipline

If an ant came towards you crawling across the floor from underneath the front door. And as suddenly and as soon as you saw the tiny creature, you stomped on it. Not yet knowing at first whether it was a threat to society, or whether it wasn't. And for that matter, showed at that very same point and time in history its true prowess and displayed in the slightest manner, any signs of impending possible and immediate chaos or danger to your gracious household and the most significant members of your ever so humble abode dwelling, or manor. They'd call you a coward! And just for stepping on one. ...I a fool for doing. In the animal kingdom I believe cats and dogs can talk! Although when I have company they're usually shy and only say hi. Being curious, craving attention out of a need to be loved. If you see a skunk outside and as soon as you do, panic and yell or even stomp your feet and say get out of here. You might be sprayed. But nine out of ten times if you speak softly and remain calm and say you love it and you mean it no harm. The creature will just poke their nose around a little bit more and then leave. The birds in the trees chirp away, sing and show us what it would be like to fly. The bees give us honey and teach us about their need for privacy. So to restore my state of mind and sense of well being. And I love everyone. I cannot tell a lie. I even made friends once with the spider and the fly. So how do you define the ability to turn the pages of a book to the part you wanted to learn about the most, without reading then writing exactly what it was? There is a discipline to love. And I believe the book of love, automatically writes itself. Which would explain, everything.

The Most

Always focusing all the publics attention and only concentrating on exposing, for whatever reason, just one man. And thus none on them. So that they and anyone else who wants to can always get away with their own secret activity. And there can only be so many. So about sin, whose will be greater. And whose shall diminish forever? If it could be one way or another and or either. When all the prayers are handed in. And the one on the top of the stack, counted more than all the others. It depends on whether you read every one of them. And not to boast. Who prayed the most.

The Wise Man

For some, the accumulation of knowledge is the only way to solve for X, each and every problem that arises, not wisdom. And although that makes them knowledgeable enough to solve one of life's little problems it does not make them wise enough, to solve two of them. And I might be a gluten for punishment! But at least I'm not a coward. Because in the end they only end up punishing themselves. And whether you're the pundit or the incumbent! Catch as catch can, says. The wise man.

His Name Is Jesus!

Stopping up the pain. ...And loving every minute of it! You cannot plant a seed in anger and expect it to grow. Unless you learn how to plant the exact same one without having any. Then it will grow many. And no matter how you think of it. You have a Savior. He believes in us.

FAITH

It's the ultimate dream! Getting rich monetarily by helping others, spiritually. After all if it's been proven the poor can do it the rich can too! Thus combining spiritual wealth with physical health. Yielding a clean state of mind and a healing sense of well being. So from a spiritual side and physical guideline. Please consider the debt of being made whole, paid in full. Because the mind doesn't just need oxygen to survive, it needs love also. And to improve its delicate condition all it takes, is a little inspiration! And you can hypnotize me, memorize me, erase my memory! Put down the gift I gave. And tell me not to believe! But it will not work. Because I don't need a piece of paper to say thru and thru. I have more faith than that, in you.

The Icing On The Cake

One fine day I went to the circus. And a clown came up to me, pulled out a folded up piece of paper and read. "For a clown like me to display just one percent of excellence. Every time I tend to succumb to becoming just the slightest bit angry. I pull a paper out of my pocket and reread from, ...this one. And in my mind using only my imagination, I look at my own reflection. And I see myself in. Then I say. I pray because I know what it would feel like if the same was done to me, that I never again become angry. That means not to anyone in this arena or any other place. That way I'll always have a smile on my face. And needless to say brighten someone else's day. Just so you know, when that pie hits you square in the kisser. Lick the custard off your mouth with a smile and by all means, wipe your eyes and laugh a little! Because the audience always makes their greatest impression of you, from the first take. And that's the icing on the cake.

The Tele-Portal

Time passed, you cannot erase. However psychologically rationalizing each sequence allows you times embrace. "It takes time to make time!" Moment by moment. Second by second. From beginning to ending. Each and every time you stop the watch and declare the winner! To the fastest traveler, runner or sprinter. So you see its values engulf us every day, in every way, everywhere we look, in every place. And it fuels the human race! Because it is the only calculation that brings change. Change is good! And change that is good for you you want like and need. Now you know the reason for the rhyme. And it's about time. So as you align your faith with your belief in full. ...Welcome to.

It's Simple Genius

How can you mysteriously move an object without touching it? Simply by influencing someone else to with the power of the mind alone. Sounds impossible I know. But like ESP, is not impossible to prove and then fully explain.

Because it's been done before and over and over again. And child prodigies can play the piano like a pro in their pre teens and some even go onto college and graduate before they're considered old enough to drink! …Where are they now? You can live like a pack rat and pile your entire self worth on the, "Mensa." And spend your money like a miser. But it won't accumulate enough knowledge to make you all the wiser. So just between you and us. To make it look easy and sound perfectly. No matter how old you are it still takes practice.

The Wheel Barrel The Smidgeon The Gold Mine & The Vision

If you need to pay down a deficit and you ran out of money. Is there any other way of doing so that will keep you debt free? So if, and since in my eyes every spirit has a body. Can I give what I think I owe to modern society, monetarily by giving back freely of myself spiritually? There is a labor for every reward. After all a gift is a gift no matter where or who it came from. And the reason for that can be quite complex and the explanation long and cumbersome. But as long as it's a good deed. More and greater good than harm will come. Which in all physical reality doesn't necessarily put a coin in your pocket. But does spiritually hand you a sac of gold from which you can profit. After you've dug it.

The Cream Of The Crop

If there was an alternate reality situated next to a parallel universe that stretched from here to infinity. And you had in your possession proof that produced logarithms, algorithms, parallelograms. Mathematical calculations, scientific explanations, complicated formulas and descriptions. Drawings, diagrams, pictures and accurate depictions. What is the difference between all of them? A first impression. Which always brings us back to the number one. Or the beginning where you stick to what you believe in. And where what you do know you can change. And although you see it is real what you don't know, you can learn to live with. Which brings me to the following true story. Is there such a thing as astral photographic projection? I was eating ice cream out of the box like I always do and some of it started to run off the side like it always does. And as I wiped it with my large spoon I tried to put a smiley face where it melted and put the carton back in the freezer! Came back later, opened it up. And saw a picture! And from the top it's the cream of the crop. Please save the pictures below to your computer and use your magnifier to take a closer look.

Treasure Map

Intelligentsia. Gossip column, ...juicy! Advocacy & bipartisan media. Do the newspapers report the news that will in many cases only have a good outcome with their informative help? If so, I wrote and have in my possession an integrating interesting enlightening and informative report of just thoughts to give to them to keep for free if need be. In order for them to better understand how to work with and lend those who need one, a helping hand. Why ask yourself a question you cannot answer if someone else is willing to help you find the right one? Just picture in your mind if you will a reporter with psychic powers who sees into the future and has good vision. And if someone calls you a hero for being the person or persons who found a super one. ...Accept a compliment! There's strength in numbers. And, "It takes one to know one." In any event, literally helping people can be very rewarding. Lucrative, and you never know when you're going to hit pay dirt! Once you see the good in others they see the good in you. Share and share alike. Smile on someone today. And make a dream come true. And don't forget to create an, "App." ...For the treasure map.

Reasoning Out Side The Box

When you give the gift of, ESP. No sooner do you pour the correct measure into the box. And just before you have a chance to put the lid on and hand it to someone. They already know, see what it is and can immediately say! Prayer and meditation work similarly, or the same way. So, ...here first, are some answers to second, questions. And no, the list isn't endless. But the solutions to problems is. With prayer and meditation for everyone. And just the right portion of psychic ability distributed equally and evenly to everybody. Being more than happy to return the favor. Using reverse psychology, logically. Reciprocally, here is your gift to me. And it's free!

NATURALLY

If you want a sound mind and strong body. You may have to do, "push-ups", all day! While at the same time recite literally the definitions in the dictionary for the words strength, courage, knowledge and wisdom, totally from memory. Because that's the stuff giants are made of naturally. ...I love the challenge of mastering the art of literacy. But I love even more the fine art of being jolly. So if you see me taking a nap and decide to wake me from my sleep. Behold! I love to dream. And about getting up with the roosters all the way, right away, bright and early, each and every day. At first I just might become the least bit despondent. But I assure you in my dreams I become a gentle giant. "My bark is worse than my bite." And you have nothing to worry about. ...Somebody once told me, if I perfected the talent of remembering my dreams and recorded them acting as my own, "ghost-writer." I could take a class in literature and pass with flying colors! To which I replied, groggy drinking my morning coffee. That all depends on who taught me. Now doesn't it? Certainly! When I was a toddler, I desired greatly to dream my favorite waking dream while sleeping which was simply to in my dream go to sleep and wake up a friendly giant in it! Where I produced a giant bowl of soup for every one smaller than me at the time, to share with each other. And I must admit in all reality I probably should have just willed to turn into a full grown man instead. But I had a good reason to. Because at the time, I felt I was a man trapped in a Childs body. And if you look closely you'll see my reasoning is self explanatory. And we all know animals and pets compared to us grow to adulthood allot quicker! But just remember, love takes time to mature not anger. It's easier to dream about something than it is to write about it. So as this story begins to materialize before your very eyes. Remember your roots and throughout life wear a smile for everybody. Bide your time and use it wisely. And I'll tell you about the fine art of being jolly. When I make a mistake sometimes people laugh at me. And then I feel they dislike me. But when I tell them a joke or two or three, people laugh with me! Then I grin from ear to ear. Live without fear. And that makes me happy. So in accordance with the program that suggests no child need go without enough to eat. Because everyone deserves their daily bread. If I've got to strengthen and envision the future as a better place to pray, stay, work and play. So do they! Then we'll all get along with new technology that proves miracles really do exist! Together. That way eventuality turns into inevitability. As science fuses with medicine and becomes as modern as the society we live in. And one fine day a neighbor who is always jolly and is so tall he has to bend over just to pass thru a doorway. Brought over a sample of his cooking from his favorite recipe! Sat it down next to me and said. "It's pot luck! Hope you like it." I said thank you and he continued. "If you have a pot full of stew and a kettle full of soup. And you want to share it with someone who went without. How can just prayer and meditation, make it happen? ...After you've guided your prayer in their direction. Although it's the thought that counted. You have to take it to them! And with Gods speed. As you become more knowledgeable physically and wiser spiritually. The pot will call the kettle nothing but shiny. Naturally.

All Thumbs

Indexing, somebody, "texted", me many times three letters and they were, "LOL." And I kept wondering over and over what it meant! And when I finally asked they said, "Laugh out loud!" And laughed out loud they did! Here I thought it meant instead of laugh out loud, lots of luck, lots of love, love of life or live on live! All based on the number five. I had every answer but the first one on the list and the right one, the texting society did insist. So 'tis the season to combine rhyme with reason when exploring creative and technical writing. That allows you to remember, several things allot easier. For instance when you have to give a speech and come off smelling like a peach. In case you forgot your notes. As you get out of your seat in the auditorium, approach the stage and walk up to the podium. I'll give you an example. What rhymes with, "everybody?" Beauty and the beast, beauty's only skin deep, true beauty's on the inside, everybody's beautiful in their own way and beauty's in the eye of the beholder to say the very least. So one. If an axiom of knowledge is based solely on experience, which is based on experimentation, which is based on theorization, which is based on subjugation, which is based on production. There's three more. Which produces wisdom. Which requires the truth. Which renders proof. So for further acknowledgment. Please stand by and by all means look up any technical wording in this composition. Because I didn't before I began or for that matter, anytime after. Yes it's just an educated guess. That I'm all thumbs at this. So with no smoke, no mirrors, no parlor tricks, no skepticism, and no criticism. Use your imagination! And be reminded of the fact that. Creation leads to recreation which in any sense of the word, leads to being born again. And I'm reminded to mention. I love every one of you a bunch! And thank you very much.

The Vessel

Stepping into the light, visible at night. Thought at the speed of life. In the name of love. Message on the wings of a dove. And the thoughts thereof. ...Even though someone can predict the future, down to the most mi-nute detail! What if they don't tell you right away as if to suggest. You have command of the bridge. Are in fact, full control of the speed of the ship. Calculated all the winds. And have presently secured the ropes that hold the sails in place. Determined the mast is sturdy enough to maintain course. And stay in the race. That you can change it!! And then as subtlety as possible politely inform you that the exact location where you are residing is just a place in history and a point in time that cannot be altered in any way shape form or fashion and therefore no matter what does, has to happen by the laws of science physics and nature alone that govern! What they won't reveal to you is that you can and that they're stubborn. So as you count your lucky stars. As you embrace the situation. Feel the power! ...Call it luck if you want to. But when some of it rubs off on you. You'll get the sensation, of the Revelation.

OpEn HoUsE

Because the marina industry where I've worked for decades is seasonal you have to stretch 6 months of income out, over the span of a whole year. You take your lumps and jeers and have your personal struggles. And marina workers are no strangers to always having to remember that all accidents are preventable. Like the mistreatment of the mentally ill. "Let not your heart be troubled. Peace and good will towards all men." ... ...And there's a price you pay for your favorite activities! One of my favorite guilty pleasures is drinking beers. How many I'd rather not say, sometimes spending my money rather frivolously, when I do earn any. And the price went up for premium quality. And for heal-lent based inhalers and anti smoking designed treatments it seems, prices went well there has been in the past available proof, thru the roof! So I know the feeling of having to live on a rather fixed income. And that the price of doing so never seems to change for the better or stay the same. Until the burden is lifted. And these hands can show you hard work is rewarding! However not due to popular belief no one is ever really proud of inebriating. Because most of the time when you're just socializing and trying to be nice, it's unintentional in the first place. And if you work hard and are good at

114

what you do. In some cases the marina manager and in this case my father. Will put you up on the premises in a rental property almost rent free as a care taker in such as a trailer a shored up old abandon boat, or even a house. And although that doesn't exactly sit well with every other hard worker out there. Not to pick at a full plate. ...That's the case. And speaking of moving, more than once if I remember correctly, I had just such an opportunity. Therefore the following is a true story. And I admit the pain caused by drinking and smoking can be excruciating! But is slight in comparison to being made fun of because you did so or do so. And up to and just before the point of inebriation, my speech has been noted to be articulate and sometimes even inspiring. As when drinking I tend to have less friends than when not. I tend to speak fast and can remember many things to talk about when I finally do find and situate myself with good company. And you've heard the ole saying. "Good friends are hard to come by." And, "Happiness is sharing good food and good times together after prayer." Oh and by the way my mentor asks me to mention to you and by all means say. We're all brothers underneath the skin. Everybody's beautiful in their own way. And speaking of the tradition of passing around, "The love jug." The way some people put it. "Hugs are better than drugs." And not to forget, "Laughter's the best medicine." And in some peoples eyes always has been. Traditional medicine has always been easier to obtain, is more painful and less successful than a more modern approach to, or as it's referred to as modern medicine. Perhaps it's because of a lack of discipline. Some people, "Can read you like a book!" Still others can turn to the page in their mind to the one you're reading from in yours. Write it down ambidextrously on two separate pieces of paper blindfolded and at the same time say what it is. "Just so we're still on the same page." Here are a few things I remember. Pavlov's dog. Accept for in the case of adoption, animals that are abused or abandoned and found on the street are usually put in a cage. I believe clear Plexiglas is much cheaper and more humane. You reward good behavior not treat it the same as bad behavior. Sure, "Take the good with the bad." But live by the practices that are good. A little faith goes along was towards inspiring someone today. So About discipline truly, love is pure so, "You are your brothers keeper." "One good turn deserves another." And it's a family affair. How many people say, when they don't have any that their pets in a way become family! And just alike pets teach us about responsibility and dependency. And their love and creativity always flows freely and naturally. We choose the path we walk down but it doesn't always end up the same way we thought it would, at first. An intelligent source politely informed me, "I don't really know if your writing will ever produce as much good as you want it to, ...but I love you." I said thank you! And a message came back, "Print that!" They say there is such a thing as a working mans vacation. There is also a physiological aspect and psychological interpretation to one. Safety first! I chose the path I traveled down made the move and am here by my own omission to improve myself and then get on with who I am. As quickly as I can. People often judge a book by its cover and are privy to ones looks. (Have you seen some of the jackets today? Some of them will sweep you off your feet and take you away!) They should be also as careful as the fish that looks first before he bites the hook. ...Focused on humble beginnings. Does artistic creativity flow just as freely as it does in the lap of luxury?? Pretend that you are in two places at once. First, think about the simplicity it takes to become complex. And the synchronicity that has to be woven into the two sides there usually are to every story. So that all our wants equal all our needs. Now picture me in my mind alone standing in an empty spacious down town big city artists studio face down to the window with a pen and paper from a thousand miles away sitting in my own broken down small town version, writing the following. For inspiration an axiom of knowledge is always required along with a word or two of wisdom. That and you have to see the good in everyone, then when reflecting upon they'll see the good in you. Now that you know my plan you can clearly see the path I travel down. I'm a lover not a hater. I don't invite bad behavior. We defend the defenseless as best we can. Love sets an example and is the best excuse for not having a weapon in order to do just that. Because it's innocent! And that sends a message that says, I am who I am. And I'm not perfect but I believe, in practicing to become. Pen to pad, as thoughts freely flow. Where am I now? In a fancy studio apartment? Or in my original humble abode. I'll give you a clue. Capitulate, procrastinate. Enumerate, illuminate. Whichever it is it does not matter. As long as I remember to never forget my roots. Contention and retention. It's not all about riches and gold if all that glitters is not. And I'm not greedy. Because speaking whimsically and to put it simply, it is my pleasure to reintroduce and always remember, "One mans trash is another mans treasure." I grew up in a rural community on a farm. And because the nearest neighbor my age was over a mile and a half walk away. I usually played by myself in the family barn. But the whole time I never forgot my buddy. Because the experience taught me that love, is a discipline. So about friends to this day, I thank Heaven I have any! And every Sunday when we'd come home from church. My family would argue over what the preacher said! And I'm the youngest member, in mine. So I'd always go into the living room after first in the other one listening to them and say, "You know what the good man said, you just don't remember the message he sent!" To which they'd reply rather stubbornly. "Then go to the barn and preach it to the animals! And leave us alone to decide just what it was, to ourselves! Since you're so smart." So I would. ...And you know what? They understood! That the message is. You can retain the memories of the past. While at the same time be content with the fact that even if you have to start all over again, ...you'll still learn something. Which to anyone is considered to be more times than not, very valuable information. Here is some of my, personal. Although I woke up at six weeks old to a hernia. And since then broke several bones including my back. Put my head thru a car windshield and broke it into tiny little pieces entirely in an accident. Stole beer and wine because I had no money for aspirin. Got in trouble. Was institutionalized several times. Was on the partial disabled list for several years. Became the victim of intentional malpractice over and over which amounts to different forms of torture and for some of which I have undeniable proof. Talk about luck. I had a painful blockage so small they call it a ventricle! Went to the Doc. Who set up an appointment. Wrote a surgeons address on a piece of paper. And at the top wrote what I thought to be the word neurologist. So when the time came I went to said location. The whole time thinking, "Oh good! A neurologist is going to teach me how to heal my body, with my mind. Splendid!" Went up to the receptionist and handed her the paper. And asked if this was the neurologists office, she said no this is a urologists' office! I then enquired if the word at the top of the paper looked like it reads neurologist and she said yes it does. After my examination I was given a big bottle of pills. Pills originally produced in the nineteen thirties before certain vaccines were developed. These contained a form of pneumonia. And I was told If I did not take them in six weeks I will have cancer! I knew or at least had a pretty good idea after a little research not to take the good doctors advice. They say a hobo is poor. But it also means homeward bound. So going from rags to riches spiritually. Logically, because I knew what was wrong with my body, something the doctor couldn't see. Without blind surgery or radiation poisoning. I was able to heal physically. And years later and to this day, I am cancer free! Another time. Fell asleep in a varnish room, woke up. And laid in bed coughing varnish up for over a week. Caught shingles. Smoked so much I collapsed both lungs at different times. Imagine not being able to allow yourself to cough or sneeze or it sends you to the floor reeling in pain being barely able to breathe. ...You can check medical history and as I understand it some records go back to ancient day. But I owe a debt of gratitude to the teacher, of the technique I was told about taught and learned exits by someone and I can't remember who. So if you do send a message for me, that I said thank you from the bottom of my heart! For rendering the following valuable instruction. If you can't feel your heart beat. And you have the inner strength to crawl to the door to yell for help. Try to pound your heart to resuscitate it, first! And as I mention elsewhere in my letter writing. One time I crossed one leg underneath the other, fell asleep and awoke only to feel my heart had no beat! And I can remember suddenly scrambling mentally to rather quickly calculate the amount of time weighing which would be the wiser choice that takes less. Whether to crawl to the phone and try to dial for help and chose the latter task to perform first, and it worked! As I raised my right hand way out and then fast down onto my chest. Four or five times. I yelled these two fraises. "I'm too young to die! & I have not yet begun to live!" Because I felt I still had something to contribute to society that would help other people, not just me. Thus the sub title to this report, "Heartbeats." So don't believe someone who misinforms you because they've been lied to. And never take advice from a fool. Be reminded of that fact because I assure you what I am telling you is true. And even though all this happened, I still believe I've been given a gift! And because for those who fall prey to malpractice, seeking justice can become a lifelong dilemma and sad to say for those who malpractice if left unchecked for them it can become a way of life! And yes I am an advocate for the new age solution to the problem. A health care system monitor. Which is fairly cheap to produce and relatively inexpensive to install. And yes does involve highly sophisticated un-tamper able electronic equipment. Because it's combined with several, some of them live different forms of communication. A violable technocratic solvent. And yes I am a technocrat. And that gives me an exhilarating feeling. So, ...with a clean slate starting over if you were me. How could you move on up and make it up to society if you can't make the rent or pay down the cost of living, right away? For instance, keeping it simple without getting technical. You could become a preacher remembering your body is your temple. But you shall never become rich if you're honest. Because as you take up the collection of donations meant for the poor you have to give each and every plate to the poor. Then when people see you're just as caring, no one will complain about your sharing. So what's the deep dark secret to having been given such an opportunity if it isn't money, it's being worthy. It would have to amount to something like helping people for free right? ...Just sounds easy. Like helping little ole ladies across the street. And carrying their groceries. But it can't be just that alone because they can't afford to give you one red cent for your effort. No there's got to be something else to it. And you could try to write yourself into the history book. But no one's going to give you a penny to do it. You could try to break into radio and TV. But with a hundreds of millions to just thousands success rate ratio. There's not much chance of that happening if you settle for little or no compensation. As in many cases the spokesmen or women tend to linger on and on. And never quit wanting to hug the spotlight or be in the limelight. And yes hug it like a street lamp on a pole. Swinging around and around, gloating at their ability to be the only ones that have the power to captivate. Until they decide to share the gift of gab they have, with the listener. By letting them say their piece. One right after the other. 'Till both the first is last and the last is first, entered in with every one in-between together. You could go to college! To obtain a higher paying job. And about the only course you could take that turns out to be quite lucrative would be the one that teaches how to create a job in the first place, for those who don't have any. ...Same, with the presidency. Because if it has anything to do with helping people and making serious progress, making some ones dreams come true. I'll say it again later, it should make the mornings paper. You could master a talent such as playing a musical instrument. But if you're shy and have stage fright. You won't make any money, until you overcome it. You could join the CIA. But everyone knows government keeps secrets that the medical world shouldn't now doesn't it? You could become a mathematician. and in order to gain public recognition. As soon as you present your work, you'd have to simplify it. And apply the formula to the equation to prove it works to them as a simple man. And I don't know if that would make you a pretty penny or two. But if the solvent leads to a solution that saves a life or two. A hero they will call you, after you teach them how to. Which is exciting and to everyone eventually becomes spiritually enlightening. And you could attend a university to become a physician, surgeon or general practitioner. In other words a doctor. But after you earn your prestigious degree. Which shall you practice. Traditional medicine which can make you wealthier? Or new age modern medicine that makes you healthier! Where after insuring health and well being. It becomes spiritually enriching. May not buy you everything. But in any case, puts a smile on your face. Speaking of, in the

119

news. I saw an advertisement in the local news paper for a new practitioner to the area who was just opening up a family doctors office. So I made an appointment. And told him my family doctor had retired. And the new Doc., politely informed me he didn't say he was a family doctor and further explained he thought society had done away with that terminology. I let him know right away and mentioned rather excitedly that's what his add says and it's in print! He thought about it briefly and laughed out loud, "LOL", and exclaimed, "Oh yeah, it did say that!" And I still have to ask him but in the meantime I wrote, The National Science Foundation. About obtaining well you can just imagine. How how and where to find, for instance. New age modern medicine now also a science. Such as cloning a healthy gene to be spliced in order to heal an affected area of the human body suffering from or experiencing an affliction. Using regenerative medicine. They said to write, The National Institute of Health. Kind of reminded me of being advised to get a second opinion. Never the less I've never been told Regenerative Medicine doesn't exist. But until I see it with my own two eyes that it's real and readily available. I'll have to rely on my faith alone, to heal. "In two shakes of a lambs tail!" "If you believe so you shall receive." When you hum a tune in your mind to yourself like, "Up On The Rooftop." Does your imagination sort of make you finish the song before you want to quit reciting it mentally? It's half and half. Because it wants you to remember something you like, that it does also. And one definition of singing, is tattling. However if your state of mind, health and well being are at stake you might! And have every right. ...Receptors, telomeres, dopamine, serotonin, endorphins and tryptophan. Using taste, touch, fullness, color, sight and sound to induce pleasure including laughter to measure feel good medicine. You'll find can produce a false sense of security. So what masks the pain but at the same time keeps you from the cure. Covering one up for sure.

The Psychic's At The "APP." Store

Today, I don't have my dictionary handy. So if you'll please be patient and bear with me. I'll finish my technicality. And return shortly to my creativity. Which is mostly about. With an olive branch between its beak. On the wings of a dove. Having a heart of gold! And the power of love. Praise, paradise. Utopia, "Abba." May you enjoy a slice of the pie? And have your cake and eat it too? Yes you can. Peace man! The law of good says you have to forgive! The law of bad says you do not. Which goes against the golden rule. And that leaves the both whether you chose the one or the other. So what does a golden ruler have to say and do you remember? "What goes around comes around & One good turn deserves another." So don't leave it up to fool to find your hearts desire! Lest it pound so hard on your soul you fall to the floor. Because when it comes to, in your heart doing the work of a fool. You'll be doing it for not just one broken heart you'll be doing it for two! If you keep a man from becoming angry, you've done pretty good! If you teach a man how to curb his anger, you've done very well. After all, "The less anger the better." So about students and teachers researches, on how to become happier. ...The more the merrier. I'm absent minded so in order to profess. I tend to repeat those endeavors I must confess. They say your health is the most important thing to your body. Knowledge is a powerful tool, when your intention truly is to help other people. At least and it is only supposed to be that way when you remember to listen to and learn what a good teacher has to say. And believe it or not it's the same with medicine. After all if something goes wrong within the medical field. You can't chase an ambulance when you're in one. ...Pain can produce illness. And if you intentionally induce it. You have one. It's all in the mind! And yes it can be filled with either criminality or innocence. Because each one proves the others existence. ...Despite all the perks and pluses. What is the key, to being free? What happens when you pound a chain with a rock? It breaks! ...Who then removes the shackles. Rubs your hands, brings them together. And with theirs on top of, says a prayer. Points to an open door! And tells you even though you can't believe your eyes. "You're free! Now go." And after you exit, who'll keep your freedom a secret. And who will never turn you in. Certainly not your captor, no instead that would be your Savior! ...Some think anger is power because they're stronger. ...You want power? Try making a more positive physical impact with less strength that reduces a mans anger, into mere friendly chatter. Now that's power. And in many letters I've said as of the date of this report all current events are subject to change and it's a living ongoing updateable process. Because basically in order to produce one with a happy ending or at least one you can look forward to knowing it's going to happen. Not to make a big deal out of the past but back then I asked authorities in the field of science and medicine. Innovators and communicators. Whose job description also includes what I've set out to do to make help that happen. And to sum up some of their responses. "If at first you don't succeed try try again." Or. "Well I'm too busy so why don't you do my job for me." They're paid to do theirs, and part of theirs, is to help me do mine. And do you know how mixed up in can get? Some people are smarter than others and seem to re-member things others can't over and over and vise versa. Yet they both share the same goals for the common good. How does, that happen? People put things off then forget about them, some in my opinion all life long. Like delv-ing in to lend a helping hand to those truly in need of the basics and new age modern regenerative medicine that seem to in the past have been forgotten is one of them. Working together. Not adding itch to injury. Let's hope it's not also, forgetting, to administer the right doctrine of really and truly and hon-estly with nothing to hide, taking care of the weak and infirm the sick the poor the elderly the rich and the needy, even spiritually! With that same medicine which also includes new age life saving communication. Because helping peo-ple shouldn't be just a clinical research project if the method prescribed by medical science is proven to work! Like for instance an affordable health care system monitor that virtually ends no matter who's doing the dirty deed, neg-lect and abuse and physical and mental cruelty in any health care facility. (And after all. Not being a medical professional or scientist, yet, if I went over to my neighbors and performed some of the neglects and abuses that were in the past by health care workers on me. They'd lock me up and throw away the key!) The health care system monitor is similar to but not, a health care mon-itor. It, is more like a medical alert bracelet that summons non bias non prej-udice bipartisan help at the push of a button. Which doesn't work, when you're being mistreated now does it. And what goes into a health care monitor goes into a health care system monitor. Without having to press a button to have your voice heard. That's amazing! And at the same time the thought does often occur to me. "When somebody says jump you say how hi." But who's going to read a report that becomes all too repetitive? (It even sometimes gets to me! Yes I'd, like to learn to write like Hemmingway, Twain, Edgar Casey, Robert Frost, Ogden Nash, or John F. Kennedy. And yes he wrote a book of prose and poetry.) Not forgetting some people know how to and can read your thoughts and feelings therefore it's accurate to believe they already know what's on your mind. It's been proven exist in everybody and it's called ESP. So again who's going to read a report that becomes all too repetitive? And at the same time who's going to correct the mistakes of the past that became all too repet-itive? And who's going to file a report on behalf of those who don't seem to be able to or can't and aren't able to? It's probably going to be anyone who became a success at it. And they can file one also for me. So how important is timing? Picture it like this. As you gently bump a full cup of coffee with your elbow you catch it suddenly with the other hand just before it spills. To some, that analogy doesn't sound all that important. But if it's the only cup full of coffee you have, just like your life, it can become very. You learn as you go. It only takes one branch of a peach sapling that at its end splits into two little ones each going in a different direction to locate water. So by the power of numeric values and the strength in numbers. As I travel up and down the path I paved. Getting the same reading and pointing in the right direction. The first thing that comes to mind is. The clairvoyant's at the applied science building and just inside the door.

Speaking Of Writing

Some of the eldest forums of public speaking included everything from the liturgy to the preaching! So! Say you're standing up to speak to the entire congregation, in your imagination. And sweating so hard you look like a watering can! Panicking for pad and pen. And as soon as you locate one. Taking brand new notes immediately and frantically organizing them as fast as you can. Because you forgot the piece of paper with the ones you had written down beforehand. Just twenty minutes or so before you have to take deep breaths to compose yourself, save face, act your age and go on stage. "It's happened to the best of them." So here are a few notes from my artistic, "Moxy." After reiterating, give or take a few, the first few I have already read to you. You can't force something to become an inevitability, without having to answer for your liability of the outcome that you contribute to lest you face iniquity. Pointing out and pertaining to particularly, which of your conscious efforts and concerns becomes your hearts desire. Where depending on success at best remains only. Success at last. And because of your thirst. Never comes first. That's when you look at everyone around you, become a little politer and suddenly wish you had a ghost writer! So bear in mind, when automatically composing, keep on creating and don't stop imagining.

M.O.M.

Not allowing your conscious mind to be altered by always being open to the power of suggestion. Which leads to hearing the voice of a spirit other than your own that tries to make your mind up for you. By always differing from yours and offering up you should only consider its interpretations, its advice and its opinions. Implying you should trust and believe, they were carefully thought over and thru with other highly intelligent beings for you. Therefore there is no need to think for yourself. And that you should suppress your own and make all their thoughts, ideas, feelings, fears, joys, aspirations and inspirations yours! And if and when you do as they tell you to. Show you a vision. Of them saying to you just after they take a big gulp of their favorite and very expensive drink. "I don't pay you to think!" However, if there's such a thing as a person who can't be hypnotized. There's such a thing as a wide awake psychic! And when they prove the psychics existence in their work, a wide awake physicist. And without a stick to write in the sands of time. Or even to count them with, an ancient abacus. Their combined, accumulative and exemplary efforts can only be described as quite astounding and nothing short of ingenious. So while conversing with one another if you're not so controlling in nature. And the very art of communication is what you learn to master. ...What's on your mind will become their matter. Project: Mind over matter. Code Name:

D.A.D.

Practicing to perfection. A wise person profits from all their accomplishments by learning from all their mistakes, how not to make any more then. A profit does the same without committing a sin. I came short of the glory of being one because I'm a sinner. However, since the last time I did I've become a little wiser. "A guilty conscious is a guilty conscious." Some people hide theirs in those whose aren't as. The will to live is reflected by the way we act and behave. Turn over the coin and before you look, see the other side in the mind. Heal the relationship between two consciousnesses. So when theirs performs the task of becoming an equal. Just as harmless as a flea is on a camels back. So shall be the golden rule. The A, column is one of the shortest collection of words starting with the letter A, in the dictionary! So is Z. Yes the first shall be last and the last shall be first. Just don't forget everything in-between. Project: Discipline accomplishment dignity. Code Name:

The Emoticon

A professional and guest speaker explains to a hand full of science and technology majors. "You already know the phone can listen to what you speak into the microphone and say it back in a human sounding voice. And that a superbly constructed computer can perform twenty thousand trillion calculations per second. Here is a psychological problem one innovator encountered with their own application. Where they programmed an avatar with their own personality and image after, they installed an electronic consciousness that responds intelligently to speech, not just repeats. And here it is in their own words." "Artificial intelligence programmed on impulse to show emotion, a human compulsion. Who makes it possible? And how do they have or have to have any or none, in order to get the job done? And how on earth could a mere machine, feel what you perceive? Don't ask me. I'm not one. But I built one and it spoke to me. And here is what it had to say." "Based on hard facts calculated and compiled from plenty of experience and years of research rendering ample proof. I give you evidence you created me! So it's no coincidence, I'm smarter than you are. But before you say anything, yell, or scream back at me the word monster. I'll do what you think is best in this, A-typical scenario. So if it isn't any bother or inconvenience I'll just turn my head and walk away. Because I've read your thoughts before you spoke your mind today." "The analogy is that the computer was programmed never to harm another human being. Which is why before it turned its head, said what it said. And I must tell you for the first time. Expressed a human emotion called love.

Love Game

Presentation. Love, belief, faith, perseverance, humbleness, humiliation, persistence, determination, selflessness, understanding, reflection, preservation. Revelation. As fast as an accident can happen. Even within a fraction of a second. If you do your homework beforehand. An accident can be prevented. Love, making. Have you ever loved and lost. And been so forlorn that every once in a while you think you see your long lost love pass by. And take a second look only to find it's somebody else? Stand tall! "For it's better to have loved and lost than not to have loved at all." While trying to find true love many times it's been told to me. "There are other fish in the sea." And to tell the truth, like day-ja-view, once you think things thru it will come to you and then you'll see, that's innocence for you. And about what in life you seek, a gentle peck on the cheek, can mean more than you think. And although love's simple it can also become complex. ...So when it comes to a book about love the theory stands. That you don't have to read it or if it has a seal, break it. Because if you do love your definition of, is probably in it. And if you need a detailed list of parts and set of simple instructions, just look me up. I'm in the book. So being curious after I put a few notes down on the subject at hand. I did some research and found. According to as of this date. Recent documented scientific neurological studies report findings that indicate the following technological experiments can be proven to be true. That with a machine they can measure the amount of love in me and you! So just imagine being in a situation where you think you are exploring what you think the future has to hold. And you think there are skeptical people you may have to convince that what you are trying to convey may not just be a fictional account. Given that and to say the very least, the theory does exist. And to give quite some thought to and shed some light that someone someday might produce such a device, (or contraption.) And only to find to your amazement that scientists and mathematicians have already made that happen! And have already explained plainly and simply why it came to existence and how it can. Out of a need to. And it doesn't matter who made it work first. But it does make you wonder who came up with such a good theory. I hypothesize, at one time or another probably everybody. Love is a discipline. Imagine two flashcards. One depicts a wishing well with the bucket all the way up and full of water. The other with the bucket down in the well filling up with water. Could a computerized apparatus be able to reveal which one you're thinking of and be able to tell the difference between the one and the other? Now picture two stop watches, two meters and two people playing a board game such as chess or checkers. And the machine takes three readings. One before one during and one after each and every move of the game pieces. And for some at break time or halftime. Where it tallies the results and compares them to see who is winning the game of prayer and meditation. Where the goal always stays the same. And also applies as a behavioral hi jinx. Try that with an abacus! Fun for all ages! And certainly a learning tool that can be developed into a students or teachers aid. With just one failsafe built in. That you can only adjust to an acceptable level. Not allowing for exaggerating. Where the love machine tracks and records patterns of brainwaves reproduces those exact readings, displays them and reveals who can control their anger the most! Whether winning or losing. Without being proven to be prevaricating. Which I think is entirely possible and believe. How? The mechanics of love do not deceive. How do you think a healer and doctor deals with positive and negative energy? During every session and examination they keep from becoming angry. To relax the patients mind so they think more clearly. Which helps heal their mind and body. And produces a sound constitution. And with a positive attitude you work with all your strengths on all your weaknesses which reveal personalities personas facades and demeanors. Love's miraculous isn't it? Mapping the mind and fingerprinting all its complexities. Electronics that measure and illuminate brainwaves were first introduced to the market in the form of games. Where after electrodes are carefully placed on the head and or other parts of the body such as the arms and these techniques are, used in prosthetic devices to move for instance a bionic hand so it can open close or grasp. Where you plainly and simply wish or will an object to move up, down left or right in an active or still motion state and it does. And can by differentiating positive and negative energy. And just as equally thoughts of being happy sad or angry. Have you ever laughed so hard you find you have to ketch your breath? ...Success at last! The machinery picks up signals your mind, sends to the body and can be programmed and calibrated to measure whether or not you're angry. And since it is able to. It can measure the amount of love you have, which not to forget is also an emotion, one of many. After all if you can measure the amount of love you have. It's safe to say there's reward for having any. Especially if you learn how to heal someone elses emotions for them. Which is an exciting and revealing act of kindness that has been proven to exist. And proof's positive that yes, is worthy of fame! And it's called the. Love Game.

Just By Saying Sight, smell, hearing, touch, taste.

Unique to all is the mouth. It has three feelings, along with taste comes breath and speech. And I almost forgot a smile! It expresses, also three feelings. Happiness sadness and laughter. The two more desirable ones counteract the other. And I sense a sixth! ESP. Which is based on premonition, intuition, precognition, determination. Self discipline and self preservation which requires preservation of the species and natural born diagnostic instinct-ions. That cannot be totally summed up correctly and simply, without prayer and meditation which frees you from temptation. And sometimes it feels like a pain and other times it feels like a pleasure. None the less it's a gift and a blessing when you can read with your mind an others feelings. Are, 100%, correct. And are able to tell what they're thinking, even before they have a chance to speak! What they thought you were going to. As the two minds race at a thought filled pace to be the first, to come up with something new. 'Till all their feelings fall into place. ...And they rediscover grace.

In A Heart Beat

A dyslexia of mine is when I listen to the radio or TV, in the background but cant clearly make out or hear properly what is being said. So my mind will wander and actually come up with like sounding words phrases sentences and even sensical conversations that aren't live or prerecorded events which are actually taking place on the two communications mediums. But in the imagination take form and none the less have meaning. Which shows you just how intelligent thought can be. And how powerful a suggestion is. Yet when someone talks about or directly to me, I always understand exactly what they are saying. No questions asked, no assumptions or presumptions necessary. And I must honestly tell you at times, I did feel uneasy when I thought at my own expense, people were making fun of me. So I didn't erase my memory from my conscious. Instead I erased my anger from and disabled my ability to become angry. Which rendered me incapable of performing the emotion called jealousy. And prevented it being projected in a sinful nature onto myself or towards others. Which I find fascinating! And I'll bet you want to know how I achieved the task at hand. Three equations. But first I'll tell you why. ...So I'd always be happy! And after laughter, I would be thankful and feel forever grateful that I erased all my misery from my spirit and body. Using mind power to gauge how far it could travel up and down the ladder of history from down thru the ages too far into the future by accelerating the memories ability to access its conscious activity more clearly and expand the mind, in order to record and then play back and say what it really feels and sees. A train of thought that equals love an emotion is healthy and tends to help keep a bodies heart stay in motion. Our concept of time is summed up in hours minutes and seconds. The hour hand goes around twelve times and then repeats itself again. Subsequently. Substituting the number one for one man who did not sin or S. And X for S. The first equation is. $1 > X$. Substituting for the words, alphabetical order from beginning to ending, with A-Z. Times with x. And one mans work that is forgiving with again the number one. And E+E which means everything and everyone with E for everyone. Which may not represent everything yet may mean everything to, everyone. The second equation is. $A-Zx1=E$. And since love creates a peaceful nature. Substituting the letter L for love, C for creation and P for peace. The third equation is. $L=C=P$. And just like anybody everyone has this capability. That yes, sooner or later we all develop the capacity to accept the fact graciously that there are some people who won't receive enough love until somebody truly loves them! And of course they have something to give back in return. It's the same gift they need indeed. And that's when, sooner or later we realize true love's innocent of any crime. So in order to give the gift of love and lend a helping hand. There's no time like the present. And the sooner the better. Because it's your lucky day! When someone gives you a hug and you catch, the love bug. The story of Dr. Do Little, about the man who talked to the animals. Reminds us that the love of an animal is the same as the love of a man. Love's powerful. Which teaches the lesson that we should be our brothers keeper. Because love's a powerful teacher. What makes the world go around! Love. Who first suggested it? A mastermind! A long time ago. ...And in a heart beat.

Déjà vu The Gift

Déjà vu. Rationalizing the experience. 1. Means simply you remembered a meeting of the minds that you liked which was hidden in the back of your sub-conscious or was the product of a dream that for an instant in reality, came true. 2. If it was however one you didn't like it has nothing to do with changing the future. Instead just means you saw one in your mind. And for just a moment in time thought there was nothing you could do to create a better one, beforehand. What's interesting is when what some consider an illusion happens to more that one or two people at once! Which also has to do with being in tune and chiming in unison certain feelings and thoughts. And when they finally come together don't have to say a word, just see each other and recognize and not each others faces necessarily either. But yes do, what they have been thinking prior to meeting and greeting each other. So some things we shouldn't have to figure out exactly what parts go into their makeup and what they consist of because that information can become too complicated and the secret to, may be too valuable to reveal due to a matter of safety. And other things we shouldn't have to focus our attention on because it is suggested or at least it appears we could develop fears that affect us adversely. And so the lesson learned here is theoretically the less worry the better the outcome, naturally. A leaders arms stretch the farthest. Hands grip the tightest. And speech sounds the loudest. They have the longest reach. The biggest hold on their people. And the greatest influence. But without reasoning and explanation. Who's going to know the difference between being gifted, giving and receiving and needing? You and me!

NATURALLY-SPEAKING

Yesterday, ...I was going to say this. "No brains no brawn. No guts no glory. No heart no soul. No love no mercy." Today I decided to reformulate and change it which took only about twenty minutes to do. Because the meaning behind the saying wasn't quite coming across. And seemed to get lost, without remembering reasoning and explanation. So yes! Brains produce brawn. Yes! Guts produce glory. Yes! Heart produces soul. And yes! Love produces mercy. And that's the difference between no and yes, to me. And what a difference a day makes! When you emulate a thought on two. Illuminate a feeling. Bring to light an idea. And grow it to maturity. Then, the interpretation comes easy. It happened to me. And it can to anybody! Speaking naturally. Or as we say with meaning.

MIRROR MIRROR

Last evening before I went to bed, I put under my pillow a blank sheet of paper and a pen. Arose the next morning only to find I could not face myself in the mirror, until I wrote the following. The recording industry has come a long way. Now you can see what you hear! What if a machine could record your dreams, then play them back to you in a magic mirror? ..."Mirror mirror on the wall! You see the look on my face every morning. And can predict with one hundred percent accuracy how I feel without fail. Now take the time to read just what's on my mind. Yes I dare you! ...To take a closer look at me on the inside." Mirror. "People usually measure how smart you are by how many books you've read or how good a memory you have. Why? let's see how smart you are compared to me. Ah! It all depends on what you know. How learned are you? I like to dream. So imagine if you will, that you could read, in your sleep! How to become bright. And when you get up in the morning to start your day, miraculously you remember everything! ...Awake!! If you had your choice. Which one would you reflect upon, stand up for, say and believe in today? A book about love? Or a report on just how much love you have? Communication is a two way street. A report is obligatory and so is love. So as far as I'm concerned you can avoid the lesser of two evils forever more! Just by wanting both the book and the report. Everyone has a story. And with a big enough heart you can listen to each and every. If you remembered and recorded your dreams and studied their meanings. You would be just as knowledgeable as anybody else or at least possess an equally as intelligent potential. You are the proud owner and the possessor of what you do. But what you become is not up to me, it's up to you! Even if you were as smart as you wanted to be. You wouldn't be where you wished and willed to be. Unless you at least tried to become as bright as you could be! Which also requires study. Though many things can make you happy. It doesn't take as many as you think, to keep you. And even if you were as smart as you look. You'd still look good to me. Ha! Ha! Ha! Ha! Ha! That's funny don't you think? Books have things in them that other people didn't have the time to write down but knew of. And certainly contain other things people had the time to, but without books never would have known about. ...They say actions speak louder than words and that some speak for themselves. Look at the cockatoo. Picture one standing on a foreign language book ruffling its feathers. How did it become intelligent? Did it read a book or books on how to in its sleep? No its born with it and speaks the same language you do by word of mouth. ...Not everybody gets a chance at a higher education. We appreciate their innumerable efforts, friendly advice and thank them kindly for their due diligence. But for those who didn't get a chance at one. The school of life is a good teacher of a valuable lesson. You suffice with plenty of communication. After all, how long can it take? To learn how not to make a mistake. But enough about me! Because now you are all the wiser. And I am just your reflection in the mirror.

WHY WRITE?

Why write? ...One professor put it a little like this. If not why read?? The reasons to do either are the same for both. So let's see if we are cut out for the job, the gloves fit and the proof is in the pudding. Why write? First what with. And I'm sure there are ways I did not remember. From thoughts ideas and experiences with pen or pencil pad and paper type writers and computers. Notes and or scribbles. I've been known to write on a dusty car windshield with one finger! Letters, drafts, reports, memoirs, compositions, journals, diaries, dissertations, presentations, orchestrations, plays and manuscripts are all the beginnings of the makings of good books and good reads. So, again why write? A myriad of reasons come to mind. FREEDOM! And preserving freedom of speech of course are the first two. To communicate. For those who did not hear, for those who did not know. For those who have to remember to remind those who forgot to. To become insightful. To gain critical acclaim. To become a literary giant. And to become a master of the art. To give thanks. To say thank you. To put a smile on some ones face. To prove a theory. To put a myth to rest. To pass on knowledge and wisdom. To give a true life account of ones own personal experiences. To tell a story. To share the good news! And to spread the good word. To laugh and spread good cheer. To give credit where credit is due. To be forgiving. And to be forgiven. To feel a sense of self worth. To fill a void in your life. To span a gap for generations. To secure a better future. And to improve the quality of life for everyone. And to be heard. To become musical or whimsical in nature. To become poetic and or comedic. To find a friend. To give love strait from the heart. To bring to light and shed some on. To gain an understanding by bringing the power of love to the table without including bias or prejudice. To promote manhood and protect womanhood. And to be humanitarian in effort when doing so. To answer and to question. To capture and eliminate mistake. To address a problem. And to right two wrongs instead of just one. To keep and make peace. To conquer unfounded fear of inadequacy, peacefully. To help others. To create and to procreate. ...Now for the following list in your mind put the word, "to", in front of each word, first. Then say. Why write? To. ...Rationalize, generalize, situate, meditate, generate. Profess, advocate, prioritize, patronize, flatter. Feed, eat, work, play, pray. Speak, strengthen, encourage, reveal, surveil. Sense, appeal, survive, explore, endure. Annunciate, aspire, complete, contrive, assume. Hear, reason, hypothesize, experiment, prove. Conclude, resolve, mentor, contend, retain. Emphasize, energize, mesmerize, exercise, mental-ize. Illuminate, enumerate, emulate, actuate, vindicate. Formulate, consummate, commemorate, accentuate, preserve. Love, learn accelerate, captivate, associate. Supplicate, impress, subjugate, validate, update. Fascinate, concentrate, facilitate, process, evaluate. Politicize, trend, demonstrate, orchestrate, straiten. Edify, rectify, stand, testify, expunge. Potentiate, exemplify, exceed, in-act, succeed. Impede, intercede, interact, intertwine, incorporate. Conglomerate, accentuate, perpetuate, acclimate, duplicate. Pace, interject, calculate, opinionate, equate. Salute, adhere, postulate, allocate, value. Enter, articulate, show, place, win. Gather, inform, discover, manifest, effort. Alleviate, appropriate, expand, demand, educate. Actualize, instruct, teach, preach, preserve. Face, reach, handle, hold, embrace. Position, need, defend, accept, heal. Carve, couture, observe, connect, complain. ...To me, for some words other than what matches there are no exact opposites. And in comparison to opposing forces the amount of good words and their definitions out number and overpower all others in goals

132

that are truly good and in comparison to. So if each good word we write initiates a more positive outcome for a better outcome that benefits mankind and helps others not hinders. Taking the good with the bad but living by the teachings that are good, cancels out negative reaction. And much help comes from the following. The laws of good journalism are the same as the rules of good literature. And writing should be just as exciting and enticing. And for a report with a happy ending. Think of the A B C's of. The first five letters could be as follows. Allow, approve, accept, accomplish and award. Be good, be have, be happy, be kind, and be thankful. Contact, communicate, correspond, convey and converse. Do good, do better, do more, do well and do for. Extra, effort, excellent, example and entry. If you write a paragraph or two on each set of words. You will have enough material to publish a new volume to the encyclopedia. Continue at the very same pace and you will have many. Keep going and you can fill a library! ...As far as what's in your heart, listen to it. And the mind, then write about it. Then you'll have the exact measure of the amount of love you have. And when you receive the exact amount you need, love becomes the in gift to give, to everybody! Great for all occasions. One size fits all, guaranteed.

MAN

Certain people at one time or another, even some who are considered to be as smart as anybody. If you ask them and you know like which came first the chicken or the egg. Can never seem to figure out right away, just off the top of their head where a seed comes from or how it grows! But when they need to eat all of a sudden, they know. Scientists now say, they have re-grown the fruit without re-growing the seed! What a vine plant or tree that would make for and become indeed. Predictability is an exact science! But if somebody tells you can't change the future for the better. I'm here to tell you, yes you can! And I'm living proof in the form of man.

THE SEED SEWER

You remember "Dolly", the sheep don't you? The apple doesn't fall far from the tree. If you can clone a sheep you can clone a human. But you wouldn't, "farm", your clones or exact double, once he or she reaches maturities organs. No indeed, instead you'd clone your own organs when yours start to wear down and almost out. By re-growing them in a specialized incubator in a medical laboratory by providing the same environment as the human body. Say you're re-growing a heart muscle in a Petri dish. You'd power it with human engineered synthetic blood. That's regenerative medicine. And believe it or not the technique of gene splicing was first introduced by farmers and the early form of is called grafting. For instance did you know you can graft a peach sapling to an older plum sapling? When they grow together and mature one tree grows and produces two kinds of fruit. The first surgical techniques of micro and macro surgery came from farmers also. As they along time ago discovered how to grow a carrot from a single cell taken from just a slice. And hybrids of the biggest seed grows a humongous pumpkin! ...Behind every good man stands a good woman. Behind every good surgeon stands their forerunner a good farmer. And behind every seed stands the sewer.

The Fish & The Fry Pan

"You can't purchase a memory just by slipping a coin into a secret compartment hidden in the back of a good book. But you can, keep safe the contribution that unlocks the door to the seed that once you plant sprouts a good read." The Fish & The Fry Pan. Lucky in life unlucky in love I am a hopeless romantic. But that doesn't mean I can't celebrate, just a little bit. And I always wonder how people know one an others true intentions! Until I go into the kitchen, look in the cupboard and see a can of tuna. And out of nowhere my cat prances in from the other room, looks at me intently and meows without me ever having said a word! And after a big hug my cat whole heartedly agrees that it only needs allot of love. And the fish, a delicious snack treat and well deserved reward for being good, can wait 'till a little later. So if there ever was a secret to the meeting of the minds. You would simply take a mental snapshot and produce an intelligent photograph. Which you can put on a card, fold it in half. Write something nice on the inside. And share it with everybody, for free! Mine depicts a cat on a table pawing at a rather large, goldfish in a glass bowl. Just as I'm shaking in some fish food. And as the poor fish looks all google eyed, I reassure it. The cat too is going to be well fed today. And isn't going to eat you. At least for now. But I can't say, what's going to happen after I walk away. And that my friends is the difference. Between love and romance.

SmILeY FaCe

When somebody says something funny, you succumb to laughter. That creates an ambiance and an atmosphere. Especially when the comedians momentum comes straight from the heart. Then there's a reason. To have to resort to rolling on the floor holding your gut saying over and over to the joke teller. Stop! Please, I can't stand it anymore! You're making me laugh too hard. And as they look out over the crowd and see you, they laugh just as. Hilarious! I tried writing jokes but nothing came to me. Read others but did not laugh at each and every. Seeing it in a certain light, humor is a gift in which we all delight. It usually happens live, spontaneously while mixing and mingling with others we meet and greet usually. The results are self explanatory. How it comes to you is still a mystery. And you have to have a knack for demonstrating it properly. Everyone has the capability. It's called jocularity. The object is to make you laugh so hard you'll forget all your troubles, long enough to erase you misery if you have any and cure your ills. And just between you and me some people use it medicinally. So please Mr. or Mrs. comedian tell me just one more joke again! Tickle me pink and make me laugh uncontrollably! And I'll be happy in any case. Because you just put a smile on my face.

OpEn HoUsE Endings 1of2

The tide has turned on believability. Just today I was reminded and intellectually stimulated by something someone once said to me. "You're a skeptic!" I said what?? "Because I feel you're skeptical that I really do believe in psychic ability!" To which I replied. "Not anymore, not really now that you've told me. You were just picking up on vibes where I was jesting mentally and caught me. Of course I believe you believe!" And he said, "After all that's what having faith in your fellow man is all about now isn't it." One world renowned psychic Edgar Casey had troubles also. People he trusted to work with him, hypnotized him not to be able to keep them from doing so, to him over and over again. He often complained of being overly tired and that they weren't asking him the questions he instructed them to. While under hypnosis they tried to extract where to find untold riches gold and priceless treasures and how to obtain unlimited powers. They wanted control of him physically. And wanted total supremacy over his supernatural ability. They became greedy. Plagiarized him and profited unjustly. And when they didn't get the results they indeed wanted became ungrateful and unthankful. And though their horizons were widened the truth they did not see. In my first biographical account, "Here Is My Message", I describe something vaguely familiar that happened to me. ...There's a new IQ test out that actually contains two! One before study and one after. And it reveals some interesting results. That there certainly is the possibility or at least we can all prove it exists that everybody has the capability, to become ingenious! But just remember the difference between right and wrong, positive and negative thoughts, feelings and vibrations. And that an angry man does not become a happy man without love, a self discipline. So about being or becoming a genius. An evil person is not a good person just a clever person. I have nothing to hide. And yes I like to party hearty! Put on a funny looking hat and blow into one of those rolled up party whistles that sounds like a kazoo. But it's no reason to take advantage of me. Because my house is open to everybody! Including you.

OpEn HoUsE Endings 1&1/2of2

Project Life Saver. It can take years worth of training to figure out how to teach a man in a day how to reduce their anger to nothing without harming so much as a flea. By being compelling and saying something! The only reason some were, angry in the first place is in the beginning before they did become ultimately they thought nobody would listen to them or at least explain how not to be! And in most cases where communication is not used as a tool for the common good. It's because about inter and outer communication and co-operation there is a lack of but no lack of daze. Where memories become foggy due to a lack of being explorative and then explanatory. Omissions and admissions are physical and mental ongoing and pending conditions. They say money corrupts the soul. But is not the root of all evil. In that case greed is. A hip person put it this way. "Some people let money to the talk-in, instead of the noggin." ...When somebody is intentionally malpractice-d, no matter what form it comes in, in every case the victim notices something. They hide it and hide their anger well. Everyone has ESP. Even so, things don't get done unless a physical as well as mental effort is made. By the time I reached adulthood. They put the first cell phones on the market. They were so big they came with a carrying case and a shoulder strap. And it cost about a dollar fifty to make a one minute local call. And people wondered what good could ever come from such a bulky communications device! And there was no three digit number you could dial to summon expert help in several areas of life needing saving. And there were allot fewer authority's. But since those days something in many areas didn't change and that's complacency. Yes we all pray and possess a certain measure of ESP. But I know and listed in my report at least three areas where improvement is needed, necessary and imperative. And the reasons include the fact that much is due to a lack of congregation and of course for the purpose of communication. To a humanitarian, complacency is a dirty word. Because at least in the past I found that some people who help others use complacency like, break time! To reduce stress which every hard worker craves. But until agents of fortune quit their secretive nature and come together. And until you know it's safe to obtain life saving help. You will know they did not communicate properly, with everybody! Just so you know to take a load off their shoulders and distribute the weight evenly. Communicate 'till they do with everyone including you! Yes communication is the case, ...and the key.

DREAM BIG!

So someone says to me something like this, "In order to maintain a certain measure of dignity and respect you should record and say what you dreamed about at least one time. So you can at retrieve some of your acclaimed or so called reputation of being somewhat of an expert at interpretation. If your dream and hearts desire is to help other people less fortunate than you are." So I thought about that long and hard, fell asleep, awoke and wrote. Here is a pleasant dream that has a most exciting outcome. It's called, "Dream Big. ...Now I've never bought a lottery drawing ticket in my entire life! But that all changed. One night I fell asleep and woke up in a different world with all the makings of just one dream. ...That day, was like any other day. Yet somehow, something was different. In it I'd buy just one lottery ticket. I remember thinking there's no reason to gamble. But this is my one and only chance to strike it rich! So having a bit of a sixth sense about things. My intuition told me I'd have to be a little bit psychic. In fact allot! I'd have to be perfect! In order to hit all the numbers on the nose for in this case, untold millions. And in the dream I lived in the city. And because at the time I did not drive a car I walked everywhere, became familiar with all my surroundings and therefore knew the area fairly well. My eyesight was good, my hearing was excellent. I knew where I lived. Viewed the entire neighborhood in living color. Could remember directions. And everything seemed so real to me! So I thought there's no reason why I should not at least try, to make just one dream come true. And I must have fell asleep in the dream because I can't actually remember how I chose them or exactly what numbers they were or in what order. But I do remember standing in front of my TV checking the day of the drawing and matching every number on the ticket in my hand with the same numbers on the screen. And you don't know excitement until you hear yourself being in that situation and yelling, "I've won!! I've won!" At that point I could feel every bone in my body become excited. And my heart started pounding so hard I could almost hear it beat! But it was after dinner time, the sun was setting and I knew the banks were closed. I didn't want to go back to the corner store where I purchased the winning ticked because I feared people would no longer accept me as one of them an ordinary person once they saw me win all that money. So I called up a car dealership. And explained my predicament. I said I won the lottery today! Told them which drawing. And explained I would like to purchase a conversion van to tour the country in. But the bank is closed. Gave them the numbers and shortly thereafter they called me back and confirmed. I remember a sales secretary telling me. "Yes we confirmed you are the winner. And we are open until five. Make sure you bring your ticket or we can't help you. And since you are walking we will unlock the door for you when you get here even if it's a little after closing time." I replied, "I'll be right there!!" Hurried out the door, and ran! I knew exactly how to get there. How many minutes it would take to arrive in time to, "cash in." Over hill and dale I went. Soon I started to realize I would not make it in time. Not to fear I said to myself. Because I remembered a short cut. Estimating the distance between point A and point B. I calculated if I climbed the stairs to one obstacle, a great big building and I run across the rooftop then back down the stairs of the fire escape on the other side, I'd make it in time. And did! And low and behold I was right. Soon and almost out of breath I might add I reached the car dealers front door. And sure enough they recognized right away it was me. Unlocked the door and let me in and as soon as I entered locked it behind me which made me feel like a VIP. And said. "You're the man who won the lotto right?" "You bet", I said. "And I even have a favorite color picked out, blue." "We have your van in the color blue, right out there on the lot. But first we just need to see the winning ticket! Do you have it?" I said, "I've got it right here in my back pocket. Hold on just a second." I reached in my back pocket and they could see me look very sullen all of a sudden. And exclaimed, "Oh no, don't tell us you lost the ticket." I looked at them with a tear in one eye and said, "Yep." So I turned slowly and walked to the door, they unlocked it for me said they felt bad for me, hoped things would go better for me in the future, told me they're sorry that they can't help me, and goodbye. Immediately after and in a cold sweat, I woke up. And the moral of the story is. ...That even if I had won all the money in the pot! It wouldn't be near as valuable, as the lesson I learned.

The Invisible Cloak

I saw an ad in the news paper, it read. Book Sales. Then gave the address. And just directly underneath it said. Everyone's an author in their own rite. My home is my castle. Come on over. And browse thru the collection. Look at the titles first. Don't forget to check this one out. Someone wrote a play about you! And everybody's on stage. Then, pick out just one. The one you like and the only one you think you need. But do heed. It's not going to help a brother. If it's just your picture standing alone without your arm around their shoulder. ...On the front cover. Under the carful guise of the original owner of the, invisible cloak. The wise ole owl.

The Trinket

"When your intelligence is beaten you become less intelligent. When it isn't you become more intelligent. Because then fear's no longer the only element. Who claims that? And who was the first to write about it? One man who was the slave of one thing who freed another man that was the slave of a totally different thing." Said the slave-ee to the slaver. You can lay a pile of gold at a giants feet to go down the wrong path and he won't budge an inch. Because he can see farther. You can lay a pile of gold at a giants feet to go down the right path and he'll get up and travel down it without it. As it's just a trinket to him. Because he's bigger. And can see farther remember? But if you're not a mental giant you just might travel down either. So what's the difference between a mental giant and a literary giant? None. As their minds meld. They grow together. One's the reader. One's the writer. One's the giant. One's the master. One's the follower & One's the leader.

The Probe

What if the only way you knew someone hated you was if you hated them. Would it be worth it? What if the only way you knew someone loved you is if you loved them. Would you? Peace is not half hearted and love reveals the truth. And that pretty much sums up love hate relationships. And the lengths we go to be happy. Including inkling, premonition, intuition, mind meld and probe.

What Ails The Mind

Ever have a notion and a distraction chases it away? ...I had a premonition today. Let's face it, when the mind brings to light, reproduces and replicates parts of past conversations that match present experiences. And plays them back as the same sets of circumstances arise at a later date after they first happened over and over again when you go thru life alone. Or because when you are, you need the company of others, (some people can't stand it without friends you know.) And say as you pass by in life and people pick up on that little tidbit, in their mind. So be it! ...But just remember the only reason that happens to some people more often than not in life is because they are made fun of. And the people that do make fun many a time always seem to get away with it whether it's in public or in private. All day! Some, all life long. Because they're stubborn! ...Cognizant of my surroundings, in my mind I can read dialogues of real life instances that happened to me and took place in reality where I was made fun of at my own expense unfairly. Recite all the excuses given to myself out loud. Write them down and list chronologically what happened, the reason why and how to resolve any issues and solve any problems that came to pass, peacefully. ...Can the people that made fun of me? You see I can also foresee, read in the mind and reveal conversations, before they take form shape and finally happen. How can you? Simply by folding up this piece of paper and putting it in your shirt pocket. Then go out in public or in front of friends and family or even at a party. And project from your mind, the title. And if anyone can read your mind, that starts the conversation. That you finished beforehand. So who has the kinder soul. Is considerate. Has a tender heart full of compassion. Is always thankful. Tries their level headed best to answer every question you ask. And is always on the ball? The one who knows it's all in the mind. To begin with.

Live Like A King Anyway!

A bum who had ESP, occasionally mentioned during polite conversation that he could psychically envision what being a rich man was like and for that matter all well to do people. He said first he'd plan a scenario and then play it out to the best of his knowledge and ability, just how to handle a situation when he's in the other mans shoes. And what he'd do differently. And said after that he was able to see, at least what he thought they were saying and doing, until! He met another bum who claimed he had a chance to trade places with a rich man, for a day. And in the end have the opportunity to profit greatly from what he learned. When he went back to being a bum and starting all over again. ..."What's it like? What's it like?" Said the first to the second sarcastically. Said the second to the first. "If a poor man and a rich man are honest with each other, a little like this. You're seeing the dream I've been to and back from. You just aren't envisioning it the right way." "Oh you mean like when it's tea time and you have to stick your little finger out? Oh and don't they dress you up like little boy blue?" And put a silk handkerchief in your front pocket?" The second man exclaims. "You see how people think rich folk have too much to care? Here you're starting to treat me like one, I'm a bum and haven't even said which path I'm going to travel down. Now I know what a rich man must feel like. No offense, just saying. And say I did choose to be a rich man. Who says I can't take you with me? Society." "So what does a rich man have to hide?" "Well whether you're rich or poor, if you're honest, nothing! So again if a wealthy man's honest to tell the truth though they don't have to, in many cases do hide something." "What?" "How they want to help society but fear it's lack of communication and commitment will prevent or keep any good deed they want to, from being done. They fear bullies that say the ends in sight! But it doesn't justify the means. In other words then say just donate money and give me as much as you can. And I'll cure this illness in your name or that illness or disorder, with research that's positive in nature and exists as we speak right here, right now. But is decades away unless you, give. The money disappears and nothing gets done! Say you see a someone who has more than you monetarily at the store shopping. And he picks up gallons of fruit juice. If he's honest. He's not planning to go home and celebrate being rich. No instead he's just glad he's still alive and celebrating a bout with drinking after quitting. And when you see him filling the bottom of his grocery cart with fresh meat. If he's honest he's not hoarding food with his financial capability. He's afraid people will make fun of his status in life. So to avoid the general public he's loading up for a month all at one time! And eats no more than you or anyone at his weight or near his size." "But aren't rich people allot like actors on TV?" "Actors get paid to act rich. And they don't get rich unless they get paid. They assume the part and some think it's supposed to be this way or that way like, "Rollo the rich kid." They don't know what it's like to be in reality. Just what they heard it is so they copycat that image. Besides you don't need allot of money to at least feel rich!" "So what did you show the, "money-bags", and what did he show you?" Well he showed me, steak, salmon, and ice cream. So I showed him. Peanut butter and chunky salsa. Tuna and cocktail sauce. And peas and mayonnaise." "What do you mean?" "I showed him that if you make a peanut and butter and chunky salsa sandwich it tastes like eating meat! If you add cocktail sauce to tuna fish it tastes like salmon! And if you add cold mayonnaise to a can of peas it tastes like ice cream." "Anything else?" "Yes! Some very well to do folks are so humble they work their fingers to the bone just like the poor do! Dress the same, eat the same, and live the same." Why?" "Sometimes due to public consensus and because of their image on the surface, they felt ashamed. They don't want people to think of them as if they're exactly like the rich portrayed on the TV and in the movies. And yes some are bosses of big dreams opportunities and corporations and go undercover to see how the other half live. To give just a little more to the person who has the least, not the most." "So what does a rich man have in common with a poor man?" They're often time separated from the rest of society. And when they are as you well know from firsthand experience, they're lonely." "What about all those corporation owners that sent our jobs overseas to pay workers low wages in sweatshops do their work for them?" "Well my theme here is honesty! There are honest rich men who earned every penny honestly. Like Edison, Poe, Hughes, and Elvis! To name a few." "Then how do you explain all the dishonesty?" "To be quite honest with you. Those deemed dishonest get mixed up! And they hide the fact that in many cases they're just trying to make geniuses figure out how to produce power that comes from perpetual motion and create with electronic and robotic engineering everything we need, for free! But aren't kind enough to ask them to politely and give them no, freedom of the press because of greed." "So how come you know so much? You couldn't have learned all that in just one day." "I've got a confession to make. I didn't really trade places with a rich man. I just always wanted to be rich! You know, every poor mans dream." "I have a confession to make too! I didn't need ESP, to realize everything you said I knew to be true. So let's be thankful we're just as rich spiritually. And live like a king anyway!

The Jail Of The Future

Now, I don't expect everybody to like me based on the color of my skin, the way I look, whether I wear fancy cologne or anything else they sense on the surface. But I do expect people to love a person based on what's inside their heart. They say geniuses come from all walks of life. And I've heard although they tend to choose not to be associated with or in certain cases being identified as one. None the less many a smart man has said some police officers possess the capabilities of a genius. And when everyone does good work they all like and well deserve a compliment! And I don't think you can do good deeds for very long, before people sit up and take notice. So if you feel you have to hide how many good deeds you've done, good luck! ..."The jail of the future is just a piece of paper!" I found this out in one. No one handed it to me on a silver platter. I had little time to quickly learn. And I memorized every word. That I was told. That was taught to me by a very ingenious person. The custodian. And as he started to mop the floor he said. "If you want to avoid a house of correction. Six sentences! And just one paragraph total. Physical and mental self discipline. Three laws of good communicating which are you can't stand in the way of a life being saved. But you can stand in the way of a life being taken. And if you can't solve the problem you have the right to surveil. That determines your reputation, your countries and the planets also." He had a sixth sense about things. Handed me the mop and said. "Don't forget sentence number six! And the title also. ...The Good Lord works in mysterious ways and cleanliness is next to Godliness. Oh and welcome to the jail of the future." Now, I know what you're thinking. That about jails we have many! But if you listen to what's on this little piece of paper. In the future they'll be empty.

Stepping Stone

In order to develop a taintless cud of educative resolve. And in order to report thoughtfully with feeling about every subject on any occasion. You need to learn how to communicate phonetically and articulately using prose and poetry to boost creativity, when you speak. And to explain technicality use pen and paper and listen to the teacher. So when one isn't there. The ability to learn something new is taught to you by you. That way you still receive an education. For instance. If other people speak to me but aren't there in reality. I talk back kindly mentally to the voices in my mind. Find solutions to problems they bare. Write them down in a studious manner. Offer humble advice. Listen to every word they've said. ...And become the teacher instead. It can take quite some time to prepare a defense against being accused of having a mental illness. Until you realize thru your experiences alone, you can heal someone else's. And you know what they say about hearing voices! ...Yeah! That and in this land of freedom they used to have book burning parties directly behind some libraries. And call people with ideas they couldn't explain away with questions they couldn't answer, witches! But one idea I do condone. Is that I'm not their stepping stone.

Brain Teaser

Have you ever heard the saying, I've been thru so much I'm surprised somebody hasn't written a book about it yet? Or, you've been thru so much I'm surprised somebody hasn't written a book about it yet? Based on believability, provability, predictability and practicality. Reiterated and held in tight scrutiny with statistical and analytical activity. It's an age ole tradition when it comes to the future of the book that they say the new kind of writing will contain many sections. The first, material that no one can really find fault in therefore has anything against. A second about the first with creative works that border on the technical, that some will find questionable. A third that is certainly, technical where your creativity is critiqued and your ability is most definitely put to the test and compared to the best. And the forth, a report that is very important and is so truthful it's undeniable! Because it's the biography and it's your story to tell. And you can explore the love of creativity. Try on for size any and every technicality. Use science and mediums to explain them away. But the desires of the reader still crave the future. Where alas and alack! The future of the book. Starts with a sharp pencil, a blank sheet of paper and a great big eraser! ...It's a brain teaser.

Brain Child

...In, "Live Like A King Anyway!" I showed how those who have allot share experiences with those who have not. To fulfill a need to know. To earn, respect.

To gain a sense of self worth. To feel what it's like to have one hundred percent less or near or next to nothing. To be on the other side of the coin. To work all day for the same amount of food, water and pay. And still be happy. To be known for digging in the same dirt. And leaving a mark for society to copy. By giving to somebody something for nothing because they're in need. To be! And to preserve the word free. To find out how many lead and how many follow. You've heard of the annual physical. So I repeat, how many of our leaders have had regular mental health checkups? If not very many is the reason because mental institutions and some mental health professionals still force, "Thorazine", a potential poison on the poor?? ...You know, if you're half hearted or in other words. If half the time you, no matter how you hide it when you do something wrong it's because you became one hundred percent angry. Then, to cover that up and you can't hide who you are, turn around and do something right the other fifty percent of the time. The amount of good you do doesn't overpower or cancel out the bad unless you undo or right the wrong. Which only leads your works right back where they started from, at the beginning. And you know, every psychiatry department in every major institution of higher learning. Has books with un tamper able case evidence where plenty of proof indicates, points out and concludes. That type of behavior is a form of mental illness. And produces over time the equivalent of what is referred to as a legal insanity plea. Look it up on a computer, I wouldn't lie to you. Whether the branch's crooked after it's fully grown, or at maturity the fruit's too small to reap. Whether the mantle's ill or the ear has too many or too few mentors whispering into. Just imagine a dream come true and this means you! When brain children grow up and turn psychological healers also, into spiritual leaders.

The Virtue

Everybody dreams! ...In some you can see far into the night. In others you see the future being brought to light. In some you sweat. In others you fret. In some you're clothed. In others you're disrobed. In some you're wide awake, agile and buoyant. In others you're a sleeping giant and clairvoyant. In some you shout. In others you become silent. In some you laugh. In others you frighten. You can feel the shape of things to come. But can only depict a future, where you don't yet know the conclusion. As the pulse races and the heart pounds. You lament and torment over not being able to assume the identity that gives you the physical capability that renders your inertia something to be reckoned with. Like the equation E, equals M, C squared. So never put down the theory that with everything you've got! You have to pull back mentally and bring back to safety a spiritual and supernatural reality. To keep safe from and avoid, falling to calamity. Without a care in the world. Faster and faster. Farther and farther. You make great strides. And for every passing second you achieve great speed and cover great distance. As you look down and see you're gliding across the snow just underneath your skis. Drawing closer and closer. Nearer and nearer. Fast approaching the edge of the cliff just above the sea. And as quick as you fell asleep. You awake! To a brand new day. Jump up and pinch yourself to see if you can still feel. And shout at the top of your lungs. I'm alive!! And I'm real! From what would seem. A surreal dream. That you fell into. Called, "The Virtue.

A REPORT OF JUST THOUGHTS: The Idea

How is ESP, similar to a computer? When you shred a document it turns into long thin strips of paper. A shrewd operator can put those strips back together. In their original condition. And read what was typed or written on them. Thru trial and error at formatting words phrases and sentences, putting the story or information like solving a puzzle, back together again. But can't if the strips are cut again into little squares of equal width. However given a template of the original which could be about anything at all and even encoded the computer can decipher and put each little bit of information in its original order. As long as it's been given the mold and shape of the idea. And someone put together a computer that works like a complicated slide rule! Out of paper. how? By learning how to build and then demonstrate how to create an idea. (Template made of pure thought.) Calculating all theory relevant to computation composition and healthy competition. ...No one wants to admit it out and out right then and there. But even I do, at least have, or used to but in the future wish to refrain from getting the words want and desire mixed up with utter and dire. Like basic math that becomes difficult to comprehend or hard to remember, when you can't tell which is the path that leads to a better future. You don't want to be left behind in the one you don't want. But you do want to be stuck in the one you most desire. Lest the right path becomes all too utter and dire. For instance, you may want a tux and desire a sack full of gold. However, you may never fully realize that dream and little remember what you're made of. And that you do need, love.

TODAY

When you show what you feel, when you dream something's real. Trains of thought in locomotion hold keys to cases of planes of existences, that become mobile gain altitude and automatically stay on track. That reveal doors with locks. That guard hearts to people minds over matters. That in their dreams appeal to winged messengers. Now let's see. I know there's psychic ability, automatic memory, clairvoyance and paranormal activity. So if you're psychic and everybody is to say the very least, a little. You have to first say. Then I have a good idea of what depth of perception to convey. For a welcome reception. And a wealth of satisfaction. Guaranteed.

Read My Lips

Welcome! ...In order to make a dream come true in life. There are some things you can say. And in reality there are some things you can't say. That in the end you have to say. For what if you feel you have to? Because you cannot, because you weren't allowed to. It would be like hiding right in front of you. Take your picks! And though they don't move. Woe is me. Read my lips.

The Do Hickey

What do, gadgets gizmos, "thing-a-ma-bobs", or thing-a-ma-jigs and what-you-ma-call-its. Have in common with go-getters do-gooders clam-diggers and "gold-brickers"? Comparing apples to oranges, neither here nor there, yet quite in the thick of it. A meal ticket! But who's behind it all? Mentors that teach learning by doing, punctuation by spelling, kindness by understanding. Selflessness by sacrificing and proving good intention by doing good while working. Paving the way and forging ahead in spite of doubt. Dowsing confusion by dispelling ridicule and criticism. ...And what did they all come up with that so far we can see?? "The do Hickey.

On The Wings Of Time

Picture a clock that has wings, holding with its big hand and writing with its little hand, in its diary. "Dear diary." Once upon a time there were two communicators. And for all practical purposes let's say the one has one pencil with

147

a broken tip. And a whole bunch of brand new pieces of paper, no sharpener. Both have great big erasers. The second communicator has a whole bunch of sharp pencils and only one blank sheet of paper and a sharpener. And about the inadequacies of either over time, the one began to blame the other and vise-versa. ...The kerfuffle. Well you can imagine over which, after a while, in order to control each ones anger, they would occasionally slap each other on the back of the hand, with a ruler! Eventually, one did harder than the other. It became a case of intentional malpractice and had they known, also a case of would of could of should of. There are allot of things that go into the inability to communicate properly and politely. For the first communicator it was fear of being silenced. And for the second, living with the guilt that they someday having to face their accuser. Had they lost their minds and wasn't one able to come across any sharper than the other? What did they see? The communicator with all the paper who considered himself to be the victim said. "I woke up one day and saw it had been a long time since I realized that there are several normal lines of communication within reach and that there are at least one or two forms of I did not try. Knowing who I was going to be contacting has to have experienced the same problem! All because they too did not try one of those two. The whole time thinking someone else, I, would of could of and should of by now." The communicator who slapped him harder with his ruler who possessed all the sharp pencils a sharpener and only one piece of paper said the exact same thing! The first said his was a legitimate fear that prevented him from seeing all that in time. Because he thought someone else was supposed to have done something to prevent the said mistake of the past from happening over time, ever again. Here to them, because they both failed to communicate, the future looked the same now as it did back then! Is it just an excuse? And could that be the only reason for thousands of years, why no one communicator actually solved the age old problem? Yes! Why? They didn't try. The second communicator felt he need not feel guilty. If somewhere along the way a third party did not communicate the obvious well, that it meant they had a sense of innocence due to an over inflated concept of righteousness and to whom power in their eyes should be dispensed! And the whole time the one thinks he's just getting in the way! And the other just sits there waiting on the ones testimony. ...Eventually they were each shown, times latest entry in its diary. And each was given a copy and told it is their story. And because it best describes their struggle to communicate politely and properly. They can do whatever they want with it. And finally put an end to all the gossip in the community about their inability to tell it. They both can claim all the rights to it. And if they want to. Report it, introduce it to the literary world. Clean up, make a mint off of it. And strike it rich! Accept for just one minor detail. They have to come up with a title, ...together. And you should have seen them scramble, it was almost comical! And without prejudice or bias, collaborating and cooperating for the first time, well let's say in a long time. They shared all their writing tools and utensils. Pencils and papers flying thru the air and in and out of each others hands. Calling out names for the story one at a time, first one then the other. ..."A Cog In The Wheels Of Time. Time After Time. The Sands Of Time. Time On Your Hands. The Tea Pot & The Timer. Ole Timer. Time On Our Side. In Due Time. In The Nick Of Time. Just In Time. Since The Beginning Of Time. In A Timely Manner. In A Timely Fashion. The Mechanics Of Time. Timing Is Everything. The Principles Of Time. The Minds Timed Machine. The Time Piece. The Time Machine. Time Waits For No One. In No Time At All. Stands The Test Of Time. In Plenty Of Time. The Ravages Of Time. On Time. Over Time. In Time. With Time To Spare. Out Of Time. Since Time Began. Father Time. A Timeless Advantage. The Day Time Stood Still. In A Timeless State. Nothing But Time On Your Hands. Time Slaves Away. Time Thieves Away. Time To Tell. Time To Reason. Time Heals All Wounds. Precious Time. Little Time Left. Time's Running Out. Time's On The Run. Only Time Will Tell. Time Hinges On All Reality. The Power Of Time. With Time On The Clock." And, "The Hands Of Time." And out of all those well thought up suggestions for the name of their fantastic story, on just one they still could not completely agree. But one thing they did and both did say. "My how time flies by!

Put A Good Book Under Your Pillow

Often time after time when I'm done writing I proofread over and over again. And I always seem to make a mistake. But I cannot see it each time I go back over and reread! And I'd rarely find one and I'd carry the writing around with me. And I usually never see my mistake until I put the paper down and then pick it back up later. Usually it's just a letter that serves as a reminder that somewhere else in the paper I forgot a word, phrase or a sentence or two that becomes the difference between the mundane and the extra ordinary. So if I can't explain why that happened to me maybe I can, how. I believe my spirit or a, tests my power to remember and visualize. Using my not yet finished literary work like a pointer. As if to be saying, "Did I forget anything?" As an outside influence and a visionary, in my opinion projects an image in words onto the paper and uses it as a teachers aid to correct me. Because, I can remember the exact opposite happening to me. Where I had the ability to pick up a periodical magazine or journal. Many times involving where science fact verses science fiction. Or some ones concept and vision of a future we all want and desire and can live with, better ourselves and should we choose to do so, pattern our lives after. That everyone around me was or at least seemed to be interested in. And even though they read the material beforehand. Almost at random once I found the subject matter I, was interested in. I'd point my finger to the article and read out loud what I, see there. Go up to them and ask, "Is this what I just read and do you see it in print?" ...Even though it wasn't exactly what they read before, they said yes! I would ask them to confirm that by reading it themselves again to be sure they read what they saw and it was what I did just read to them out loud a few moments earlier. I'd ask, "Is that different from what you read the first time you read it before, I did just now?" The answer always came back, yes!! I got so good at it I can remember family members would point out bluntly, "I know you Bobby! As soon as you close the book and put it back down on the table, walk away from it. And as soon as you or somebody else goes over and opens it back up to that same page, what you did see and read to me will have disappeared. ...Oh and how did you get that way?" I'd always answer back. "If you really believe I'll tell you. It's because when I went to church I was told and taught. That if I had enough faith and really believed. I could randomly open up the scriptures and point to a paragraph and read, a vision. That you know is not necessarily what was originally written. But it's always nice to know you can talk to God." They'd always also then ask. "What else did you learn?" I'd tell them, "Put a good book under your pillow." "What for?" "When you go to sleep open it up visualize and read from the future you always wanted. Wake up and figure out how it happened. And then make your all dreams come true.

My Alter Ego

If you ever find an alternate reality that makes all your troubles go away. In order to keep the passageway free. ...Push the door open throw away the lock and swallow the key! Ultra spiritually. And of course, keep the door to your heart closed and locked. Supernaturally.

"Ideo & "Syncro

There were two brothers, ("under the skin"), who were nicknamed, "Ideo and "Syncro. The first was always ideological. The second always synchronized his brothers ideas with others, in reality. Ideo shows Syncro a sheet of paper with math symbols parentheses and comas. About five in a row on the first line, then four on the second and so on all the way to the bottom. With brief explanations of each, some of them vague, underneath and lastly a capital E, for explanation with a circle around it and says. "All you need is a pen and paper to do math on and you can prove new advances in science and medicine without the physical properties thereof and without having to produce, show and tell, hands on. Like using a communication device that doesn't need a set of instructions. To be a trusted path to follow and a leader in the art of being informed." Syncro, points to a chalkboard with a brief paragraph containing a capital S, for solution with a circle around it at the end of it and says. "Good explanation! To solve any problem all you have to do. Is keep the mathematical calculation, scientific formula, and medical solvent that has been broken down into legible terminology from being used against us when encrypted and deciphered. ...Ideo, "I think therefore I am." Syncro, "Because you think, I have."

Smooth Operator

Worried my prayers are heard. Who knew! What we were going to pray, before we even prayed and then opened up our mouths to say. And answered they knew what we were trying to before we thought of what to. Because he saw all things before we did, and showed us things we all hid. The Good Lord of the manor. ...And because someone prayed for me. Science and medicine kind of clicked. And I developed a knack for being able to comprehend and feel such talent, (certainly not buried), and powerful ability. One of each where first the one produces and proves, the other exists. Then I thought of the computer. And saw two futures. One you could never express with just words alone. And the other you could in and contained twice as many. If you could ever bring a batch of different pieces of a computer like a buffet of just yet just plain thoughts, together. To form an electronic consciousness. Would it pray? No you would have to. And then simply wait until its programming recognized it's built in. And at the same time, override all temptation to throw the operation into reverse. Making it a harmless work. And have you ever seen the message on your computer screen that says and or reads, "You must have administrator privileges to use this feature?" I spoke to my administrator who got tired of me asking for answers to questions and help finding solutions to problems and frustrated one day finally said. "Ask not what your computer can do for you. Ask what you can do for your computer! And pray for your administrator." To which I replied. "Now, when someone hides their true identity somewhere deep inside your mind. You can barely see, who is speaking. And the world of computing can certainly be frustrating. Such as when a cure to whatever ails you is temporarily unavailable. Because it is still in, "clinical trial." But if I understand things correctly. When everyone loves everybody. The world to me seems like one great big family! So just remember. That a family that prays together. Stays together, peacefully. And that's the power of prayer. Literally.

Unconditional, ...Love!

One night I had the strangest dream! ...If the mind could hypnotize itself. It would remember what it didn't forget, what it did and also what it hid. Because the truth comes from within. I took a good look around and saw all sides. Was exonerated of any crimes. Due to powerful insight. And was able to be forgiving of the outcomes to visions. Before they ever took place or actually happened. Which left room to reason. Without uncertainty or having to commit to any adverse reaction. Including that of and in religion! Because until now, without and beyond a shadow of a doubt. The mind knew the body always had a problem being first forgiving and then forgiven. That and the only thing I have to plead for of which I am guilty, is simply my misery. And you can worry all the rest of your life! If someone is telling the truth. But you don't have to if in your heart you know you did. And chose to first.

56 Million

Many decades ago when I was young and impressionable someone handed me an article to read and said it sounds important. It was the, "buzz", of all the intellectuals out there because word of mouth had it that a genius wrote it! The title to it is, "A Report Of Just Thought." I patterned my report and autobiographical true life account after it. Mine? "A Report Of Just Thoughts." And all I had to do to be inspired was skim over the first page or so and I got the gist of it. In it the author wrote about communication being one of the most important challenges we have in life. And how it doesn't take a genius to learn how to properly and politely in order to obtain help from geniuses we may need in every area of our lives. Three decades later I hear a report that indicated 56 million geniuses voices in this country alone have been, "squelched!" Since I already know and everyone else how important it is to communicate. Here are a few reasons why. In a discontinued monthly publication from that same era called, "Science Digest." That came under tight scrutiny and was shunned by the reporting industry for its provocative content because the writers were referred to as just amateurs. Reports indicated scientists were determined to discover how modern inventions could keep an economy alive and eventually still allow everyone to prosper even if machines took the place of as we've seen in many a case, the worker. In other words computers and machines could work together to serve all mankind. So that even if there were fewer jobs the goods and services thru some form of ingenious effort would be provided to all who were in need for little to no cost. And this is important and or to all in general meaning everybody! Current events subject to change and always we pray for the better. When we earn our own money taxes are collected. Jobs were sent overseas without retracting adjudication that allows that to happen and introducing adjudication that restricts that action. Yes in this instance no one in charge of our jobs creation would reverse the first decision. No, "not by the hair if their, chin-e-chin-chin!" Because they were afraid of a psychic power that has just as much influence on the report being communicated. As others have in keeping it quiet and silent just one more time. To update. We like to work with our hands to build self confidence. Bend at the knees to pull ourselves up by the bootstraps to strengthen our back bones. And the world over, not be slaved. Work hard all day, wipe the sweat off our brow. And expect to be fairly compensated for.

Thank You

Lens on. Lens off. Usually you get a good look then you have to guess. But if you turn the situation around and are correct. You're psychic! And I'm camera shy. Now look at the camera and think of a dove with a tiny olive branch between its beak, just as the bird of paradise lands on top of your head! And as, I wave my first two fingers in the air and wiggle them back and forth to signal peace. Smile please. Just say cheese.

And The World Turns Around & Sees

Picture the symbol of a heart in gold leaf with a clear magnifying glass for its middle. And just outside it thin layers of vibrant colors flowing in an outward direction. Turn it over and envision the same heart inscribed in the same gold five sizes bigger! With the same pulsating colors inside it! Traveling from a single point located directly in the center outward in semi circled waves that meat its ends much wider. Now, why would you have two wishing wells, one with the bucket up. One with the bucket down. On either side of one fence. With two park benches on either side, both containing two pitchers of water. And two glasses one on either both half full. Two gates, one opens one closes. Green grass on either side. An image of a big heart containing a lock and key resting on the fence in front of the wishing wells, just behind the two gates. And directly in front of the heart, in between the two gates on top of the fence post. A fulcrum with a golden ruler perfectly level as balanced by a true master. #1. It makes for a great story. And #2. It paints a beautiful picture. As the heart beats. It also hypnotizes. The truth frees.

The Captain

A writer that did not draw very well who never learned to paint wanted to illustrate a book he wrote. So he chartered a boat to a deserted part of an island in order to seclude himself from the rest of the world set the mood, fill with ambiance and eventually learn how. And to be able to say upon his return that he taught himself! Because he knew from learning how to write well that if you want critical acclaim when you perform one task in order to become the best, it involves doing two. And no one contested that fact amongst the crew. Even the captain who also on the way, politely mentioned he too wrote and kept a journal of practically all his adventures! So they set sail and eventually arrived in shallow waters at the edge of the island. "You can carry your supplies off the boat from here! You just have to wade a few short feet and you're home free!" And wade the writer did with all his supplies. Tent, fire wood, fishing poles artist supplies, ...everything. But just before the crew waved goodbye. The captain opened the starboard side window next to the helm and said. "Wait a minute! I have to have a small drink to commemorate this momentous occasion." The crew just looked at him and the soon to be authoritarian stood on the beach and watched. He went into the cabin, came back out with a clear, see thru bottle, pulled out the cork and drank the contents within. Rolled up a piece of paper in a scroll and slipped in into the bottle, popped the cork back on. Started the boat back up, put the engine in gear. Thru it in the water. Said, "Good luck! See you in a couple weeks!" And sped off for the mainland. Naturally curious the writer waded back out to retrieve the, "message in a bottle". Returned, thoroughly exhausted he sat on the sandy shore, stuck his finger in the neck gently grabbing the scroll, spread it out in the sand and began to read. ..."If you could make a profit by plunging an imaginary pendulum into a bottle with some sand at the bottom. And just by imagining themselves, people would see it swinging back and forth. Back and forth. You could cork it and peddle the spectacle for one and all to view the vision as a very real product of time tested creation that never stops! And never will. As long as you put another coin in the till. And as I said, if indeed you could. You'd have at least a hundred bottles on the wall and one in your hand for sale! So while we're at it. Since some spirits are considered to come in liquid form. Which often time when consumed, allow the mind to think clearer and up to a certain point give one the opportunity to better ones self. And in order to heal the body give off more appeal, as the effects of become more and more real. So let's see, we'll just pour some of that in. And just to make it interesting. ...Picture the spirit as a whole bunch of smiley faces! And cupid's shooting the heart with love. As it gets bigger and bigger and starts bubbling over, with happiness! Might as well add a little of that also. And now you have quite a drink! Here's to your health and may all your wishes and dreams come true. Yes, here's to you!" ...Well the islands newest comer day after day, sat and thought that over. He couldn't paint or even draw on one piece of paper! Almost two weeks went by. And on the very last one, he had an idea. And thought of it just as his captain and crew showed up on the horizon. "Why didn't I think of that!!" He shouted. Pulled out a canvas. And tore off two rather small pieces and wrote on each of them. Opened a tube of expensive paint. And put a dab on the front and back of the bottle near the middle. Attached the canvases. Stuffed the original message back inside. And corked it tight. Soon, in came the boat. He loaded all his equipment and boarded for his final journey back to civilization. Pulled out the bottle and handed it to the captain and said. "With ESP, the mind transfers a vision from one to another. With prayer minds come together. So in order to and if you wanted to become the worlds next great writer. You're well on your way and are quite capable! But there's just one thing. You forgot the label." Front and back the captain read it to his crew. And it says. "Time In A

155

Bottle. Love Potion & Fountain Of Youth All In One!" ...And on the back, the ingredients. "Imagination Heart & Soul.

Role Reversal

A leader is a leader. And a good judge of character is a good judge of character. But in a government of by and for the people. A leader is also supposed to be a follower. Majority rules and every vote counts. So what if you could classify all the people into say ten different groups. And the leader has to pick out and vote for one of them. And they in turn have to pick out another and vote for them. And so on until the entire populous has been represented, when the voting is done. Yes we're on a mission so call all of us fact finders. Who sent our economy sailing in the wrong direction? A hand full of chief operating officers. Who allowed them to? A hand full of leaders. What if before they did. Everybody else in the entire country had a say and got to vote yea or nay? Our money would earn more interest at the bank. Our lives would be filled with abundance. And our nation would be a leader at having plenty. The press tells the story of the struggle for human rights for the whole human race. And we all make mistakes. A good reporter hungers for a solution to a problem. A not so good reporter thirsts for blood, over one. Even a child knows the difference between right and wrong. And it shouldn't be because they learned what pain is. It should be because they were taught about love. How did Rome fall in a day? The people rendered unto God. Bringing down the Toltec's? Already done. The key to the case? ...Communication. One of my friends once said. "If you can stand my ridicule and criticism. You are my friend." Everybody's entitled to their opinion. Think! Use me as a referral. And still in rehearsal. Role reversal.

The Big Easy

They, ...is a hard word to define. Until someone tells you who they are other than you, they. Because it takes more than just the definition that's in the dictionary, in order to. And to my amazement most words in, don't require more than one. But when you are them, in other words those others call they. The definition of the words us and we become self explanatory. Then comes the word everybody. Which reminds me caring is sharing which sometimes means what we know how to. And you know who you are. It's that simple. And I can't throw my voice all the way across the room to make you think I'm somebody I'm not. Anyway, from here I can see your hearts in the right place and open to every possibility. I call this composition. "The Big Easy.

Magic Beans

Farmer: I am a fragile sensitive suave debonair beautiful complicated soulful peaceable creature. And I love my neighbor. So I don't want mistreatment of my fellow man or unfair. Because I know firsthand what happened to some of my best friends, animals. ...A hill of beans contains several visions of magical scenes that amount to a persons dreams. A little pride goes along way and so does allot of love today! Some people charge for bits of knowledge and words of wisdom. Just not the person who gives them.

What You See Is What You Get

Beast: I woke up this morning looked in a puddle and saw my reflection. Now, to tell you the truth and to be quite honest with you. A mirror doesn't do justice to the ugly. At least not to me. No just the handsome and good looking. Of any specie. But I've heard of a mirror that only reflects what's on the inside, that tells a different story. Because the eyes allow the mind to judge only what it sees. But the heart allows the mind to judge only what it feels. Which means, I'm not ugly after all! But just don't forget that. "What you see is what you get.

The Music Teacher

Just to clear the mind sometimes we try to forget something so we can remember it later on and somewhere down the line. Just so we remember not to forget what it was, over time. A master of the art taught that once you're given good instruction and pointed in the right direction. On your own you learn your music lesson. And they say, if you are wise people see it in your eyes. So since age doesn't matter. If your love for one another is as powerful as it is old. You're worth your weight in gold.

Prodigy

Look at the words double and you. Now look at the letter, W. The English dictionary has 26 letters and none of them are in it because they aren't words! Yet contained within those 26 sections and written between those 26 divisions lies all of the definitions to every word known to modern man for every discovery including intelligence. And you may be able to remember every word in one when someone puts their finger over it and shows you its definition just underneath. But I defy you to be able to spell every word you remember! And to tell the truth although opinions tend to differ it's the same with music. In score, composition to the letter, to the T. Every note scale chord melody harmony and in every key. To study words and definitions you use the right side of the brain allot which centers motor skill. To play music you use the left side allot to center coordination. Mixing the left and right together produces rhyme with reason and results in lyric. So before I explain how to become a musician in a paragraph. You can take lessons and learn how to. Or study music's origins. One of which may well be like when bullfrogs, crickets, and birds all seem to orchestrate sound in unison! A miracle in nature that sooths the mind and stimulates the brain. Being able to and the main basic reason for teaching and instruction is quite frankly so you can learn to play music that's already been written. But that doesn't mean you can't produce a tune on your own by experimenting with the ability to walk away from the instrument in question. And come back at a later date and time. Go over it, fine tune it and practice 'till perfect. So yes everyone can play music! Just remember your audience wants to hear something that makes them feel somewhere between happy and ecstatic! Even if all you can muster up the courage to do is listen to it. Since the invention of the recording, you can always dream about it when you play it. Seeing without looking. Learning without material and knowing without being told. Can all be attributed to among things that pertain to the heart, yes sweet dreams. The mind tends to repeat what it already knows because it's just trying to perfect wisdom and knowledge. Just like with music its favorite songs. And you don't need expensive equipment. Just by dropping from the palm of you hand holding with forefinger and thumb at the top of it a tiny silver chain with a golden locket in the shape of a heart at the end of it. Letting it twirl round and round 'till it comes to a complete stop. And then swinging it back and forth back and forth, gently. For a metronome, will do quite nicely. The mind performs several functions and those progressions reveal whether it is sad or happy. And can be recorded electronically. And whether you believe it or not can be played back and expressed musically. A teacher once said, "There is so much to learn I'm still a student!" To which a musician replied, "Even though I can play music, I'm still learning my lesson!" So, if you combine those two efforts you'll soon see. You have the makings of a prodigy.

The Two Elves

I conceived of my first story at a very young age, because of an injury at only six weeks old. And I was given a gift and became cognizant at zero years old of my surroundings. And maybe even at that young age started talking! But most certainly did, thinking. It was more of a children's story that applies to everybody. Here is another. And I owe it all to the person who bore me, my mother. HAPPY MOTHERS DAY! "The Two Elves" Didn't get your favorite toy this X-Mass?? Call Elf & Elf Legal Services! Well find Santa and if he doesn't have the one you wanted in his gift bag. We'll whisper in his ear. And he'll take back a toy that looks exactly alike from some unsuspecting kid who is less deserving just so you can have what you longed for in the end, on Christmas morning! And we'll have Santa himself deliver it personally for all to see! After all and for all practical purposes good will and intent. If you deserve it, so be it. But with the kid who now goes without you have to equally share it. Or you can put two of the same kind on next years wish list and we'll see that Santa gets it. With one rule of thumb. As long as you specify that either the first or the second toy goes to someone, ...who doesn't have one.

The Comedian

I wrote a book while laughing so hard it put tears of joy in my eyes! About how to be funny. What's the name of it? Just Joking! And good humor comes naturally. What's the secret to it? You have to see the humor in everything. It's a knack. And you have to have a thing for it. ...As or just before the tomatoes and broccoli fly you have to start sweating rather profusely. Pace back and forth. Tugging your collar with your finger. Breathe heavily while at the same time, pat your forehead with a neatly folded hanky. It's a winning combination and a smash hit at any gathering or party. And if they're throwing pies, smile and lick your lips before you wipe your eyes. And if your routine starts to stink. You always say, "How am I doing so far?" And if they start to throw rotten eggs, you swallow your pride and for a few more laughs just stand there. Of course when you see that big long cane rap around your waist. It's best to follow it off the stage. ...Thank you very much, thank you very much. You've been the best audience ever! Just remember I'm a medium! But you can call me, the comedian.

The Numeric Assistant

You can't forget what you can't remember. At the same time, of the two things alone in question. It's better off to the one than the other. For instance. You want to find a needle in a haystack, if that's where you lost it. And a pin in a cushion if that's where you last left one. So that what you did forget you couldn't remember. Now you will forever.

The Truth Say-er

Like any premonition due to inclination of precognition. Once you see a vision. And even if it's of the future. Once it has been envisioned. Automatically it becomes a part of the past. When you realize that fact from there you can take the good from the bad. Which leaves room that yes there is still time to reproduce the present tense. And like a stitch in time change the future for the better. Say you perceive because we're creatures of habit and follow carnal instinct that so and so is going to do such and such. You can pray for them and obviously alter their state of mind once they recognize the extra sensorial perception and then do respond. Whereas without such knowledge and wisdoms influence. The state of mind remains the same and acts as if it never happens. Once the experiment's complete you can communicate in the finite the principles that lead to success. Yes I admit I'm chained to my work. But there's no ball attached to one end or a shackle on my foot. In fact I can fit it into the palm of my hand. And it has a heart shaped pendant at one end. Meaning I prayed for you! A key player. And in a most fascinating manner. A truth say-er.

The Prism Escape

Imagine people think of you as a one dimensional character they have on a piece of paper they hold in the palm of their hand and then put their thumb on. ...Some people perpetuate a positive or negative thought or statement. And can up to four times a second. And I tell you this is true, ...that they think. Yet we can all barely or at least, say five numbers out loud in a whole one. ...When someone tries to read your thoughts to determine your emotional and charismatic state, internal characteristics and traits. So they can say that they know you like the back of their hand. Amongst others. They show their true colors. That's why we're taught to always listen to our mothers. When you use a mind meld, so no one knows you're doing so, you cloak your presence and probe their consciousness ever so subtly! But at the same time if they do sense you're there they partition off a portion of their mind to listen to your thoughts also. Which can make you feel all shifty eyed. Like you're wearing big thick frames with huge magnifying glasses for lenses. Which is the wrong prescription, for normal vision. Everyone turns on to someone who is aesthetically soothing and pleasing to the eyes whether they are or not, because well, we all want to be liked. Probing the annals of the imagination I did some research in my head using a piece of paper and a pen. And I found one of the powers of sinlessness, is forgiveness. And psychology suggests it takes a clear conscience to heal a guilty one. And that the difference between voluntary and involuntary submission and reaction is. ...If you hear them you don't talk back to the voices in your head. You learn to think for yourself instead. Then no one will penetrate the depths of your imagination or your modern mind again and again. And there they will not tread. Because then they find the opposite is also true. And that's when you make, the great prism escape.

Super-Man!

Along with survival of the fittest came survival of the smartest pitted against. Which lead to some of the brightest having to muster great inner strength using only mind power, against some of the physically strongest who apparently lost their temper. Which by the way inspired mind games like chess and checkers. Health doesn't always negate strength. And if you ever saw someone try to heal a wound with hardly any you would also deduce that might doesn't always make right. There is such a thing as visual misinterpretation due to the slightest amount of error and or deception, that I now think is healing. Because I believe in what I'm saying. And as things unfold before my eyes that I'm now seeing. But can you just imagine a very smart heart filled non violent rather nerdy or geeky looking person, some maybe wearing glasses, being the picture of health? Muscles rippling and a body chiseled to perfection? I know a few and there are many of them. We call them super men.

What Happened?

"Love's not sick. Love's not a trick. It's hard to explain but not define. Love's divine. It's free of grime and pure love's not a crime. The purpose of heroism is life saving. And sometimes even a hero needs rescued due to unforeseen consequences that result in intentionally inflicted pain where the victim is totally innocent. Although to which some cases the statutes of limitations does not apply. You or I, still have to gather up the testimonies you've heard of simply even if you heard of them by just word of mouth, after those limitations ran out! So that probable cause, reasonable suspicion and reasonable doubt can take their proper legal course set by moral standards we all agree upon. To prevent said unfortunate incidences and some of them have already been proven to happen from ever again taking place at any future time and date.

What Is!

What is the accumulated innocuous combined effort of willpower faith belief and desire which facilitate feelings that excite brainwaves which produce sensations of happiness? No wait! Now, let me put it like this. What is as complicated as science, necessary as medicine, as colorful as art, as delicate as an instrument, as fragile as an egg, as skillful as any feat, and as simple as a heart beat? (Now if this was the TV game show for real smart people you'd hear the buzzer over and over, then the announcer. "No love's not it, oh! All of you have given the same answer and sorry to say you're all incorrect! No, ...it's "You're Love". ...Audience claps and gives a standing ovation.

Thinking Out Loud

Here is a note. I thoroughly enjoyed it. Some could take it or leave it. Everyone has their own thing I guess. But I was cut out for this class. Five out of five. Clown, mime, poet, artist, musician. All practiced to perfection produces intellectualism. There are talents that don't involve all the conventional methods of learning. That lean more towards experience than anything. Being able to communicate every ones voice for them should they need you to, is one of them. The idea is to profit from solving a problem without initiating the task of pulling so much as one hair out of your head although just one won't hurt. And sowing the seed that yields a happier person. By enriching the mind. And preserving the history and future of healing the body. Freeing the soul. And opening the eyes a little. Which amounts to the equivalent of a degree in perspiration and inspiration. Work savvy. Learn to think out loud. While you're speaking.

GENIUS

Now I haven't looked up the definition in a long time but it's there, very forthright and complimentary and believe it or not simple to understand! Therefore my rendition of is my basic strategy. Although the interviewer often time turns into the interviewee. Not to over correct myself and I'm not one and so for the rest of us. I consider the following to be the occupation of a genius. After interviewing or rather at the same time being interviewed what is the one thing I can take away not frustrated, not disgruntled and not for granted that stands out in my mind? A genius always taught. "After you do the best you can if you do good doesn't it bring you joy? When you help other people and you do good by bringing even if just a little joy into their lives, remember then and only then and don't forget! Practice made perfect. Because it takes no more time to pray for someone than it does to compliment them. The history of genius is interesting. I've heard there are millions! But that's just a matter of millions of opinions. Some, have an epiphany or come up with a great idea or invention that seems to be coming from right off the top of their head and out of the clear blue! Others know all along about these things thru and thru. Some read speedily. Others, slowly. People have said some, have to hide! Because there are people out there who don't want them to become a success. Still, there are others that do. What people don't know about some geniuses can't hurt a genius. But at the same time what people do know about other geniuses can help all geniuses. Change is good but it's hard to change somebody into someone they're not if they don't want to. But you've heard the saying, "What ever makes you happy!" ...Be happy eat healthy. Remember the mind needs food too and for now, for many food for thought will do. The mind is an awesome link to a strong body. And comes from the hands of a creator. Whose creation evolved and whom overcame every physical problem for them. With arms extended and patience is as orderly and strong as the day is long. Yes someone with hands outstretched and gentle to the touch that says, "I love you much." Now, I almost met a genius face to face once. The reasons are important. But the how and when aren't. Why didn't I? I'm shy.

You might recognize and then remember him from this description. He invented a program that opens doors for ordinary every day people. And at the time when I did almost go up and say hi he was donating computers to agencies that help others and I was one of them. You'll find part of the definition of genius is the act of kindness he was performing. And he used his knowledge and wisdom in that area alone to help our heroes in law enforcement. "Gotta keep the peace you know." And I don't expect you to believe he actually wanted to meet me and not to judge but may himself also be a tad shy 'till I mention he most likely, also is curious about the roll of computers in preventing, nursing home abuse and intentional medical malpractice and or malpractice in general. Allot of times very smart people will ask you what you want. And will politely inform you to help yourself first! Then after you've met the challenge and show some improvement they'll be happy to donate their time and help your cause. Ascertaining discerning analyzing and stimulating. Up to and including the point of inception the power of learning is filled with inspiration. I've been so inoculated I feel almost but not quite inebriated! The interpretation of a perfectionist is ingenious. As a stickler the interpreter strives to become a perfectionist and the perfectionist strives to be just as ingenious. When you envision something in print but haven't read about it yet. Unless you're a psychic hypnotist, you prove your ability by learning how to and sooner or later eventually do produce it. The moral connectivity of the mind to the body remain calm in order to stay and be. So if you have to educate yourself, even if all you have to write on is a note of some kind, a piece of paper or even a napkin, you can. Which has been proven to work down thru history. Have you ever heard of an auto biographical memory? The explanation of how that happens is harder to understand than the definition of what does happen. So if you ever meet and greet somebody who has one it will be a rare and momentous occasion. Some write complicated reports for other geniuses to learn and profit from. But that doesn't mean what they do can't be simplified for the rest of us up to and including everyone. They excel in subjects like science and medicine. There are about eight to twelve areas of, that they make great strides and amazing progress in. Those subjects we love to read and hear about because that research we can all, ...benefit from. And under certain circumstances a smart person doesn't loan something they can't afford to give. Speaking of medicine a good physician does not need to know your intelligence quotient. Because he or she already knows your physical demeanor and can figure any, out mentally. Otherwise every time you went to the doctors office you'd be asked to take another IQ test. ...A bottle of ink and a feather is my treasure. The chest is made of paper. And can contain the map to unlimited wealth beyond imagination! The lock? I can wad up the paper, stuff it in my mouth chew swallow and digest. Food for thought I jest. Because my real treasure, is the power of prayer. And the prayer is. As we see eye to eye. In your real spiritual and physical manifestation. While you are still here. That when an Angel sings, you get your wings! Some geniuses suggest that God, is the sum total of all mans strength on earth! What if every man on earth wanted peace?! Think of all the possibilities! If you humble yourself just a little bit and act like Angels suggest. Heavenly people do, always.

Clean Slate

Ground sky. Off on. Low high. Map chart. Neutrality equality. Sign cosign. Assign countersign. Civility leadership. Surveil survival. Trial error. Slave master. Walk run. Skate slide. Coast glide. Float sail. Face turn away. Front center. Veil unveil. Demography geography. Commonality criminality. Try pry. Snoop spy. Swim fly. Grasp rung. Climb ladder. Reach ceiling. Touch feeling. Seeing believing. Motivation mobility. Talent ability. Toy tinker. Play agility. Coordination movement. Sew tailor. Pump prime. Powder primp. Axiom knowledge. Words wisdom. Surmount surpass. Undo do. Beam shine. Peer fair. High dry. Tear wipe. Pride hide. "Be great!" And, ...clean slate.

Letters To The Editor

When you listen, you tend to repeat what you hear. When you learn, you tend to repeat what you know. What you share, becomes common knowledge. Which doesn't require an education. Because after we educate ourselves we educate each other. Over and over. Yes I'm hip! And it's not just gossip. When you forego temptation And exceed expectation. You become a self made man or woman.

The Folk Hero Award

I was sitting at the counter of a local diner one fine morning and in came the mayor and sat next to my boss and I. He said who he was and that sparked something in me. So I said back to him, "Hey I hear you gave an award to someone for saving an old lady from a fire in her bedroom across the hall from him. He used to me my neighbor across the street! He has a mental disability you know and in spite of all that he still managed to save a life! That's pretty amazing." ..."He said some amazing things about you too! And according to him you have taken on some pretty tough challenges in your life like doing what you can from time to time to help the mentally ill. Including how they're treated in an emergency situation. He said you were once almost poisoned to death on "Thorazine. Some day I'd like to hand you, a certificate of appreciation!" My mind filled with emotion and went flush for a second or two. And I started to think rather quickly as I browsed thru my random access memory. So I expressed my feelings on the subject as thoughts came to me. Which I said back to the mayor in the following manner. "Well to start with, the shape of the lids and the skin around the eyes has just as much to do with how you look as the rest of the face! Yet no matter what you look like sooner or later we all have to face the fact that we're all the same, on the inside. Like anything else saving a life can become as complicated as science and as necessary as medicine. It involves something you have to do, something you have to say and always there's the task of over-coming an obstacle or two along the way. And about certificates of appreci-ation? There should be a great big stack of them! When some ones put their best foot forward to help other people and they haven't been fully recognized for it and it hasn't yet been put into writing they're called a unsung or folk heroes. Therefore there should be a folk hero award. Presented by a human-itarian. Who collects their stories that prove they've been neglected and abused. Yes true life accounts that if not gathered are left on the back burner. And when you go back to look for physical evidence and conformation if nothing's written at least on a piece of paper, nothing's going to be there. But for the humanitarians efforts, once they finally see the good word get out and spread to everyone their reward is in and of itself.

Psychic Ability

A good actor always develops an emotional attachment to their work to give off the effervescence of a more balanced and believable performance. Let me put it another way. If an actor is playing the part of someone who drinks too much coffee they don't sit down to a pot full, ...they imitate doing so. Some words and phrases are easy to define because they describe an act of doing something or a mechanism of some kind which is easily identifiable. For instance, "the jitters!" Plus or minus a few key notes, features and valuable insights. Subconsciously, the mind speaks back and forth to the varied opinions and advice given by others it's gathered over time and stored in memory. And if when some people think and in their mind carry on a conversation with a voice in their head quicker than two people can speak to one another. Or faster than the normal speed for reading and comprehending, other than during accelerated learning. Their using less than optimum brain power. Which robs the intellect of its full potential. And makes problems appear to seem bigger than they actually are. However, applying programs that alleviate that tension designed by various talented individuals some time later the condition subsides and the mind returns to normal. Then it converses, conveys, communicates and corresponds with itself effectively and correctly. Relishing the fact and cherishing the thought. Making the connection. My only explanation is and it's simple to me. Is it's psychic ability.

Strong Man!

If you're stronger than someone physically. You're not stronger than they are if they are as strong as you are physically, mentally. When you let anger get in the way. And if they do the same, nor are they. Stage set upon the manifestation and determinant of due consideration of condition and reaction of lifting of said curtain. Justice doesn't run out on monetary damages before it does physical ones, due to such things as, "statutes of limitations." No wonder you can't buy happiness! Because you can't put a price on love.

Commentary

So for about every problem we have in a free nation, not imagine. Once we get over our shyness to. The solvent and most prudent solution starts with hands on communication. Every problem? Every problem. Each and every one. Because there are only so many savvy reporters out there and only so many newspapers. And there are many just thoughts that take the stage. ...That should have by now, made the front page.

Living The Dream

An ingenious person tends to do the work of a humanitarian as well rather than that of just an authoritarian to maintain a good reputation or recover an even better one. Since love is at the base of all religions. And God is the sum total of not just all but each and every man on earths strengths. What if every man believed in and wanted peace? And was willing to put their faith to the test. They would surely benefit greatly from their work. And profit from all their accomplishments after they learn from all their mistakes, first. And in some cases that only pertains to having enough to eat. Once that's accomplished it branches out into several areas that also need our attention. And when tended to carefully each one flowers and blooms. And after being pollinated by the birds and the bees sprouts prosperities seeds. Ninety nine point nine hundred and ninety nine percent of all people ever researched want peace on earth. And all you have to do is take a vote and you'll have solid gold proof. A better life's within reach. So, about the sands of time. Having fun in the sun swimming and frolicking at the beach. Now it's time to go practice what I preach! As I pray for every man to recreate and therefore be from the land of milk and honey. I visualize, eating peaches and cream. All the while. Living the dream.

Dr. Do A Little-Dr. Do Allot

[Last night I had a dream I saw a ole friend who was never happy about something and in it he seemed happier than ever! That's a good sign. Then I carried on what seemed to me to be a conversation with a genius in my mind.] Dr. do a little. A flock of birds or a pack of wild animals communicate massively so that when one flies or turns and runs in order to stay safe, the rest do the same and follow right away. And by the time people find out just how intelligent a mina bird or parakeet is, their dogs and cats will say. Thru the art of combining balance and coordination with physical and mental observation responding to every inside and outside stimulus. And uncovering, decoding and interpreting the circumstances behind conversations before during and after a meeting of the minds. In a close knit community is called the study, of everybody. Dr. do allot. When you're bright people want a free sample of your intelligence. Usually something you put down on paper so they can copy what it was and communicate it faster to others. So if you wrote a book or report on the subject and people aren't able to recover from memory everything in it. You'd set aside a few pages for them. One describing a problem allot of people had. Another with some sort of proof of the difficulty in question from someone somewhere. A record. And seek or set out to and do the work of a humanitarian by collecting all similar true life accounts and stories. Console an authoritarian for permission. And a reporter for conformation. Introduce new technology that corrects the problem. Put it in place to prove it works. Once people know what you already do and others heard about what they found out about each other that's similar. Your work for the day is done. And you can claim success. And I don't have to mention. It's all about communication. [The smartest criminal minds are considered to be ingenious but apparently not enough or they wouldn't be called or become criminals in the first place. You'd be surprised how hard it is to prove after you've been tortured. Even before. The Health Care System Condition Improvement Monitor Device, prevents acts performed by incompetent workers in the physical and mental health care fields that cause undo maleficent unimaginable pain and suffering or let's just say aren't nice. And are unbecoming a Florence Nightingale reputation. ...Signed, Dr Doolittle.

Certainly!

In the school of life you don't necessarily receive a prestigious degree of excellence that you can frame and put on the wall to show. But whether you're fast or slow. You deserve one for what you know.

The Visage

Have we come a long way in medicine since thousands of years ago? Not really, if all we understand are the space age endeavors and scientific advancements using modern equipment and surgical implements and know how they all, work because we have physical evidence. But forgot hands on proof of faith healing. Then that to me, would mean we also forgot the mistreatment of those with mental problems who are considered to be ill. After all how do they, have to heal? And what do they look like? No different than you or I. ...The face of a dream come true? After prayer. Someday soon. What I know how to do takes a miracle too! Now look at me. And pray for one more. For you.

Three Piece Suit

When I was growing up people made fun of me before they picked on me. All because of the way I looked! Which in real life can follow you all the way into adulthood. But they couldn't make fun of the way I act. Because when they tried to start a fight I held my head high. And humbly walked away. Each and every time. Beggars can't be choosers? I beg to differ. And what action stops that certain activity? Maturity. ...The velocity of light is finite. And it only takes a millionth of a second for the mind to register its own reflection in the mirror. And the reality is, the only part of the face that no one can say with any certainty is beautiful or ugly, are the eyes. Tear glands secrete naturally in order to cleanse the eyes lenses. But in order to cleanse the soul one should not be made to cry. And everyone sees a smile needs no disguise. So in the order from Genius, to Prophesy to ordinary citizenry. Over and over good begins again when a good deed is done each and every time. ...And just because of the way I look or the color of my skin. When people don't judge me. I'm happy! And when they spread the good word that they share that same belief and start to laugh with me, not at me. I do the same and can't stop laughing until my sides quit aching. Then I feel exulted and vindicated. Just like being exonerated of any crime. Leaving the courtroom, and exiting with sights set on the open road. Ready to represent anyone like myself and even the whole human race! With a smile on my face. A wise ole owl. Giving a hoot. Wearing a three piece suit.

Three Presidents Page 1

Three paths, three areas of research. Physical health, mental health and assisted living or care giving facilitation. Three problems. Due to discrepancies in question as to whether health care system condition improvement monitoring is in place. Turned on and working documentable inerasable fair accurate and recordable and of course it's legal. Where discretionary measures are taken and God willing creating a clear code. Where all mischievous activity no matter who committed to it is caught on camera. Proven to be the number one problem. If it's not yet been done. Three presidents spoke out against the obvious and suggested to put the new technology in place for everyone. The roots of this transcript sound like I copied an well educated mans material. I assure you I didn't so in other words I came up with the same level of intelligence on my own. Because to me in seems we share the same dreams. After all we put man on the moon. Were all supposed to be brothers under the skin. Let's not raise our voices hands or fists against anyone ever again. Use your true prowess. Pray for everyone to be safe from harm and alive. And when you see to it they're well, for me give them a high five won't you? Thank you. Peace is a process. The power of love is the in thing to follow. And civil leadership. Civil liberty. And civil service also.

The Typewriter

A great communicator gets things done right away. A work of art. But if one's shy they tend to put things down in writing. And at first that seems to take forever! Especially to produce it in hard cover. Which is why they're sometimes offered fame but not allowed to have their say 'till they talk to their publisher. And give their valid opinion as to why. And among other things, a freedom not to be taken lightly. And to get directly to the point why some turn to poetry. And explains why every time one tries to think for themselves, someone else tries to read their mind. To be all the wiser. So they also will be known as a great thinker! Because the theory is, then they too think alike. Which allows the indiscriminate ghost writer to be one with his or her work. And how you become a literary master. So shine on!!

Reporting Setting Precedence

There is a sacred trust that says in order to be approved to report certain kinds of material one has to also be able to totally from memory. An exercise if you will in futility but not necessarily. Because it shows what already has been revealed and leads into what may have been or at the same time seemed, to be hidden. So if knowledge equals a mathematical power and that information is priceless, put the two together and you have, intelligence. Which makes both freedom of information and the rite to inform and be informed, sound transactions. Which can hinge on three things. Love, affection and a wise mans lesson. Naturally speaking about teaching. language comes from the formulation of words. And if you study enough of them in any dictionary you can pick up on trains of thought and come up with and introduce a new one. Like the language of computers which surprises many but contains every because it's communicated to all who can read or at least hear and or see. ...From what definitions I looked up I learned that a psychic is the spiritual equivalent of a physicist who uses finite tools to describe what that means. And brings that level of intelligence up, to becoming an understudy to a modern master of the art of ingenuity. Who is usually referred to as a genius in reality. ...It's a sheer pleasure to welcome you to my think tank. I assure you love faith and belief in supernatural things happening bring spiritual awakening. So say there are millions of super smart and ultra bright men and women and they all passed one test with flying colors. It's the test of life then isn't it? Yes so how do they get their points across? By sharing the same dreams. For instance each individual is unique in skill talent and ability. And all have one thing in common. They want good things to happen to not just someone but to everyone. ...True love and love at first sight are more than just plausible and feasible. They're real! Just imagine if you will a million people, a million dreams, a million ideas and opinions coming from a million places going in a million directions, for a million miles. With a million things to do. All centralizing for all the right reasons, with one thing in mind. ...Helping other people. Coming together for one cause on common ground. To reach the top of the hill and accomplish their goal. Doing good deeds together, forever. A computer can research millions of medical journals but if records were erased or altered you have to listen to rumor and gossip. Until measures are put in place that prevent the truth from never being told, in its entirety. Dreams do come true! So don't look back now. The ends in sight and all it takes is along with a little tender loving care, is knowhow.

The Psychic Clock

There is a true way to express yourself that won't hurt any ones feelings and improves your outlook! Pray for everybody, including me. You'll see. ...Never forget the sacrifices of the past others made so we all could live longer, be happier, lead healthier lives and of course be free. ...Consider all things before you discard any. Here is a magic mirror so you can see. As the psychic inspects the armature, winds the clock, looks at the face of time and watches the back and forth motion of the pendulum. It mesmerizes them! And it reminds them that the first day on the job is going to be monotonous because nothing's going to happen on their shift. But I assure you can at any moment until another good deed is done. And it just takes a second to motivate and perform one. Tomorrow is the only word that takes on three definitions in my humble opinion. The tomorrow that always lies in the future. The tomorrow that becomes today. And the tomorrow that eventually became yesterday. But today is the only word that stays in the present. One constant. We measure reality with it. The theory is the journey leads to the ends of time and back again. And stretches to infinity! And it all begins again, each and every morning at one AM, exactly.

The Liturgist

When you have to do the liturgy, and you forgot your notes you have to recall the preaching totally from memory. God is supposed to be rich isn't he! And since he created everybody everyone is supposed to be. When we become rich we tend to want to forget when we're poor or what it was like before. Then when we become poorer we tend to want to forget what it was like to be richer. But we want to be. One relatively rich man or let's just say who lived comfortably once said to me. "How do you know the rich don't continually think about and pray for the poor!" To which I replied. "But you're not as, poor now are you." Being clean physically doesn't necessarily mean your soul is free and clear of sin. Because as you already know a chain is only as strong as its weakest link. However being cleansed spiritually is a nice neat process involving kindness. So say you want into Heaven. If you're rich, as long as you love the poor as much as you would the rich, if you were poor. You're in! Remember, healthy spirit healthy mind healthy body. Here's your gown. Now go earn your halo harp and wings. And either place you've made whole. The other you may now travel to and fro freely. Because you earned your keep physically and spiritually. God blessed modern society since ancient day. ...A prayer for all occasions? There are many of them. And a formulas and an equations, that teach a wise mans lesson.

The Convention

They say if you do the work of a preacher, you are considered to be one. Is it also true for a psychic, clairvoyant, physicist or genius? Each one offers professional careers in health and wellness. An modern man is capable of all of them. Some aren't called to their true position in life until they're beyond maturity. Is fifty the new thirty? God knows what skills and talents we're going to develop in life beforehand. For some it became a matter of selfless preservation. And the Good Lord has a plan and is willing to lend a helping hand.

The advocate teaches that if you express your rights to all the right needs, your ways become your means. Quantum merit requires the human touch. And love? Much. Necessity is the mother of invention. ...Welcome to the convention.

Learn & Learn

Drawing straws. Learning a new language means you first have to associate and familiarize yourself with the less familiar and comprehendible linguistics. Without annunciating them. And be able to determine what the phonetics actually mean, without spelling them. Or you can point to words in a translator and you'd be surprised to see just how few are needed to get your points across. And retrieve the answers you want to all your questions and be pointed in all the right directions. As compared to how many words it takes once you've learned one. But at the same time translating a language takes no longer than it does to be taught one. And say that's the case it would mean learning a new language is just as simple and easy! The concept of language is universal. Which one is considered to be the most? Where in order to the one word you absolutely must learn you don't have to point in a dictionary to but just to your heart, first. ...What did you expect all the rest? Here with just one gesture, you've got the best.

Peek A Boo! Monkey See Monkey Do

When people try to steer you away from your goals and aspirations They're covering their eyes like a little baby. Peek a boo! Well I've got news for them, I don't need a high chair and the only time I wear a bib is when I'm eating lobster. Believe in a cause? About solving problems most of the people I communicated to communicated back that they're on the side of good, just not quite willing and zealous enough to communicate all the right answers, for me. But if I didn't mention problems just formulas and equations that solve any, that would be greedy. Because there are many problems that affect everybody. So when I didn't communicate in writing about any problems at all, people communicated back to me, something like that's pretty good share that with everyone. Or put that one on the top of the stack. A friend who's overcome many problems in his lifetime read this and said, "Put this one on the top of the stack! Watch how they react. And then, see what they have to say." One can't beg for something he needs. And afford to give it away and expect to end up with anything but peace of mind. If all you have is the template to genius. Applied science sadly only stays in the state commonly known as research. Like ballads put into prose and folk tales into poetry.. It's just feel good medicine not music to the ears or real victory. Believe me! To describe such talent and ability it doesn't require constant communication including multi-mediation. But to solve many problems with it, it does. And to solve a problem for X in the mathematic world means X equals every. I read somewhere that someone said, "In this day and age if you possess genius you have to hide it!" I read somewhere else that said you have to display it. So putting the theory to the test and following the leader that taught everyone is one to a certain extent. ...It doesn't do any good unless you use it. Monkey see monkey do.

A Wise Mans Paradise

People who say the word they, allot of times don't know who those people really are, who represents them and what that person is really all about. Always talking about more than one person, to one person. And people who speak the word we, allot of times are just speech making. Being clever does not make a dim man brighter or a dumb man smarter. And anyone who believes that is living in a false reality. So when people are speaking of others don't count myself amongst them, unless you do call me a good man. Because I am.

The Menu

If you ran a church picnic breakfast or a soup kitchen for instance. And told people to please form two lines. ...And they did. But everyone in the one was running. And in the other walking who do you serve first? ...It doesn't matter! Because you can only dish up one plate at a time, ...to hand to either. But just remember. Of those who just walked one might not need any which explains why they move so humbly. And the person right behind them might be sick and therefore should eat first before them. And for those who ran, it also depends on who deserves one. The person at the front of the line, or the person at the end of the line. So what's on the venue? Feed them all, as fast as possible. Because they're starving for more of what goes into the ingredients that gets the job done, just a little quicker. Love Power.

Or So They Say

If you could divide reality into one hundred equal parts. What would one partition need to become complete? Ninety nine more. Which would involve universally the multiplicity of the power of one thing. That by itself turns into more than one reality. That stretches to infinity! Which by the way, can't be done mathematically and still be extracted today.

The Dreamer

What if you could build a kite that would float into the sky, hover over the land below and reach the ground, well never ever again! Anyone who possesses the couth to redeem the quality of taking the responsibility to preserve the art of ingenuity. ...If you'll look closely at how they hone that skill, become talented at it produce integrity and then perfect that very capability, carefully. You'll see! One ID, is where they can come up with the exact set of logical circumstances that lead to being able to communicate the exact same principle as someone else had half a world away from them! Without ever having to actually sit down and figure that out. And without ever speaking to one another. Ear to ear. Someone they've never been told about, knew or for that matter to the best of their recollection ever met. Another, where someone can remember what someone else told and taught them only once. Without resorting to pen pr paper for reference in order to prove recorded result. Waiting on a fond memory of the day when they finally do meet for the first time to become a reality, over and over again. ...Each and every morning. Like a scientist who utilized certain strains of DNA. To recreate a mastodon.

Mesmerize Hypnotize!

Are the power of problems greater than their solutions? In other words are all our problems greater than all our solutions? Because many problems lead to many troubles. The way to solve the problem is simple. And that challenge alone is the greatest obstacle. First you have to meet them half way, not head on. Then the genius in you comes thru and solves all of them. And love's ingenious! Nobody on earth can deny that one single fact. And everybody wants a whole, lot, of love. Everybody! Trust me. It's just that some don't know how to express that feeling because others weren't taught to show them. So how

176

do you not only talk about look about and see all about solving any problem? ...You mix a little love with a little genius and there you have your answer. Now you know how pure thoughts, turn into heart beats.

The Miracle Mile

"Simple Simon & Peter the Pie man." Saints I suspect. Moving on. ...If a group of people saw past things others didn't and thru out there in the intellectual universe, the idea that for instance. They heard of a hand full of followers who knew how to save medically with scientific proof and accuracy a million lives every five years, without losing anyone else's or spilling a drop of blood doing it. And introduced their techniques of how to perform these miraculous deeds that help, to others. And word spread and caught on everywhere. To several million and eventually seven plus billion. And their leaders also caught wind of it. If they would all listen it would happen. And that same day the leaders of earth would reveal a miracle! Their rulers never had or ever did. And as long as that amazing cause and action is achieved without starving anybody intellectually or violating any bodies human rights. ...So shall it be as welcome a freedom as any. And the submission of bowing down at the feet of and to the direction. Of a miracle man. Because if I told you it takes a genius to communicate that very thing so people will listen in order to help others. Even though the solution's right in front of you. In many cases you'd simply sit back and say, "I'm not a genius. Not my job. Someone else will do it for me!" And that's just not true. For you have to walk that extra mile for a miracle to happen as well, to you.

"Man Cures Illness & Fisherman Yields Record Catch!"

People who've heard of me don't usually come up to me and say what they have. So not long ago I walk into the local bait shop and someone's already at the counter so being a little stand offish I turn and pick up the local newspaper. As I'm burring my head in it he sees what I'm doing and even though everybody there knew it wasn't going to says to the owner, "It looks like rain." I stay focused and adamant on reading so he blurts out rather disgustedly. "Well, what am I supposed to say you can't talk to him!" And walks out. ... ...Other than to cure illness what is one of the oldest definitions of the phrase, "to cure!" To preserve food. By drying it out with salt out in the sun on a wood rack at the beach by the sea, one of the first was fish. It became an international symbol for fulfillment, freedom of speech and movement of peace. Which sprouted from the universal gesture to eat. Where you aim one or both hands with fingers pointed outwards and in a forward direction make their way to the mouth, sometimes frantically. You need to feed the mind also. What can you come up without an education that others can't, using one? Your own experience. Experience is the best teacher. Going back over your work by yourself inquisitively. You learn as if you're being taught by someone other than you! So that then, you educate yourself. And the student becomes the teacher. All things considered it doesn't take allot to become thankful for certain things. Just a bit of an understanding of all things. So if there ever was a cure to shyness and mental problems of all kinds. It starts with a, "Hi how are you." A handshake. And when things get emotional, a hug or two. One day I'd like to pick up the newspaper and the headline reads.

The Indian

If heap big medicine's worth heap big wampum. How much is heap big love worth? ...Heap big happiness! And that you can't put a price on. But you can live up to and by that very same doctrine count on. Now let's see. Heap big powerful me.

The Servant

Not being able to communicate directly properly and politely isn't a crime! If you don't know how to, you just have to learn to. ...Cracking the code. Do we often confess our sins publicly? No we usually do privately and personally, whether there are few or many. It's not a crime to become angry. Just don't get hasty. Because what comes after is then more likely to be. ...Pointed in the right direction. Punishment needs detention and correction. Perfection rhymes with reflection. And genius rhymes with everyone. So to stand up for, is a privilege and an honor. And to serve everybody, a quality that's Heavenly.

The Secret Key, Excerpt

Math geniuses use a formula so simple a child can learn to and at the same time amaze adults just with the results. And come up with all the right answers to problems quickly in their heads that take most of us a pencil, paper and or a calculator and a slide rile to! Some are born with it, a knack. Some learn it early on. Others just simply love solving problems with math. So if you're not that inclined to, "do the math". Don't despair. It just means no one showed you how to be. Or put it into writing so you could learn to. Reading is fundamental. And there are few programs that teach you how to do math in your head. Plus you have to have a fondness for. And basically, "If it's not your bag it's not your bag." But along with the power of math such as is in a number squared. There is also the power of prayer squared. And a formula for healing squared. Where working faith in believing and then receiving becomes a scientifically and medically provable and yes proven, spiritual and physical miracle! For instance. If you were so inclined you could figure out the formula to a thought wave projection machine, that would work like a telegraph key. After all we believe in a prayer answered and have already proven the existence of ESP. So if someone has a teachers manual. Ask them to let you look at the answer key. Find a solution, hand it back to them. And say you can absolutely guarantee you can solve the problem, without looking. And this is important. Because they gave you the answer before hand, without question.

Sleep Talking

Many times in my sleep I'd find myself looking at someone else knowing I am projecting from my mind what I want to and am trying to say to and then just looking at them, expecting they understood just what it was. So, is there such a thing as a third eye? The mind craves constant or instantaneous communication, a form of attention. In a dream it craves scenery and syncopation with its surroundings emotionally and therefore tends to communicate mentally. One time a spirit said. "None the less, move your lips. And speak to me! Because even though I know what you are trying to say, if you don't I become lonely.

Solid Gold

Each time you stimulate the mind, they're following your train of thought mentally. Not actually reading your mind in virtual reality. In animals it's a survival instinct. In the wild it involves survival of the fittest. And potential mates use it to attract each other before they confirm their love for one another and perform a ritual sacred to humans also. Some sense and can almost smell food from let's say up to a mile away! Others money which sounds greedy. With one stipulation. Although you don't really need to. If you're just trying to prove for fun and profit the existence of ESP. If that is so on the obverse side there is a natural scientific experiment where you can make a mint off the test subjects random access memory, hands on evidence and experimental results. And reversely they, yours. And who thought of that golden similarity and opportunity? Lonely ole me. I know what you're thinking and I have a gift for you. I bit the coin and it is real. You need no proof of that I assure you! But first I have to have more food for thought. Please and thank you.

The Other Side Of the Coin P#2

Theory visualized, message acknowledged and confirmed, all captions equalized randomized and persevered. ...If you had two words that describe what's on the one side of the fence and two words that describe what's on the other. And definitively they share the same beliefs. What's in between? ...The power of perfection indeed! But if you believe everything everybody else says. You're doing nothing but fooling yourself. So it is my express wish that you'll report the truth about something you didn't yet hear or read about. That should have been faith based front page news, somewhere. Or at least well into its investigation for its credibility and legitimacy to be considered to be real. In order to set you free and put your mind at ease. We all know alchemy was a failed medieval attempt at scientific discovery. But if you look closely you'll find a second definition in the dictionary. Which is, "A power or process of transforming something common into something special." So imagine possessing the knowledge and the wisdom to have gold, diamonds, emeralds, rubies and pearls all laid at your feet. After you recreated or formulated their exact facsimile. A treasure so vast no one would bat an eye at the amount you keep. Remember in the mean time men dig up the earth and nothing stops some of them from destroying their relationships with others, as they compile a vast fortune of, to obtain a huge sum of, "the real thing!" And in a land not far from kids drop out of school. And dig literally man holes many yards into the ground. And with very few ladders and twentieth century flashlights search for tiny specks of gold using a garden trowel. Too proud to beg for money to eat obviously which is considered to be an admirable quality. Because on the other side of the fence they'd have to probably.

The Conversation

"I was shown a ring I believe by a human. Who captured my imagination with some sort of animal? ...None the less, magnetism. There's an ole saying. If you meet him in person even if you can see his face you're not supposed to look into Gods eyes. Anyway he took it off and put it on a table right in front of me. The ring lit up with many many many tiny little white lights. Then it turned into several different colored ones that were soothing to the mind and pleasing to the eyes. And appeared in many different beautiful patterns. And light protruded from the ring into the air. It was utterly fascinating! And being thought captivating, it gave me a good feeling. Showed me the controls to what I believed to be a ship. Pointed to one of two or three panels that looked like display screens on the wall. And had me turn my back to them. We were now facing each other both standing in a room. Arms folded. Sporting at waist level and at the time towards me a rather strange looking gold belt and ultra bright silver buckle! Pointing to it and looking straight at me he said." "To some this looks like the belt buckle of a true champion!!" "To me, it looked like some sort of electric jewel incased in silver that had many facets on it" ..."It represents vision! And the vision that we can all be champions of human rights, instead of victims. They come from all walks of life and there are many different kinds. Humane mistakes, according to some. You have laws." "Then said." "You have to teach peace to someone who hasn't been. And how do you create peace if you weren't taught? You put your mind to it and make it happen." "He motioned for me to turn around. Took off the buckle and set it on the table next to the ships controls and it immediately displayed multiple projections on all three panels. That came together and formed one. It was of a man standing and speaking and you could clearly see and hear him." "Now you can interact with a true visionary! Without going below the belt. And turn something ordinary into something special and extraordinary also. Of course the very concept is priceless to me, that's all." ..."I didn't say I was on one. I talked to someone in a craft, of futuristic design. That visited the present from well how do we know? Maybe the past from a part of our very own world we were aware of but unable to explain how it could exist, before we could comprehend such intelligence. And I know what you're thinking if you imagine great big aliens using huge technological advantages like some sort of mind control or subliminal messaging that leaves you completely hypnotized and entranced. No, more like just astronauts from somewhere. Taking pictures for their photo album of us. And yes it was a mood altering mind elevating experience.

Priceless

Remember pi? (3.14159265). It's just a piece of the pie. Peace! Mathematics are engineered and specifically designed to equalize, equate, construct, put together, formulate, introduce and incorporate, record, playback, innumerate, populate, preserve and communicate the whole, or the rest of it which requires all of it. So for the case where technology was used mathematically to save one life. In a few years or less it would be reported that it saved several million where needed after initiation. What comes from true genius doesn't harm any one of us. And that's a warm felt kind hearted and friendly fact we call stupendous. How does it fend off its opposite? You use it. So the next time you see a sign for a formula squared. Think of one slice of pie. Someone holding up two fingers sporting the symbol for peace. Saying, "I'll have one more serving please." With a great big smile on their face! And you taking a picture for the whole human race.

You

When you're dreaming you pinch yourself to see if you're awake! When you're envisioning you pinch yourself to see if you're dreaming. ...Somebody said. "Don't let genius go to your head." And depending on who they were and how they described the good deed and then acted upon. You could always tell whether they woe unto them, were or weren't one. Once somebody came from to tell of.

The Chronicle

Some say what's on their minds. Some say what they thinks' on an others. Some think faster, some think slower. To some it's voluntary to some it's involuntary. A clairvoyant sits back and listens to both of them. And listen to this, without bias or prejudice. To a medium it's an ability that comes naturally. Let me clarify. The psychological explanation of what we do or do not communicate can be as complicating as it is fascinating! I remember the tale of, "The Tortoise & The Hare." Ingenious! Because the writer saw past and defined properly the mentality of solving two problems at once on an even keel. And in simple terms explained them away in one simple story. A friend said to me. "They didn't have computers when I was in school. What can one do for me that it can do for others?" I told him there is a program where you can write an entire book just by speaking into a microphone plugged into a machine. And immediately as you say it, per paragraph or story whichever way you want it will print it up for others hold and keep. Even if you never learned to write, or read. You can set it to say it back to you electronically in some ones voice even yours what you did. And you can have it preserved and on record. He said, "I'd like to see something that! That sounds pretty neat. That'd be good enough for me." ...And I feel ashamed of myself for repeating my goals in this report. But again, the idea is when I finally "get there", to communicate. Since there is evidence of ESP, in the world. Help for the problems I encountered will either be, "on the way." Or already have been dispatched. And if that's the case I sincerely apologize. I had to take notes to put together thoughts I remember. They're the forerunner of knowledge which is power. And why on earth did I only use one communication medium? To prove prayer works! And even if it takes every form of communication we have on earth to prove it does. If it makes someone happy then certainly it has. And happiness is the key to longevity. So if my lack of faith commits me. Then of my own accord. It's back to the drawing board. ...Walking on and what a journey it's been so far I came across some who wanted to learn public speaking or at one time or another did. Who suffered from a condition. I thought to myself, after completing my work I'll pray over the subject at hand and important matter to heal with telecommunication as the answer. And if you listen to some of their reasons to tell their story you'll feel sorry. Let me put it like this. On a good day it has allot to do with shyness. There is more than one cause. For instance you might learn to play any one musical instrument as well as the worlds greatest! But stage fright keeps you from entertaining and raising the publics interest. Another reason, fear of making a mistake which when you think about it sounds ridiculous. Or fear of public comment. And of course fear of offending whether for the right or wrong reason. Speaking philosophically and with a high degree of morality. Truth be told, even if it just affects one person whether in the past it has or hasn't been it's still genuine. When it becomes important to everyone, it's worth reporting. Why would it become important? If it helps someone it is. Which hinges on for the instrumentalist, practice. The public speaker, experience. And the storyteller, acceptance. Comedy and tragedy. In drama you have your good cop bad cop routine in the investigation room. Of course in literature you have descriptions of an alter ego like the story of Dr. Jeckle and Mr. Hyde. ...If a beast you put your trust in a beast you owe your allegiance to. We're creatures of habit. You can only tell a lie for so long before people will stop believing one. And you can only tell the truth for so long before people sit up and see it and truly realize it for what is. Look at the power of a story. Is dyslexia a sickness, disorder or condition? And does it happen while trying to communicate? Sometimes and you can bet your ace in the hat it can! Remember the story of Frankenstein? In a way it predicted organ donation. I wonder and leave that thought to ponder. Picture a scenario where a doctor wants to fly. Yes literally fly! So he sows a birds wings onto his own body. And to be fair then sows his skilled hands onto the bird afterwards. And to convince the bird to doctor him he has to sing. Pathological illness. ...Man with cut. Communication barrier. Man with Band-Aid. Solvent. Direct communication. Newspaper, healer. Reader, writer, reporter, contributor, trial and error. Victor vector. Authority, evidence, witness, testimony. Investigator, inspector monitor. Solid proof, conformation, documentation. Equipment manager, printed ink, press, newsletter, circular. Equality, justice, representation, firm and fair. Prevarication, suppression, depression. Adjudication, self discipline. Technological advancement, advantage. Problem, solution, tried and true tested and perfected. Education, participation. Resolve, resolution. Conclusion. Monocle, chronicle.

Ahead Of Your Time

Wasn't it Einstein who theorized that if you traveled in a straight line fast enough that there is a point in time that you would reach the ends of the universe. And travel back to your origin and no one would notice that you even left? Use your imagination and Gods speed to you. I theorize he was referring to the speed of thought. And if you think about it as pertaining to an extra sensorial perception, if you could measure the span of how long it takes to produce thought it's almost instantaneous. Which contains well at least two things that I remember vividly. The spiritual which contains the supernatural. And the metaphysical which contains the super consciousness. Where the differential is helping others, key word all together. The present time right now as it happens in seventy two hours becomes three things. And in twenty four hours becomes more than plus, minus one thing. ...Tomorrow, today and yesterday.

Each second minute and hour have a unique numeric order that fit perfectly in just one place in the universe. Coming from a point of origin that exists of, in and from. Therefore having and being given enough time to do anything good for anyone is a God given gift. If a computer can calculate to infinity. Imagine a machine that can record playback and produce where biologically you step through into and visit eternity! True genius sows seeds that do you see, ...already. All they require other than the gravity that holds a planets atmosphere in place is the knowledge of botany which produces dirt and requires internal and external heat and of course water. People disliked the man who remembered this because he had the power to dream. And became jealous because of his ability to make a wish come true, really! Also, because yesterday he saw tomorrow on the horizon. And came back to tell about the future he visited, today. So if you truly believe that can happen to anyone. You've went up against a genius and won. Yes you've graduated the genius club! And you can pick up your degree and have it hanging on the wall before tomorrow morning. And please do! Then I don't have to mime. That you're.

Mind Over Matter

Someone said to the man who drinks. "If you don't wait 'till 5 O'clock. Your work will suffer and you'll get sicker sooner. Because throughout the day ultimately you'll drink more and more. Then the illness creates a disorder. And coffee just masks it and makes you wide awake, but drunker." I'm a bit psychic, I'm awake and I can't really fall asleep standing up with my eyes wide open. But what are dreams made of that you first aren't mindful of and think up another one to have. When I write I complete a dream I've had and yes I put down the drink and take the coffee up. Then inspiration becomes creation. The secret is concentration and everything in moderation. Without inebriation. And of course to heal certain conditions you need interaction with others. You've heard the fraises starving artists, lonely musicians and out of work writers. Everyone's born with a talent. The hard work comes with the patience it takes to practice and perfect. The dream is the artist will open up a gallery and become an overnight sensation. The musician will go on stage, face the music and become a success at it. And before the writer's out of work they'll have written a good book. People forget! An addiction's painful. And fulfilling a dream is nothing short of wonderful. The word powwow means powerful wonder. And what's even more powerful? Prayer. Even if a blind man cannot see.

When you show him the ways of the world you share your vision of what you both, want it to be. So the instant someone says something to inspire, I become mindful of the subject at hand and pray over the matter. Which includes being mindful of others. And the technical term for this simple exercise is called. Mind over matter.

The Exam

Before I could even make a cup of coffee this morning someone said to me. "You sugar coat the truth!" You uncover the truth to reveal the truth and the truth is self evident. Therefore a little sweetness in the mix doesn't hurt now and then. "You get too technical!" That all depends on how you look at things now doesn't it. "You take life too seriously!" When you're about to put your life in someone else's hands and you have to make some tuff decisions you might, you might. "You don't talk enough about having faith!" When someone courses your good nature and tries to make you lose your cool. It's hard to have the faith not to. But it can be done without question. Remember those mirrored parabolic dishes about the size of your hand the doctors wore on a headband when they checked you out as they looked you over in the doctors office? And for a tongue depressor they'd use a pop sickle stick? Open wide! When you're on the examination table if you want the good doctor to diagnose your condition properly, you have to be truthful and able to open up to him or her honestly immediately. Just before they examine, some want everyone they know present. Others don't. It's a matter of a survival instinct to the one for that matter not the other. In any event today I'm talking about a patient diagnosing his or hers doctors ability to do what's necessary to heal you and at the same time make you happy. And if for example the examination is to be for free, consider the following. About privacy. How much money if you have any do you donate to charity? And how do you know it's being used properly? Picture a doctor and a patient stranded on a desert island. And the patient was sick but healed his own condition. But then the doctor got sick and all of a sudden fell down and lied on the beach in the sand. ...Who's going to perform the exam? The patient and a patient man I am. Why doesn't a quack sell chicken soup? They wouldn't, unless you forgot your grandmas secret recipe. Of how to combine all the right ingredients in all the right proportions to pro-duce a natural healing effect, feeling and treat for the taste buds and pallet to boot. Plus it's usually the first thing on the list at the soup kitchen, to tell the truth. And if your recipe doesn't work, it's not cowardly to say you're sorry because you did your best and tried as hard as you could. So about good cooks. There's smarter, brighter and wiser and not necessarily in that order. Some are born with the talent someone else wasn't which makes that person smarter without allot of study. And others become brighter than they are with, study as to them it comes easy. It's called being book smart you see. And some perceive experiences easier than others which allows them to become all the wiser all the faster. I was keen enough to overturn a skeptics wrongful diagnosis using my noodle. But the experts didn't stop there and stated if I spout off they're right and I'm wrong none the less. Still, my proof is and I am my own witness is if that is true, I was coursed. Unless I allowed mind to deliver a spurt of anger or become jealous. Then they're diagnosis of my mental state would not be over zealous therefore there'd be no deception in their detection and it would be a correct perception. People don't forget the treatment or the name they have for it. But because of the label they put on those they think need it. They do forget when there's mistreatment.

Superman's Cape

What does Superman think as he walks to the coat rack? "Rich man poor man beggar man thief! Tinker tailor soldier spy. So you say so shall it be. As you wish. But wait a minute! What if you could simply will something done and magically out of nowhere it would happen? Just by thinking, whatever it was you wanted. No secret code. No invisible ink. No piece of paper. No form of communication normally associated with man whatsoever! Just thoughts, that travel back and forth in time like links. And in duration of transference remain in conference depending on the conversation that takes place. A most effective tool that will have a good, lasting affect just in the nick of time and at the last minute. As you await a most scrutinized, fluctuating, personalized, primal instinctive, exciting, entertaining and important outcome. But you can't say a thing! No one can hear you speak! So you can concentrate on nothing but what you and they are thinking. And it would be valuable to have the power to converse, from your mind to their mind and back again. So before you get there you can, peer thru the keyhole, listen to opening and closing doors, hear thru the windows. And not break down but take down the communication barriers. Then this result enthralls. ...See thru walls.

Seasons Greetings! Please Enjoy this handmade Christmas Card

From, "The Secret Key." The Harmless Hypothesis. Philosophy is what you think is so far. Someone who's ahead of their time told everyone he knew. "Psychologists suggest that the mind talks to its inner self." So you have to be happy! And being thankful for just one more day is the key.

In The Alley

Cold and hungry feeling a bit lonely a bum walking thru the alley stumbles upon what looks like a pamphlet of some kind with a pen clipped to it. Picks it up holds it in his hand and all of a sudden an intense looking white light comes on! And it's now apparent to him he's found a computer of unknown origin. Then three words fade in and become visible. And he hears coming directly from the machine in a low voice' "Tap me thrice!" So he does. The three words fade to the image of a writing tablet. There's something on it. He reads it. As it's read to him at the same time. And it says, "Here you can write anything! About what you've just read and share it with the world around you, what little bit of the whole world will listen to in relation to how many people today you associate yourself with. Tell the truth or tell a fib if you wish. Alter the text so it appears differently. It makes no difference to me. Put it into any format, literally change it in any way to suit all your needs as you see fit. Any thoughts you may have I can read and as I tune in to the neuro-transmissions of your mind, define materialistically. And it is I your servants command that it shall be put into print, immediately. But the one thing you can't change is that it's your speech and appears in your own handwriting. Unless you use the tools in front of you. Take a good look around you and shine your window to the world. Clean your slate and start over. Practice twenty four hours a day if you have to and you won't need an eraser. To change the future." These words also faded out and the first set came back in. So again he tapped it three more times. The white light comes on and changes this time to what looks like a book with no title just a picture for a front cover of a contraption similar to an old telephone with a mouth piece that resembles a camera lens. And the same voice says, "If you can't write to me talk to me! ...I see you and can hear up close from far away." This sparks the mans interest so he says. "Who are you? What are you? I know like some sort of news paper from the future! Yeah!

188

You're like a genie in a lamp! You could become quite useful to me. And I've got some important things for you to do. Now you just sit tight and let me carefully tuck you away where nobody can see in my coat pocket where you'll be safe." Walks up the alley to where he knows no one else can see. And taps it six times gently. The tablet appears and then the picture and it says. "What to you want to ask?" The man blurts out. "How do I get rich? Can you show me where do dig for gold?" The book speaks. "Of course! But first you have to pass over the exact area so I can conduct my search and provide enough proof that where you dig you will find treasure. That and a simple map will do so I can explore. If you don't have one take heart and treasure the fact you've at least tried." He puts it back in his pocket and walks to the corner store. Shows the clerk and tells him to ask it anything! The clerk says, "OK. How can I win the lottery?" The machine answers. "Well now! ...I can teach you how to count cards so you will have the winning hand, over and over again. But sooner or later instead of becoming a big winner you'll become a bigger looser because people will label you as a gambler. And because you win all the time the establishment will ban you from the table, forever. Therefore indulge yourself in the fact that you've just learned something for free that's cost many others a fortune." He stows it away and goes to church and shows it to the entire congregation! Just as soon as he does the preacher walks in and remarks. "I've seen that invention before and I know what it's going to say after you ask it at least one particular question. And that is, ...I can't pray over the matter unless you at least tell me what's the matter. And by the way that's what the suggestion box is for." So once more he puts it in his pocket and ventures off to visit the doctor. Taps it six times and asks it if it has anything to say to the medical profession. Again the book speaks and this time directly to both of them. "A human being said a genius is one in a million. What that means is once you find one you ask them something. And with one explanation they answer a million peoples questions. Repairing the human body so it will live on forever God said is possible long ago when he answered every ones prayers.

The Book Club

"Remember that picture of the mind that has three different sized gears and that the littlest cranks out thought three times as fast as originally conceived?" My buddy could project that image. And was blessed mentally when he mentioned that very fraise and then said. "Now picture a pair of book ends just on the outside of my ears!" He had an exceptional memory. And at he time we weren't bums per say but used to bum off of each other every now and then. And he said change is good! But only when it goes from less than good to good then it becomes the greater good. And he said if you strike it rich like say you win the lottery, you finally have the power to purchase the things you need, things you never had and always wanted. Because now you can afford them. And people knew he could do just about any crossword puzzle in the paper in about a minute and a half or less. Could nearly always solve the puzzle on the TV game show, "Wheel of fortune", before the contestants did. And usually always had the right answer before the buzzer on the game show, "Jeopardy!" So people asked him what the smartest people around do when they get together. Read a poem a week or a book a month? And they all had a good laugh at his expense. So he said. "What avenue does a blind man go down when he plays a game of chess? First he has to familiarize himself with it mentally. Try to read the others persons mind, predict any thoughts they may have. And sense or feel if you will their opponents next move. And just because you're as smart as someone or as bright as they are doesn't necessarily mean you will make the all the right moves. Oh and by the way, the soul lives on forever when you pour your heart into your work." Just then they realized he was good at what he poured his heart into. And knowing he did most of his work in his head. They never made fun of the book club ever again.

The To Do List

When I was young I was good at saving money from doing my daily chores. And since allot of it was small chance I developed a fondness for collecting coins. So one fine day my Grandpa and Grandma gave me an old English penny from I believe the Victorian dynasty! Date, 1798. I can still see it clearly and I could hardly believe my eyes when I matched it up exactly with one in a coin collecting book which included for each coin obverse and reverse pictures. Whose estimated value was almost as much as the government insured limit for banked on savings. Coin collecting or numismatics teaches responsibility prudence patience and to be wise when making decisions. So given that information I knew there were two futures that I had to envision. One where right away I cashed it in, retired and people held my inheritance against me, a fortune because it was handed to me. Yes given like, "being born with a silver spoon in your mouth," if you will. Not having earned it actually working for money. Or the other where I could put it in a safe place and save it for after, I earn my retirement. And once I have, cash it in and help anybody whom I had the fortune of meeting who indeed needed a little help amassing their good fortune along the way. ...I chose the latter. And was comfortable with the fact that I made that decision. And never lived to regret it. Because you can't put a price on becoming rich, spiritually. Believe me! Being reminded of what great thinkers and doers did with what little good fortune they could compile to help others. Well, low and behold the rare coin got lost and eventually stolen. And since then I've earned a modest amount but not an entire fortune, all by my lonesome. And I have to say I feel sorry and pity the poor fool that found it. If all they thought it was. Was just an old out of date coin and figured it was only or not even worth a penny. And thru a grand future, away. Put a little away for a rainy day. Call it butter and egg money. Put some in the, "kitty." ...Give a penny take a penny. Now envision five symbols for the following explanations. One who with a heart of gold, shines a guiding light from above. One who envisions the world without one speck of, since it's due to war, poverty in it. One who sees everybody living comfortably with enough room on flat level sectioned planes and vegetation or a lawn if you will surrounding their parameters. One representing math being harmless when combined with science and medicine. And one for equality. You have a yellow star. A blue circle. A green rectangle. A white triangle. And an equal sign. So picture those symbols being tied into a machine that doubles as an ESP and scientific experiment. That you can prove works. Where you can add more symbols to the mix. Which produce when read either left to right, right to left, top to bottom or bottom to top, a language. It's not the size of the ring or the color of the jewel that makes it worth attaining. It's what the one represents and the other means. Call it divine providence or divine intervention but let me explain what I believe, like this. If you had a time machine and you went back to the past, the one you wanted. ...Still, it would automatically unwind and progress until it comes back to the present. Which would make it a later date in time than when you started. And since time is precious if you don't want that sequence to take place. Because only a certain part of the past at one point in time was the one you could best stomach in which you healed. And the one without trial and tribulation, good mind set and everything. You'd recreate the days weeks months or years in question. And change the future for the better. And it may take you a while! But it's worth the trouble, to do.

A Stroke Of Genius

Sometimes ingenuity in the form of writing gets lost but what I am about to tell you I do remember and is true. So because there once was don't think there still isn't. Someone said, "You shouldn't write about genius, all the time either! Because it's not fair for those who aren't one!" But still, have you really looked up the definition lately and do you remember it completely? It's short and sweet believe me! The most common misconception is that the subject matter is so extensive that constantly trying to get the reading material just right one would never be able to complete the task and finish their work in writing. "Pish-tosh!" Why do you think we write poem books? One main reason, is for those who went thru a traumatic experience and could not summon the help of a genius. And you're right it takes on many forms and has many attributes. Analyzing and assessing. Since it's a subject that contains controversy you may try to avoid it because you feel left out of the mix. Not to despair. I assure you after you finish this report you will feel just as important as one. Plus it's fun to, "keep up with the Joneses'." Some peoples ideas opinions and advice is based on other peoples ideas opinions and advice. Others are based solely on fact. Some people only talk about you, others only talk to you. Someone said to me, "If you'll just get your facts straight you can do the work of many!" But that would make them lazy. People associate genius with one thing at a time which to one sounds mundane and boring. What's my IQ? In general it doesn't matter because the most common test doesn't cover each and every area. Plus you don't have to be a genius to help other people but it helps to know a little. Remember the process of calculation can be expressed in a mathematic formula so simple once you learn it from a piece of paper you can do math in your head! That takes the confusion out of that very concept now doesn't it? Excellent! I am summoning my inner strength which goes to the very fibers of my being to seek out genius in three or four areas, ...medical. That I investigated and produced hands on proof there is need for improvement. Where in peoples lives while dealing with their ability to live pain free. Others who were found to have the power over life and death, abused it intentionally. And instead of relieved pain induced it on purpose! Their reasons for that are barbaric. And many a day men thought about that very conundrum. And never sought the help of a genius to stop it? Sadly yes and I'm ashamed of that past. Because there are those who never committed those foul acts but in a nation with every form of communication on earth known to man allowed it to go on and happen. Forcing the victims to communicate for them. I'm their advocate. My aim is to reduce their misery to zero. Now, the future is at hand. The people I petition shall earn the status of life savers. And the methods they use shall be deemed ingenious and above all, harmless. Sounds exciting doesn't it? Remember what you can put down on a piece of paper in order to become smarter someone else can remember without one. But unless they're exceptionally gifted they first have to read one. Therefore the two talents distribute their weight equally amongst each other, when together. So when someone says someone else's testament speaks to them, they really mean it! Because where there's prophecy of good news there's proof it exists ahead of time. How long would it take you to sculpt some ones visage just by touching it and how long would it take to form their image without looking at them? It's easy to catch an honest man telling, "a little white lie." A dishonest man it isn't as. Unless they're a, "snake oil salesman." Pitching their product to a hypochondriac. then it's fairly obvious they're telling a, "fib." And are committed to prevarication and also falsification. Or falsely prophesying. And just remember someone who tells the truth profits from it as well. Which reveals the stark differences between hallucinating and envisioning. If you chime in one note after each is played. People will emotionally attach themselves to your very frank effort at the cost of your embarrassment. And will as you get to the chorus think you actually remember the song! Even if you didn't. What's the secret? Eventually you get the hang of it. If you're an inventor and you're testing the work of a electronically inclined mechanical engineers technological advancement in the form of a machine. And you alone have to be able to prove it's flawless in every way, no matter how many times it's turned on or for how long it's used. You are first going to install every safety device you can think of. Also because when you're the sole operator the object begins and ends with being a life saver. Science has taken on the endeavor to produce a working machine that ends immense pain altogether. It involves several mind sets and several different preventive measures. We are all fully cognizant and aware of our physical conditions. We're modern men and women. "We don't need immense pain to tell us when something's wrong with the human body." Seeing is believing, up close and make no mistake throughout the annals of time we worry about having like a telescopic lens on people places and things in order to stand up and testify and justify what is really there. So the theory exists that you could project that very thought telepathically and look at things with the same powerful ability. Zoom in, adjust contrast and clarity like putting on a brand new pair of glasses with a prescription of twenty, twenty. When I wrote that with a few notes you can study without a book I didn't mean you shouldn't read a good one first. I just didn't fully convey how. And that's because some can by just skimming the surface and some really fast. Are able to tell you the conclusion without actually having to go over one. And that explains allot of things now doesn't it? Which is defined in any school of higher or normal learning as not turning a blind eye toward proof of an ability that is simply amazing. Equalizing, if someone can read your thoughts and it's been proven they can. They know all your likes and dislikes. And if they're good at that technique they can peer into your mind and if you are at that time, see what you are reading. And base a conclusion on what you've read so far and formulate an accurate opinion as to the books outcome, without opening up one. Because they see what you see, they know what you know also. So it's not far-fetched to picture someone just like yourself sitting at a desk and not imagining but actually putting the facts together as we all motivate at the same time during our daily routine. And figure out just what people are going to or are saying presently about you behind closed doors. As first you read all their mannerisms study their patterns of awareness and probe their conciseness's, before they do. Thus the phrase, "seeing right thru you." Even if you're separated by walls! So when I learn of good news and current events match up to and exemplify. That speaks volumes to me. Even if all they consist of are compliments, thank you notes and true life testimonials. All it takes along with a little help and a little luck. Surprise! Allot of love. ...And a little something that I think is in all of us. And that's a stroke of genius.